OCEANS AWAY

SKYE MCNEIL

For information, contact the publisher, Hot Tree Publishing.
WWW.HOTTREEPUBLISHING.COM

EDITING: HOT TREE EDITING
COVER DESIGNER: SOXSATIONAL COVER ART
FORMATTING: RMGRAPHX

ISBN: 978-1-925853-38-4

LIST OF BOOKS

<u>ATLAS</u>
HEARTS ABROAD
OCEANS AWAY

<u>THE MOBSTER FILES</u>
APPOINTED BY FATE
EXONERATED WITH LOVE

<u>THE COLLEGIATE PEAKS</u>
TIMBERLINE
ST. ELMO

<u>STAND-ALONES</u>
DONUTS, DIAMONDS & ASSORTED DETAILS

For the dreamers stuck in reality.

CHAPTER ONE

"You're going to miss your flight home," the driver pointed out.

Ireland Leighton studied the serene view of the Atlantic Ocean in the distance. "They'll hold it." Barbados felt more like home than the multitude of places she'd been in the last six years. But now she was on her way to the first home she remembered: Iowa. The thought scared her more than the paperwork sure to pile up during her short stint in the States.

Closing the door, she grabbed the handle to her suitcase and walked toward the private entrance of the Grantley Adams International Airport. She straightened her shoulders and entered the side of the airport she never thought she'd set foot in. Waving to the woman at the front desk, she took a seat and perused an airline magazine.

Only two other fliers were waiting for their flights. She recognized one as a businessman from Venezuela. The other was in the African trade industry.

"Miss Leighton, your pilot is ready," a flight attendant said, walking over to her as a younger man followed and grabbed Ireland's luggage. The woman with gorgeous black hair and tanned skin grinned. "Going back to the States so soon?"

Ireland nodded and fell in step with the one person she knew almost as well as her personal assistant. "Yes, Darja. It's been too long."

She slipped on her sunglasses when they walked to the runway, deciding not to include the part about her parents demanding a visit. Apparently, her recently engaged brother, Zavier, had a request that could only be made face-to-face. Without hearing it, Ireland knew it had something to do with her world-wide connections. Though her degree was in business, it didn't take much to figure out that Zavier and his bride-to-be wished for a tropical wedding and honeymoon. Well, she didn't mind. He was her only sibling, after all. His timing, on the other hand, could've been better.

Let's hope he doesn't want to get married soon.

"What projects are you working on now?"

Eyeing the private jet still in the distance, Ireland slowed her gait for the shorter woman. "A new orphanage in Melverton is set to start construction next month."

Darja beamed at her. "You do so much good here. I don't know how you manage it all."

Tucking her hair behind her ears, Ireland shrugged. "Lots of help."

"Have a good time," Darja called as they reached the

steps to the private jet.

Ireland glanced back at the island one last time and hoped it'd only be a week or two before she'd return. While she adored her family, she loved her life away from cornfields and pig farms. The Leightons understood and encouraged her dreams, no matter how farfetched they sounded. It was something she hoped to someday, somehow repay them for.

Taking a seat, she waved aside the flight attendant's offer of alcohol. Any other time, she'd agree, but she was on her way to Iowa. She'd see *him* again, and that was a recipe for disaster.

Buckling up, she reclined her chair and grabbed her sleeping mask, not wanting to watch her home disappear among the clouds. She'd built an empire in the Caribbean, but now she'd have to face her past.

Millions of dollars in a trust fund helped set her up, but the millions in the bank now were all due to her dedication and passion to help others. *Well, a few lucrative business ventures didn't hurt either.* She soon discovered that in order to continue her charity work, she also had to put in plenty of hours in her biological family's businesses.

As the plane taxied the runway, Ireland snuck a peek out the window. The last time she was in Iowa, things hadn't gone so well.

Here's hoping just over half a decade made it all better.

In her heart, she knew it wouldn't happen. *He* was there. He was the neighbor next door who'd asked her to stay. And he was also the same man she'd rejected. She kept telling herself she'd done it because of her duty to her biological parents long dead. That wasn't the case, though. She'd asked Gideon Taggart to move overseas with her, but he wouldn't budge. His was rooted in Iowa, whereas Ireland always knew she belonged somewhere else. Her heart had shattered that day and she didn't want to trust another man with it again.

Letting out a frustrated breath, Ireland sat up. She'd never get any sleep while she thought about the heart of the Midwest. She grabbed her carry-on from the seat beside her and pulled out the portfolio her assistant created the night before. An investment for an up-and-coming cybersecurity firm in Amsterdam looked promising.

She glanced around the plane's lavish cabin. *Something has to pay for all this.*

Flipping to the first page, she focused on her ultimate goal: to make the world a better place. In order to do that, she had to be savvy with her business ventures.

***

The comforting hum of machinery and voices caused a smile to cross Ireland's sun-kissed face. The inner workings of Des Moines International Airport looked the same as when she'd left. The strong scent of coffee mingled with the Americana grill near the terminals. Cornfields could be seen from any window. It was Iowan to a tee, something she didn't think she'd ever miss.

Ireland's light brown eyes flicked to the few terminals as her phone rang. Digging the smartphone out of her purse, she answered the call from her college best friend. "Krista?"

"Hey! I'm so glad you answered!"

Moving out of the way of oncoming foot traffic, Ireland cleared her throat. She hadn't heard from Krista in nearly five years. Not since her friend decided to pursue her teaching career.

"Yeah, me too. So, what's up?"

"I met someone."

Ireland rolled her eyes. The woman was notorious for hopping from one guy to the next. *Not that I was much better after I left.*

"Oh yeah? That's great."

Krista giggled. "You know him fairly well."

The breath in Ireland's lungs deflated. *Surely, she doesn't mean....* She couldn't finish the thought.

"Really? Who might he be?"

An announcement over the speaker system cut through the conversation. Grinding her teeth, Ireland glanced at her watch. No doubt one of her family members would pick her up, and she shouldn't keep them waiting.

"Look, Krista, I need to run. I'll call you later, okay?" She hung up before the other woman could reply. They didn't have many friends in common anymore. The one summer Krista spent with the Leightons after college was the same as when Ireland had left. Not long before, she'd received correspondence from France. Her entire world changed that July day.

Ireland checked her emails and saw one from her grandmother. She put that one aside for the time being;

there'd be time to catch up later.

Starting through the airport, she paused at a rack of magazines outside one of the shops. *Damn.* Two covers had her face splashed on them. Hoping no one recognized her, she moved farther down the hall. The fame was still something she was getting used to.

Being adopted as a baby, she'd never given much thought to the parents who she assumed abandoned her. Well, she knew better now, if she was to believe her father's mother. Her biological parents died on their yacht when a swell in the Caribbean overtook them. She'd been an infant at the time, awaiting their return in St. James, Barbados. But they never came back, and she'd been thrown into an orphanage. Things may have been different if her biological father hadn't been cut off from his family and her mother's parents weren't dead. She stayed at the home until the Leightons adopted her.

It was a lot to digest at twenty-two-years-old. So far, six years hadn't helped her accept her true French origins. It was ironic that the Leightons chose her name based on a country—just the wrong one.

As the heir of the Bourgeois companies, her paternal grandmother, Fiona Bourgeois, expected her to return to France one day soon to take over the family estate. She sighed at the thought. Planning out her life wasn't what she wanted right then. Enjoying all the world had to offer was more her style.

As the one and only heir to a massive fortune spanning France, the Caribbean, and the UK, it was her destiny to settle down somewhere. At present, it was Barbados. Her grandmother owned several lucrative businesses on the island, which Ireland had taken over one by one during the last few years.

Her true calling was the charity works her biological parents started, though. Those were the best parts of being an heiress. It was easy to fall into, since the director of the orphanage that'd taken care of her was the first stop on Ireland's list to visit. Since then, she couldn't think of a better use of her free time than to help children in need just as she'd once been.

After being extremely stupid, that is. She shook her head to rid herself of the memory, not wanting to think about the dumb things she'd done right after finding out her origins.

A click of cameras caught her ear. She glanced around suspiciously, expecting a paparazzo to be lurking somewhere. When all she saw was an elderly couple attempting a selfie, her heart rate slowed. *Maybe the paps won't follow me here.* She'd left explicit details regarding a story about flying to Europe for her assistant to give the photographers in hopes to deter them. Her family didn't want the hassle, and they didn't deserve the invasion of privacy. After being harassed the summer after she left, the Leightons opted to not join her on any other family vacations she offered them after that. It stung to hear their excuses, mainly farm obligations, but she understood. How could she not? Her family didn't want the limelight and she wouldn't force it on them. From then on, it was safer to keep her distance. Their weekly Skype conversations helped, but it wasn't the same as being home.

Their schedules never seemed to mesh. Whenever she had a day or two off, her dad or mom would have an event, or the fields were ready for harvest. As badly as she wanted to see her family again, Ireland couldn't bring herself to set foot in Iowa. *Until today.*

She scanned the airport, but only saw tourists, businessmen and women, and airport staff. She was safe. *So far so good.* She made sure to post a check-in at one of her hotels in Rome before she put the phone away. As far as the world was concerned, she was on vacation.

Ireland neared the steps to the arrival area and knots fill her stomach. She didn't know what to expect. When she'd left, she'd been alone. Not even her brother had driven her to the airport. Then again, she'd just broken his best friend's heart and snuck to the airport in the middle of the night to catch the first flight out to France. Not the best idea, but she'd been young and dumb.

Reaching the stairs, Ireland couldn't see the waiting crowd members below thanks to the low beam. It'd been six years. Surely the butterflies in her stomach were from seeing her family again.

She rubbed her lips together. Who did she want to greet her? Her brother? Her parents? Gideon? A Starbucks barista with a venti iced white mocha? She tucked her bra strap back under the tank top. While her favorite coffee would be the perfect start to her stay in Iowa, she didn't think she could keep it down. Her gut was too jittery. She stayed in contact the best she could, but her conscience still nagged at her. Her family didn't like to travel, but she should've come home sooner. The Midwest morals the Leightons ingrained in her ate away and she felt bad for not persuading them to visit her in Barbados or even France. *I can make up for that all now.*

She couldn't regret leaving Iowa to pursue her dreams upon her inheritance. *No, partial inheritance.* The certified letter from a bank in Paris burned a hole in her bag even then. It seemed her elderly grandmother was more than eager for Ireland to take over the estates, but there were strings attached—business strings with a fellow millionaire. She swallowed the bile in her throat at the responsibilities Fiona mentioned. The timing would never be right.

Focus, Ireland. Worry about that stuff later.

Her line of vision cleared and she glanced around the small crowd. Roughed-up boots and denim jeans caught her attention. She swore her heart stopped beating. When she noticed a man standing behind one of the posts, reading a sports magazine, she took a deep breath. As she drew closer, her excitement went in a different direction.

"Hey, little sis," her brother greeted with a cheery smile." He tossed the magazine to a nearby chair and wrapped her in a bear hug until her toes no longer touched the floor. "Man, I thought you weren't ever coming back."

"Z, you're going to kill me," she squeaked, sure he'd squeezed her lungs dry.

"Oops, sorry." He set her back down and looked her over. "Well, somebody got extra tan when she was gallivanting."

"Yep." Ireland jabbed him in the side. "Looks like somebody put on a little weight while I was gone too."

Zavier rolled his eyes, a dark shade of blue. "Yeah, yeah. Come on, princess. Let's get your shit and go home. Mama's been beside herself since you emailed your plane information." He glanced around and lowered his voice. "We all thought your private jet would drop you off on the front pasture."

"I only do that for galas," Ireland teased and playfully punched Zavier. Not once had he ever seen her as anything but a sister. She'd figured out her adoption early on when the entire Leighton family mirrored each other except her. The naturally tanned pigmentation of her skin also clued her in to the news. They never made her feel unwelcome or unloved, though. The Leightons accepted her from day one.

They walked toward the baggage claim, weaving around frequent fliers and first-timers. "Why didn't Mom and Dad come?"

"Dad had an appointment and Mom wanted to make your favorite for dinner. Plus, Mom was worried they might end up in the paper if they picked you up." He glanced to the bay window. "Looks like they were right."

Turning toward the wall of windows, Ireland cringed. *Damn, so much for the decoy.* A dozen local reporters hovered outside the doors, waiting to get the inside scoop about the hometown farm girl turned heiress. Her face had been plastered in local and global gossip magazines when the media caught wind of the newfound Bourgeois heir who spent her money traveling.

Well, that was all she'd give the paparazzi. They didn't care about the other things she did with her money unless it made a scene and sold magazines. The constant flashes didn't happen as much in Barbados, and she'd hoped Iowa would be the same. *Forgot about the local stations.* They were pleasant and polite compared to the international ones but weren't fun to deal with nevertheless.

"Sorry about them."

"It's all right. You're home, that's all we care about."

Zavier stopped at the baggage claim and rested his thumbs in his belt buckle. Though they lived in Iowa, her brother had thought he was a cowboy since they were kids. He even held a twang to his words, though she blamed their mother's Southern background for that influence. Plus, he went to Tennessee to visit that side of the family as often as his farm duties allowed.

"So, anything new?" she asked. The conveyer belt hadn't budged yet. It had stayed the same over the years. The Des Moines airport was great, to an extent, but it never changed enough to warrant a speedy arrival pattern.

Zavier scratched his chin. He'd grown out his facial hair since she'd seen him last. He didn't look half bad with the scruff either. "Not much. We expanded the fields another hundred acres for the cows. Bought more livestock. Building repairs. Good crops for the last six seasons." He swung his eyes to her. "Could've used your help in the fields. You always had a knack for farming."

"And risk chipping my fake nails?" she teased, holding up her nails that were in more need of a manicure than anything. Succumbing to all-things plastic wasn't her thing. Even though she had money, she didn't want to spend it on such things. Not when the funds could be better used elsewhere.

He chuckled, then rolled back his shoulders. "It's cool. I get it. You traded your boots for something better. Can't fault you there."

"I'll come back for the next harvest if I can swing it."

He merely nodded.

Farm talk was what she'd grown up on. It was part of the reason she'd left Iowa in college for the study abroad programs, then again once her bombshell family news showed up in a bank account. She adored the great outdoors, but cornfields entertained her for only so long. She had a future outside Iowa. One that cemented her in the charity field for good. She'd worked too hard abroad for it to be for naught.

"So, are you going to tell me who the lucky lady is?"

A brief smile lit up his face, but he quickly disguised it. She made a mental note to come back to that. It was why she was in town, after all.

"How's your business stuff?" Zavier asked.

Ireland couldn't help but laugh. Her brother attended ISU too, but for agriculture, not the study of international business like her. Zavier never understood her fascination for travel and charity, even when she'd volunteered around the Des Moines metro. She'd known back then that she was meant for more than the farm. "It's great, thanks."

The belt started up and they stepped closer. Her phone vibrated, but the text messages from her assistant weren't what she'd hoped to see. They offered her no distraction from the fact that somewhere deep in her gut, she wished someone else had picked her up from the airport.

"Tagg's working the fields today," Zavier stated, not looking at her.

She stilled at his statement. Tagg was Gideon Taggart's nickname ever since their teenage years. As to why only he got the nickname and not his older brother, Lance, she didn't know. It just stuck one day and never stopped. She'd never called him by the name, though. Gideon was much too unique in her opinion. "What? Why would I—"

"Ireland, we all know what happened before you ran to the airport," he cut in. "Tagg told me about it. Hell, the whole town knew, so don't act like you didn't want him to pick you up today."

"I didn't. He's in my past." He gave her a disbelieving glance. "There's my bag." She pointed at the brown suitcase and Zavier retrieved it.

She didn't want to discuss their Taggart neighbors. *I'm not even sure what happened.* One minute she and Gideon were making out, and the next she was hailing a cab. *It's all a blur.* She couldn't recall all the details about their fight, but the main issue was her surprise cash in a French bank account. He hadn't taken it well.

Opting to go around the news reporters, they walked through the entire airport until they were sure no one followed. Zavier's old truck sat nearly alone in the covered parking garage. It was a welcomed sight despite the rust on the rims.

"You still have this thing?"

"Of course." He patted the side. "I don't give up on a good thing."

And here's the guilt trip.

Zavier coughed. "Shit, sorry. I didn't mean—"

"It's fine, don't worry about it."

Once he tossed her bags in the bed, they climbed in, and the engine spouted diesel smoke. Zavier might live in Iowa, but he was more Southern than Midwestern.

Turning up the radio until a country station blared, Ireland sat back and slipped on her designer sunglasses. Their relationship had changed. It was bound to happen over six years, but she could sense that Zavier was upset at her for pursuing a life outside Iowa. It hurt more than she expected. She cursed herself for the tears forming in her eyes. It was her own fault for the distance between them. Clearing her throat, she reaffirmed her goal for the trip and that was to make amends for the time lost.

They made it to the interstate before he spoke again.

"Tagg's still single, by the way." He glanced her direction expectantly.

"Oh my God, seriously? It's been years, Z."

"Yeah, I know, but—"

"No buts." Ireland furrowed her brows. "You really think I came back to Iowa to get back together with our neighbor? I'm not the same person as when I left."

"The paparazzi pictures tell another story." He chuckled. "I love you, sis, but you're a flirt. A flirt with money. You have good taste too, or at least that's what—" He stopped himself and cleared his throat.

"You were going to say your fiancée's name, weren't you?"

He smirked and kept driving. "Maybe."

"Well, I've settled down in Barbados, so the paps won't get any juicy stories from me."

"Mmhmm, sure."

"They won't." She pulled out her phone to check messages. The conversation was ridiculous no matter which direction it went, but it felt good to tease each other again. For now, she wouldn't mind being his little sister who used to annoy the crap out of him.

She tried not to think how the constant stories of her travels and photos of the glamorous life didn't help matters in Iowa. She'd been stupid when she first found out, partying harder than anyone in Iowa alongside other kids from wealthy families. *I know better now.* The slew of risqué photos that graced the internet forced her grandmother to visit her after one of the parties. *Man, she was pissed.* Ireland quickly learned the consequences of having money. Boozing her way across Europe only happened once, and she swore to never do it again.

Hopefully I can mend a few fences with this wedding. She had several ideas but needed to feel the situation out before she'd mention them.

He focused on the road. "Right. Well, I know you have a busy life and all, but can you promise me one thing?"

"Anything, Z. You guys are my family."

He tightly gripped the steering wheel. "Come home every Christmas. It's Mom's favorite holiday and—"

"Done."

He looked over and grinned. "Thanks. Now, is there anything else I can persuade you to do?" he teased with a wiggle of his brows.

"Taking advantage already? That doesn't sound like you," she teased back.

Zavier chuckled and flipped to another radio station. They still had a few things to work out, but Ireland was positive this trip would help their family come together again.

She sat back and watched the buildings fade into fields. She'd missed the simplicity of Iowa. Dirt roads, lightning bugs, and sweet corn were among her best memories of the farm life. Her love for animals didn't hurt things either. She won more 4H projects than her brother and the Taggart boys.

Those were the good times.

"In case you were wondering, Tagg took over the farm. Lance helps too, but it's mostly Tagg." Zavier grinned and pulled on his camouflage sunglasses. "Thought you might want to know before you see him again."

Ireland held on to the door handle as the truck took a sharp left turn. "What makes you think I want to know that?"

Zavier let out a hearty laugh. "Just wait and see, girly. Just wait and see."

Deciding it was best to do as he suggested, she settled into the passenger seat and watched the cornfields overwhelm both sides of the road. Even if she was only in Iowa for a few weeks, she'd enjoy the scenery.

And hopefully, steer clear of Gideon.

CHAPTER TWO

Sweat slid down Gideon Taggart's back in a steady stream thanks to Iowa's humid temperatures. The earthy scent of soil clung to his weathered work gloves. Planting flowers wasn't usually on his list of things to do, but he couldn't turn down his mom when she'd asked.

He brushed a bead of sweat off his brow, no doubt smudging dirt with the action. Glancing at his jeans, he chuckled. The rest of him was covered in mud, so why not his face too?

A cloud of gravel spun in the distance, summoning him to stand. Only two families lived on the road, his and the Leightons. The bright red Dodge truck drove into view.

"Looks like Zavier is back from Des Moines," his mom pointed out from her perch on the porch swing.

"Why was he there?" he asked, pulling off the leather gloves.

Frances Taggart stood and offered him a glass of

lemonade. Grabbing it, he took a big swallow. "To pick up Ireland from the airport, of course."

The sour drink lodged in his throat. Coughing, he handed the glass back to her. "I didn't realize she was coming back."

His mom eyed him quizzically. "For a man who's been in love with Ireland Leighton his whole life, you sure don't pay attention."

Gideon took off his green baseball cap and pushed his fingers through his wavy brown hair. "I'm not in love with her, Mom," he growled.

The truck drew closer, and he suddenly didn't know what to do with his hands. Opting for his usual stance, Gideon shoved them in his front pockets as the vehicle rolled by their front yard. He couldn't see Ireland, but he'd be damned if he missed the boyish smirk on Zavier's face. It was one he knew well. He swore the truck slowed ever so slightly as it passed them. Raising one hand, he waved at Zavier. His best friend saluted, and Gideon swore he saw a flash of Ireland's long hair from the passenger seat. The truck continued toward the other farmhouse and he let out his breath and watched the dust cloud the road.

"The Leightons are having a get-together tonight," his mom stated. "A homecoming of sorts."

Gideon turned toward her and lifted his brows. "I thought we were celebrating Zavier's engagement."

Frances chuckled and wiped her hands on her summery dress. "Both, sweetheart." She moved to the screen door and eyed him warily. "Maybe shower before she sees you again. The poor girl probably didn't recognize you covered in tattoos and dirt."

Looking down at his shirtless attire, Gideon let out a grunt. His abs were speckled with mud, and his chest held streaks as well. The colorful half sleeve on his left arm was nearly unrecognizable thanks to the muck. When he worked, he got dirty. It was the only way he knew to do something—all or nothing.

"Yeah, I suppose I should." He waited until his mom went inside to curse profusely. "Of course you look like shit when Ireland sees you for the first time in six years." He gathered the gardening tools and walked toward the shed. "She doesn't want a muddy guy. She wants some exotic guy. Or business guy. Or rich guy. I'm none of those."

Putting the tools back in their places, he looked in the Leighton farm's direction. He'd never been unsure of himself when it came to life until Ireland flew to Europe. He'd always wanted to take over the farm and stay in Iowa. Before that, the one time he'd doubted his future was when Ireland smiled his way. She was a sweet country girl whether she'd admit it or not, and he'd loved her since first grade.

No one believed it at first when Ireland went out with him in high school. He'd been the envy of every guy at their small school. Ireland was popular, gorgeous, and a bit spoiled in his opinion, but damn if it didn't make him count his lucky stars every time she kissed him.

From the beginning, it was obvious she was different. When she found out her true parentage, it all made sense. A French heiress matched with how the Leightons had treated their baby girl since her adoption. He should've known a princess didn't settle down with a farmer, no matter how much he loved her.

Gideon moved to the barn, weaving around the multitude of barn cats and impish kittens. He loved the feisty felines almost as much as his dogs. Animals of all kinds were his life, ever since he brought home strays as a kid. The farm never had more dogs, cats, and even squirrels. From a young age, he nurtured abandoned or hurt animals. Helping them was as much a part of him as farming—though he preferred the animals more.

After Ireland's departure, he'd focused on college. She didn't know his side job, and he wanted it kept that way. He was glad his brother hadn't completely left him high and dry with the farm. Gideon wouldn't have been able to run it and maintain his small vet clinic without Lance's help. If he had his way, he'd let his brother handle the farm while he worked full-time as a veterinarian.

Grabbing a pile of reins, he smirked when one kitten followed the trail of ropes in his wake. He made it to the front door at the same time the kitten pounced on the reins. Ireland always loved farm critters too. She was incredible with cats, dogs, and horses. It made sense how she'd beat them all in 4H competitions. She was a wonder—one he thought was only his to discover.

Sunlight glistened on his arms. They were a nice shade of farmer's tan, and the rest of him looked the same. Going to the gym wasn't something he had time for any given day, but like his brother, Gideon had plenty of things to do on the property that kept him in optimal shape.

After untangling a knot in one of the reins, he adjusted his trusty hat and leaned his back against the side of the barn. From there, he could see the Leighton farm in its enormous glory. The Leightons owned most of the farmland north of Polk City, save the Taggart acres. If their family friendship didn't go back two generations, the Taggarts would've been out of a place to live and work long ago.

A balmy breeze swept his curly hair across his forehead. Gideon scratched the back of his neck and stared toward where Ireland slept on the second floor. Many a time, she'd snuck out the window and down the emergency ladder to go night fishing with him. As she grew, so did the reason why she chanced the dangling rungs.

He smiled at the distant memories. Ireland was a girly girl growing up, but she also had a little tomboy in her. His smile waned at the thought that all the time across the world had changed her. But despite the fame associated with her inheritance, he wanted to know her again, mostly to see if the flame he'd kept hidden away for her was worth the effort or if snuffing it out was in everyone's best interest.

He may have still been the neighbor next door, but he was much more than that now. He had dreams and aspirations of his own. She'd inspired him to look outside family traditions, and he was damned glad he did. It was the family loyalty that kept him from leaving. He couldn't, not until his parents and brother were secure. He may have been the youngest, but he was the responsible one of the two.

The lowing of cows met his ears. For today, he'd take care of the livestock. Afterward, he needed to check in on the "vet barn," as he called it. He didn't have enough money to build what he wanted for a clinic, but he had a steady stream of clients he visited on a weekly basis.

Hanging the reins in their rightful spot, he kicked at a rock. He'd shower and decide if a visit to the Leighton house was a good idea. His heart said yes, but his mind wasn't so sure.

Walking toward the newest barn on the property, he saw his two dogs running at full speed in his direction. The red merle and blue merle kicked up dust when they skidded to a halt. Tongues hanging out, the Australian shepherds wagged their nub tails and fell in step on either side of him.

"C'mon, Diesel. Let's go, Dallas," he called with a whistle. He took off at a sprint, both dogs barking and whining as they caught up. The Ireland conundrum would be dealt with in a few hours. It was good enough for him, even if his gut told him different.

***

Ireland opened the truck door and smiled at the homecoming party. It was the same as when she'd returned from Madrid her junior year of college, both parents in the driveway with ecstatic faces. Only now the years had slowly worn on her loving mother and protective father.

"Ireland, I'm so happy you're home," her mother, Joanna, said, pulling her in for a hug.

"Me too."

Her dad, Kenny, wrapped his long arms around both of

them to make the hug last longer. "Good to have you back, princess."

They made their way into the hundred-year-old farmhouse, not a thing out of place since last she saw it. The burgundy couches sat beside a pair of handmade rocking chairs, all of which faced a large television set. The scent of pie lingered in the air and made her stomach rumble. She grinned at the pile of kittens perched in the enclosed porch on the back side of the house. Their little faces were pressed against the screen door, loud meows accompanying them.

"Looks the same," she commented, setting her purse on the kitchen counter.

"Just about." Zavier nudged her with his elbow. "You want this all in your old room?"

Ireland turned to see him teetering on the first step with her luggage. "Yeah, that'd be great, thanks."

"So, Ireland, tell us all about what you've been doing," her dad began.

Joanna shook her head and handed her a glass of iced tea. "Oh no you don't." She wagged her finger at her husband. "She needs to tell everyone once they get here."

The glass paused at Ireland's lips. "What are you talking about?"

Zavier bounded down the staircase. "We're having the Taggarts over later, sis."

"What?" She swung her gaze to her parents. "What's he talking about?"

Kenny scratched the bald spot on top of his head. "I think it's time to check on the pigs. C'mon, Z."

Before she could utter another word, they escaped the room and the conversation.

Turning back to her mom, Ireland gave her a pointed look. "I just got home. I thought we'd have a chance to catch up before…."

Joanna took a seat in one of the rocking chairs. "I'm sorry. I know you're probably jet-lagged and all that, but the Taggarts care about you. They want to know what you've done with your new, uh…." She paused and bit her lip. Talking about Ireland's biological parentage had never come easy to Joanna. "Family business."

Taking a sip of tea, Ireland reminded herself that the whole situation was different. This wasn't like the time she studied abroad in college. She'd left for six years and hadn't returned until now. Sure, they kept in better contact than when she was in college, but it wasn't the same as seeing each other in person.

"Plus we already planned Zavier's engagement party—"

"Will someone please tell me who he's engaged to?"

"Krista Kellogg."

Ireland spat the tea back into the cup before she could stop it. "My old roommate, Krista?"

Joanna shot up and grabbed a napkin for her. "Yes, dear."

"Wow. I missed a lot." Ireland dabbed at her lips. *Well, the phone call makes sense now.* She couldn't wrap her brain around all the changes. *First, we drive by the Taggart farm and Gideon looks like a freaking model, and now Z's engaged to Krista? What next?*

"She's a perfect fit for Zavier," her mother continued.

"They'd be cute together." She thought back to the summer before she left. Sure enough, memories of the two flirting flooded her mind. Feeling a headache creep into the front of her skull, Ireland stood. "You know, I think I'm going to lie down for a while until the festivities."

"Oh, of course. I understand." Joanna hugged her once more. "I'll call you when they're all here."

"Thanks, Mom." While she made her way to the stairs, her mom resumed her role in the kitchen. Ireland stood and watched for a moment. Joanna Leighton was a whiz when it came to baking and cooking. It was a wonder they all didn't roll around the house from eating all the goodies she made.

Seeing her mom so comfortable in the kitchen brought memories to the surface. Joanna consistently made time to teach her daughter about baking, cooking, and even sewing—though that last one didn't stick.

She marched upward, intent on carving out time to spend with her mom. *I could use a mother-daughter afternoon. It's well past due.*

Opening the door to her bedroom of years past, she grinned. Nothing had changed since she left it. Plopping face-first onto the twin-sized bed covered with a quilt, she breathed in the essence of her childhood home. It smelled like lemons, freshly cut grass, and a hint of honey like she remembered. She rolled onto her back and grinned. The stick-on, glow-in-the-dark stars were somehow still on her ceiling.

Glancing to the shelves along the room, trophies met her eyes. She'd bet the farm that they were free of dust too. Joanna was a cleaning guru. *Well, her cleaning lady is.* Though most were for 4H and National Honor Society events, she couldn't believe her mother kept them displayed so proudly, alongside her collection of pony figurines lined up in a small cabinet with a glass door.

She was thankful they hadn't changed her walls. They were covered in maps just as she'd left them. It'd always been her dream to travel the world, and her parents let her take school trips and encouraged her to study abroad. They were nothing but supportive when it came to exploring outside Iowa. Once she learned her parentage, the travel bug made sense. She didn't need any additional incentive to plan trips.

Ireland smiled, recalling the hours upon hours spent poring over the atlases. She mapped out tours of Paris, Florence, and London long before she visited them.

A lump lodged in her throat and she held back tears. She loved the room, but at the same time, she regretted the wanderlust. It'd taken her away from her family and friends. She'd been to almost every place she'd ever dreamed of, but it felt hollow in a way.

She turned her thoughts away from travel and back to Iowa. After seeing Gideon shirtless, bearded, muddy and covered in tattoos, it was a wonder she could speak at all. That was not the same guy from six years ago. The tattoos were a nice surprise. She always did love art on a guy. The added muscles on his torso definitely were new too.

She pursed her lips. *I wonder if he has more ink on other places.* The thought made her shiver, though she couldn't figure out why. She was long over Gideon. *I think.* She'd never really had the chance to get over him, now that she thought about it. Her life had changed so drastically, and it was a whirlwind she was still caught up in.

From the edge of reality, her phone rang. She dug through her Chanel purse and pulled it out.

"Hey, Toby, what's up?"

Her assistant cleared his throat on the other end of the line. "You had a conference call thirty minutes ago."

Looking at the cartoon cat clock above her door, she groaned. "Shit, did you cover for me?"

"Yes, and rescheduled, but your grandmother was off put, to put it lightly."

Ireland unzipped her carry-on bag and pulled out the information on the investment company. She and Fiona chatted weekly about business, and that afternoon just happened to be the never-ending appointment. "Thanks. It must've slipped my mind. Toby, you're the best."

"I know, I know. So, are you going to tell me how Podunk, Iowa, is or what?"

Grinning, she moved the curtain away from the window, but no vibrant greenery met her gaze. From her guess, Iowa was short on rain that year.

"Well, I found out my ex is super hunky now."

"Oh my!"

"And then there's my brother's wedding. Still waiting to find out when the big day is, but I'm guessing soon. He's marrying my college roomie, Krista Kellogg."

Toby gasped. "What? No! Really?"

"Yep." She fluffed the pillow behind her head, instantly missing her pillow in Barbados. *Should've brought it with me.*

"Hmm, well that's all fine and dandy, but I'd rather hear about your muscular neighbor."

She smirked. No doubt her extremely attractive and gay personal assistant was drooling at the thought. "What's there to say? Gideon was covered in delicious tattoos, a beard, and all muddy when we drove by. I almost didn't recognize him."

"Okay, you really should've let me come with you," Toby complained. "I like hotties. Both thermally and otherwise."

Ireland rolled her eyes. "Try to keep it in your pants, Mr. Huong."

"Hey, you're just as dirty, so don't act like a blushing virgin."

She couldn't argue with him there. A steady boyfriend wasn't how she'd spent the last few years. One-night stands were all she could handle with her schedule. Plus, getting attached to someone again wasn't something she was interested in. Her one heartache kept her from moving on.

"If you need anything, I'm just a plane ride away."

Studying the faded carpeting, she sighed. "I might need you. I'm not the best at wedding stuff."

Toby snorted. "I wonder why."

Before she could respond, Joanna called up the stairs. "Ireland, the Taggarts are pulling into the drive."

"All right," she hollered back.

"Is that your mum?"

She stood and rifled through her suitcase. "Yes."

"Make sure you wear something cute. They haven't seen you in years," Joanna yelled next.

Ireland groaned when Toby made cooing sounds over the phone. Her mother was dead set on the Taggarts and Leightons eventually merging. Since she was the only option, they'd been thrilled when she and Gideon dated. Their breakup hurt both families, but the mothers seemed to take it the worst.

"Ugh, she still thinks Gideon and I will get back together."

Toby clucked his tongue. "And is there any chance?"

She quickly sat up as three truck doors closed. "No. We're over."

"Hmm, too bad."

"Plus there's the whole merger set to close—"

"Remind me again why your grandmother's business partner has to go to Iowa to meet your family?"

Picking at her thumbnail, she thought about the man her grandmother introduced her to six months ago. "Because I guess he likes to get to know his partners and their families. I don't know. It's not really a big deal. It's a lot of money at stake, so him wanting to make sure I'm not a crook isn't far-fetched."

"I would pay good money to see your family's reactions to your—ahem—partner. He sure gets my engines revving."

"Ireland!" Joanna said again, louder that time.

Ireland rolled her eyes. "I'll call you later, Tobes."

"Mmhmm, you better."

She hung up and tossed the phone to the bed. Smirking, she hoped Toby would stay out of trouble. He was her travel companion and best friend ever since she met him in the London airport straight off the plane from Iowa. He was smart, quirky, snarky, and kept her sane. His British accent, pristine fashion sense, and business intellect made him the perfect combination of personal assistant and friend. Even her grandmother liked him, and that was saying something.

Changing into a lightweight dress, she checked her reflection. The jet lag was evident around her eyes, but at least her honey brown hair was straightened to perfection despite the humidity.

With one last pat of the long silky tresses, Ireland slid mint lip gloss on and bounded down the stairwell. The alluring smell of pot roast, potatoes, and cooked carrots filled the refurbished farmhouse. She was glad her parents didn't tear it down and build a new house after she paid off their mortgage. There was too much history to destroy it.

Following the sound of voices, she turned toward the formal dining room and simply watched the hubbub from the shadows. Her parents chatted with Frances and Walt Taggart like old chums. Once upon a time, Joanna and Frances hated each other, though that obviously didn't last long since they were bridesmaids in each other's weddings.

Ireland leaned her cheek on the oak doorframe. Zavier tipped back a bottle of beer with Lance Taggart, though she hadn't seen his face yet. The hair so black it had streaks of blue in it was recognizable anywhere. He looked the same, if that was possible. The expensive sedan in the driveway caught her eye. *Always the farm boy wishing he was a stock trader.* The dark-wash jeans and button-down shirt looked good on him. Back in high school, he hadn't been her type—his younger brother by two years took that role and ran with it. *Speaking of, where is he?* She glanced around the room but didn't see him yet. It wouldn't surprise her if he opted out of the shindig. He wasn't big on awkward confrontations when they were together. She smiled at the memories of her time with Gideon. They were all happy, save one.

Stomach growling hungrily, she realized she hadn't eaten all day. Seeing the group perfectly happy talking amongst themselves, she retreated to the kitchen and opened the refrigerator door. A slice of apple pie sat all alone on a plate and she couldn't resist. Her mom made the best and it'd been years since she tasted it. Grabbing a fork from the drawer, she took a giant bite and moaned at the burst of apple and cinnamon.

"I'm glad to see you still like sneaking dessert before dinner," a man's voice teased against the back of her head.

A shiver ran down Ireland's spine at the husky tone. His voice hadn't changed one bit, and it still sent her stomach into a nosedive. She almost didn't want to face him again. From a distance was one thing, but up close and personal was bound to be a disaster.

Turning around, she pressed her back to the counter, pie instantly forgotten. "Gideon."

She silently swore at how breathless she sounded, but how could she not lose her breath when she looked into his electric blue gaze? He'd combed his beard since she saw him shirtless earlier in the day. Her fingers itched to reach up and feel the bristles herself. *He was always clean-cut. I wonder when he started growing it.*

Gideon grinned and looked at her lips. She inadvertently licked them, and a light sparked in his eyes. "You look very nice. Can't say I've seen that outfit on girls around here."

"Thanks." She glanced at the fashion designed by a French artist she'd met two years prior. "It's from Paris."

Taking off his hat that he wore like a second skin, Gideon chuckled and smoothed back his curls before he replaced it. "Hmm, I'm surprised you don't have a fancy new accent after traveling the world for all these years."

"Nah, I have the same boring Midwest accent." Ireland tried to move, but Gideon placed his arms on either side of her and her pulse quickened.

"Good, because I like you," he said, leaning close. His eyes searched hers, and she couldn't move if she wanted to. "Just the way you are."

Ireland inhaled, the act shaky at best. *What the hell is wrong with you?* Gideon's musky scent added to the light woodsy hints of his soap and sent her mind into a spiral. His eyes pinned her feet to the hardwood flooring. This wasn't the same Gideon she fell in love with as a teenager. A man stood before her now, and every fiber of her being urged her to lean forward and see how his beard felt against her lips.

"Ireland, there you are!" Lance said, breaking into their moment. Ireland managed to set down the plate before he pulled her away from his brother and wrapped an arm around her waist, hugging her. "It's great to see you. God, you smell delicious."

Ireland's face heated. She glanced to Gideon in the doorway, then back to Lance. "Um, thanks."

Lance kissed her cheek, his overpowering cologne filling her nostrils. "Man, we've all missed you."

She untangled from his grip to greet his parents. "Me too."

"Ireland, tell us about your businesses. I've read quite a few articles about Bourgeois Investments being the front-runner for the year," Walt Taggart said after greeting her.

"Oh, she doesn't want to talk business," Frances cut in. "Give us the details of what Barbados is like, and all those other fancy places you've been."

Taking a deep breath, Ireland started in on the details of her life. She made sure to leave out the details the paparazzi enjoyed flaunting.

The entire time she spoke, Gideon didn't take his eyes off her. It was unnerving and endearing at the same time as he just stood there, nursing a glass of lemonade. It was obvious he wanted to talk to her alone, but she could never manage to escape without a familial escort.

An hour and too many questions later, Ireland sipped on a bottle of beer and listened to everyone else speak for a change. After a hearty debate about international stocks, her voice was ready for a break. Sure, she loved the business side of her life, but it wasn't something she wanted to constantly discuss. The fact that none of them brought up her charity work unnerved her. While she was more than willing to talk about work, she'd hoped they would've seen through the paparazzi debacles and want to discuss her main passion. They didn't, which was fine for the time being. Part of the draw of charity was being anonymous.

Joanna glanced toward her son. "I think Zavier has an announcement to make."

All eyes swung to the farmer by the front door. Zavier grinned and his eyes met Ireland's. "So a few years ago, my sister came home with a friend for the summer. As most of you already know, she never left."

Ireland's palms started to sweat. She knew the ending already. While she loved Krista, it was bound to be weird to see her on Zavier's arm.

"I've said it once, but I'll say it again because I'm so damned excited." He opened the screen door and pulled in the blonde beauty. "Krista has agreed to marry me." He paused. "Next month."

A chorus of congratulations filled the living room, but Ireland could only manage a smile.

"Surprised?" Gideon asked, somehow beside her.

Glancing up at him, she nodded. "Yeah. I mean, they flirted a ton that summer, but I never thought they'd end up together."

Gideon looked toward the happy couple showing off the engagement ring. "Well, you left before they really started heating up."

The underlying bitterness in his words wasn't lost on her. "I've never seen him like this."

"Funny how shit happens when you aren't looking for it," he said before walking toward the couple.

Her scowl didn't reach Gideon's gaze, and she quickly replaced it with a smile when Krista looked her way, moving forward to join her brother and his fiancée.

"Hey, I really wanted to tell you, but Zavier made me keep it a secret." Krista grabbed Ireland's hands. "Are you upset?"

The focus of the room shifted to her. "No, of course not." She hugged Krista. "I'm very happy for you two. You're perfect for each other."

Zavier beamed down at Krista. "Well, I'm glad you think so, because we have a favor to ask."

"Uh-huh."

"Krista's always dreamed of a destination wedding," Zavier began, his blue eyes looking at her hopefully.

Putting the rest of the pieces together, Ireland chuckled. "Barbados?"

Krista nodded enthusiastically. "It'd be a dream come true. We have all the money, just not the connections."

For a millisecond, Ireland hated her college roommate. Krista had her happily ever after and she didn't. That moment passed rather quickly when Gideon poked her side and brought her back to reality. "Oh, um, yeah. I can get you guys set up at one of the resorts, no problem."

Krista and Zavier sandwiched her in a hug. "Thank you so much!"

Pulling away, she forced a smile. "It's my pleasure. My big brother only gets married once, right?" She eyed the rest of the living room. "And there will be plenty of rooms for family and friends. Let me know how many you need."

Krista's excited squealing sent Ireland racing toward the kitchen. She suddenly needed space. *Married. Z's getting married. To Krista.* She leaned her hands against the sink. The fact that they waited for her arrival to ask a favor suddenly irked her. Zavier wasn't the kind of person to take advantage, but Krista was another story. Then again, it had been six years. She'd changed, and if Zavier was in love with Krista, maybe she wasn't the same girl who used to write IOUs on the grocery list.

"You all right? You look kind of green."

Ireland stared at the duck-shaped bar of soap on the counter. "I'm fine."

Gideon carefully turned her toward him. She avoided his gaze as long as possible, but when he tilted her face up with his fingers, she couldn't resist. "No, you're not." His eyes searched her face. "What's wrong?"

The tenderness in his touch and words brought back memories she'd long buried. It took all her power to keep from falling into his embrace and staying there. It'd be too easy. Instead, she moved out of his grip. "Nothing. I already have Toby working on the wedding details."

Gideon frowned. "Who's Toby?"

Before she could respond, her mother stepped into the kitchen. "Now, Frances and I will do dishes and—"

"Oh no you don't," Walt interrupted, waving at his wife. "Kenny and I will take over the duties for the night."

"So long as there's warm cherry cobbler waiting when

we're done," Kenny teased, coming into the shrinking area.

Using the distraction, Ireland walked out to the front porch. Matching rocking chairs sat to one side, and a wooden swing swayed slowly in the breeze on the other end. If there was ever a time to be alone, it was now.

She sat down, closed her eyes, and inhaled. It smelled like her childhood. A waft from the pigpens came to her next and she scrunched her nose. *Yep, definitely home.*

The screen door squeaked open and the swing rocked slightly as Zavier joined her. "What do you think of everything?" he asked, tickling her side. "A lot to take in, I'm sure."

Flicking open her eyelids, Ireland pushed at his fingers. "I was her roommate, Z. She's great."

He continued to tickle her sides until she squealed. "Thanks, she really is."

Ireland caught her breath. "I never imagined she'd settle down."

"Me either. I guess a farm boy is all it takes." He crossed his ankles and looked at her expectantly.

"Yeah, yeah."

They watched fireflies light up the yard. Chickens clucked in the distance, and a horse whinnied from the barn. It couldn't have been more Iowa unless a combine drove up the road.

"I hope you don't think we're taking advantage of you."

Ireland turned toward him, and all her uneasy thoughts disappeared. "You're my brother. I'd do anything for you." Already, she knew what to get Zavier and Krista for their wedding present. While she'd planned on helping out the newlyweds with the wedding anyway, Ireland wanted to include something they couldn't get without years of saving. She made a mental note to put together a yearly honeymoon trip for the happy couple.

Gideon stepped out on the porch and smiled at them.

"You're the best," Zavier said, then added under his breath, "And so is he."

"What?" She stared at the yard but felt Gideon's gaze on her. After a minute, she looked over at him. "What've you been up to, Gideon?"

Sitting in one of the rocking chairs, he tipped up his cap. It was the same one he had years before. "Just keeping the farm running. Not much to report."

"He got another dog," Lance shared, joining them.

"Oh yeah? What kind?" she asked. Gideon was an animal whisperer. It was why no one balked when he attended undergrad for veterinary sciences. It made sense with his career as a farmer to know everything about his animals. *I wonder if he ever finished.*

"Red merle Aussie," Gideon replied, leaning back in the seat. Gone were the torn jeans of earlier, and Ireland immediately missed the shirtless torso. He had more muscles than she remembered.

Or maybe I chose to forget.

She smiled. "Aw, fun. I'll have to swing by and check him out."

Gideon nodded. "Anytime, darlin'."

Ireland bit her lip at the nickname only he called her. From the looks of it, everyone else outside caught the slip too. It was his pet name for her when they were together. *If awkward could talk....*

Silence simmered around the four, and Ireland used the waning sunlight to her advantage to study the Taggart boys. *Men. Let's be honest here.* Lance fiddled with his cell phone, as dapper as ever. Gideon watched the sun sink over the horizon, a content expression on his bearded face. They were both so different, yet the same.

"So, did Tagg tell you about his—"

Gideon jabbed Lance in the gut with his elbow, silencing the rest of the question.

"About what?" She quirked her brow at the two brothers.

"Okay, kids, dessert's ready," Walt called from inside before anyone could respond.

Zavier stood and pulled Ireland up with him. "Maybe traveling the world didn't make you happy for a reason," he whispered.

"Who said I wasn't—" She stopped when he walked away and left her with Lance and Gideon. Smiling, she pointed to the door. "Yum, cobbler."

She inwardly groaned at how dumb she sounded. *I'm anything but dumb.*

Evidently, when Gideon was around, her brain went the opposite direction.

***

She's spectacular. In his opinion, Ireland had always been gorgeous, but the way that dress hit above her knees and the deep shade of her tan made her exotic in only the best way. Her skin was always a few shades darker than any other girls at their school, but now she was the definition of Amazonian.

His heart pounded like a drum whenever she looked in his direction. It wasn't as often as he'd like, but he'd take what he could get from the brown-eyed beauty. For once, he was thankful his older brother stole her attention; he was enjoying simply being in the same room with her again. Although, if Lance bragged about his luxury car one more time, Gideon was going to blow a gasket. A farmer didn't need a swanky vehicle, but Lance was always about money.

He sipped his coffee with cream, no sugar, and watched his brother make a fool out of himself. Well, in Gideon's opinion, anyway. Though from the looks of it, he wasn't the only one who thought Lance was a cocky ass.

Blowing on the coffee, his gaze met Zavier's. The other man rolled his eyes before he guzzled a bottle of beer. A part of Gideon wanted to join in on the pastime, but he'd sworn not to after wrecking his truck back in college. It was stupid to drive drunk, he knew that now. His one salvation was that no one was injured. If anything had happened, he'd never have been able to forgive himself. Ever since that night, no alcohol of any kind passed his lips.

Ireland giggled at Lance's story. That didn't bother him, but when she full-out laughed and snorted, Gideon felt his jaw tighten. She may have sounded ridiculous snorting like a piglet, but he liked it about her. It meant she was enjoying herself and not pretending.

He gripped the ceramic mug harder. Watching her pat

Lance's arm and laugh was his own personal form of hell. He never truly had a chance at a life with the smartest and prettiest girl in school. He was biased, but she got a full ride on her wits. *Not that her parents couldn't afford the tuition.*

"What's up with Lance tonight? He's extra douchey." Zavier moved to the spot beside Gideon.

The clock struck ten at night. "No clue. My guess is he came to see if somebody was interested." He nodded at Ireland, whose eyes eluded him yet again. It was as if she was purposefully ignoring him.

"Aw, come on. She'd never fall for him." Zavier took a pull of beer. "Plus, I think being away changed her."

"Let's hope not too much," Gideon muttered. His pulse quickened when Lance leaned over and kissed Ireland's cheek. "Motherfucker."

The look on her face reminded Gideon of the first time she caught a fish: uncertainty and terror. She politely smiled but didn't encourage Lance's affections. *Thank God.*

"So, should we believe all the gossip about you or what?" Lance asked, loud enough for everyone on the front porch to hear. That took balls. Big, brass, idiotic balls for his brother to ask such a boldfaced question. No one spoke about her party girl photos or the tabloids. From what he could tell, she was done with all that. Evidently, his brother was wondering for selfish reasons; Lance had always partied hard, and that hadn't changed with age.

Ireland floundered for words, opening those pretty rose-colored lips and then clamping them shut. Her gaze met his, and Gideon was certain he'd break the mug from gripping it so tight. The hesitation in her eyes gave him pause from spilling the coffee on the floor.

Finally, she spoke. "You know, I'd rather not talk about that stuff. I went through a phase and it's over now."

"Aw, why not? Was it true?" Lance whined.

She stood and twisted her diamond stud earrings. Real, if he had to guess. Another habit of hers that Gideon loved to watch. "The paps tend to exaggerate, and I've grown out of my past."

Leaving the bowl of her dessert uneaten on the coffee table, her footfalls echoed through the house, then through the back door.

It was right about then that Gideon craved a stiff drink. She'd matured, that much she'd proved then and there. A part of him still wanted to know more about her "wild side," as the press dubbed it. She'd never done much in high school party wise, so when her face popped up with headings about drugs and booze, he hadn't believed them.

Maybe some were true.

Zavier cleared his throat. "Well, that's not going to be weird for years to come." He patted Gideon's back. "But hey, at least Ireland's not into him."

Gideon ignored the slighted remark. He needed to get out of the house, now. As much as he wanted to ignore Ireland's direction, he couldn't. His brother tended to screw shit up, and he had to clean up the messes. This one in particular wasn't one he minded in the least.

Sneaking out the back door, he breathed in the humid summer night. He glanced around but didn't see her anywhere. Following his instincts, he walked toward the horse barns. She always had a soft spot for the equestrian arts.

Rounding the house, he sighed when he saw the side door of the barn cracked open. He stepped over the threshold and listened to the whinny of horses.

"Ireland, are you in here?"

"No."

He smirked and followed the smell of her vanilla perfume, leading him straight to the loft full of hay. Climbing the ladder, he paused at the last rung and took in her fashionable clothes that definitely didn't belong in the barn.

"What's going on, princess?" he teased.

Her eyes whipped to him. "Please don't."

Gideon took a seat next to her and pulled a piece of hay from her hair. "Aw, I'm sorry. I didn't realize teasing was forbidden these days."

"Sorry. It's not." She pushed back her hair and rolled her eyes. "Guess I should've seen Lance's question coming, huh?

"Hmm, I don't know." He folded his arms over his chest. "But we're all pretty curious about what you've been doing. I mean, you find out your birth family is loaded and left you money. The next thing we know, you've jetted off to Europe and God knows where." He paused. That last bit hurt more to say it out loud. "We can ignore the tabloids, but only for so long. You need to give us something."

"Ugh, I probably sound like some spoiled brat." She chuckled when he shrugged. "Nothing new there, right?"

"Hey, you're not a brat. But you always were spoiled." Gideon's stomach jolted when she tucked her hands in her lap. She looked so proper and poised. He immediately wondered if her biological grandmother sent her off to some etiquette school, because she was the epitome of a lady. "Any explanation you can give would be great. If not to me, then your parents and Z. Your departure hurt them the most."

"You're right. It's difficult, as I'm sure you know." Pulling the hem of her dress over her knees, Ireland took a deep breath. "I grew up thinking my biological parents didn't love me. One day I find out they loved me so much they left me millions. Honestly, I don't believe it some days. I want to make them proud. It's probably stupid, but I hunted down any person who may have known them back then." She smiled sadly. "I didn't find what I wanted. In the end, I made a few friends along the way and that's just as good, right?"

"I guarantee they're proud of you." He reached out to touch her hair, then pulled back. He wasn't her boyfriend anymore; he needed to be careful around her or his feelings would resurface. He suddenly remembered seeing an article about an anonymous donor from France give money to aid the homeless shelters along the beaches in the Caribbean. Without a doubt, Ireland was the reason behind the decline in homelessness.

She smiled up at him. "Thanks." Her small heeled shoes slid beneath her dress. "Do you think I'm crazy for ignoring Lance's questions?"

"I think you'd be crazy if you answered him. It's your business to share when you want." He laughed when her brows rose. "He's my brother and I love him, but he's kind of crazy."

"I don't know. He's such a dreamboat," she joked.

"Yeah, maybe, but he's not the guy for you."

Ireland tilted her head to the left. "Oh yeah?"

"Yeah."

"How do you know?"

Gideon bit back the reply he so badly wanted to say. Instead, he went with the safer option. "I just know."

She nodded and grabbed a handful of hay. Tossing it at him, she laughed. "You and your sixth sense."

Ignoring the way the hay stuck to his beard, Gideon smirked. "It works for animals so well that I had to extend it to humans."

Ireland wiped her hands on her dress. "I should probably get back before our moms start looking for us."

Standing, Gideon helped her up. He wanted to say more, but it wasn't the time.

Walking to the ladder, she turned around. "Hey, have you ever been to Barbados?"

"Do I look like someone who's been to Barbados?"

Ireland started down the ladder. "Good point. I guess you'll get your chance for Z's wedding." She eyed him from head to toe. "You'd look good on a beach. See you around."

He waited until she was securely on the barn floor before following her. If he caught up, he'd have no control over his actions. All he wanted to do was crush his lips to hers and whisper that he didn't give a shit about some stupid money she inherited or gossip blogs. She was the only thing he cared about.

Damn, I guess I never stopped loving her.

CHAPTER THREE

Ireland spent most of the next day in the house with her mom baking all sorts of goodies, and she was glad they had time together, just the two of them. Their bond was so special, and she'd put it on the back burner for reasons that now seemed juvenile. Once they finished baking, she managed to catch up on her emails, reports, and even made a few international phone calls. After chatting with Toby, he'd promised to pick up the slack for the wedding preparations. She'd need to fly back to Barbados later in the week to iron out last-minute details with a nearby island orphanage, but then would return to Iowa for more time with the family.

Ireland helped her mom ice cinnamon rolls before she snuck out of the house. Her clothes smelled like nutmeg, but she didn't care to change. It reminded her of her childhood. *Just like everything else here.*

The bright sun warmed her within seconds. She caught

up with Zavier long enough to hear him say the Taggarts were in town. Breathing in the late July weather, Ireland set her gaze to the main barn. She was in dire need of cuddly kittens and whimpering puppies. In high school, there wasn't a week that went by without her stopping at her local animal shelter to volunteer. Most of the time, she cleaned cages and walked the dogs, but every now and then she tried to sneak in playing with the puppies and kittens.

Ireland smiled at the clowder nearby. One of the first things she'd done with her inheritance was anonymously donate money to help rebuild the decrepit shelter. *I should stop by and see the place.* Her mother had mentioned the reopening two years back, and Ireland couldn't wait to see how they used the money. If she had her way, she'd give all her money to needy animals and humans. The trustee to her bank account didn't see things her way, though, so she helped when and where she could.

Opening the side door, she waved at two of the hired hands who worked the farm, then steered toward the back of the barn. She'd long ago dubbed the area the "baby pens." It was the warmest part of the big red structure, which made it ideal for livestock who weren't ready for the outside world yet.

Poking her head in the first stall, she grinned at the mass of kittens meowing. Careful not to let them escape, Ireland closed the stall door and settled into the yellow straw. The mother cats purred and jumped on her lap while the kittens followed suit. Soon enough, she was covered from head to toe in a blanket of cats.

"Probably not the best day to wear shorts," she laughed at the constant kneading of claws.

"But I bet they look good on you," Gideon said from the door.

Ireland whipped her head up and locked gazes with him. Those sky-blue eyes were quickly becoming her favorite part of being in Iowa. "Oh, hey. I didn't know you were here."

He rested his forearms on the door. "Your dad asked me to check in on the baby calf." He jutted a thumb over his shoulder. "He was a little underweight."

Ireland nuzzled her nose to a mama cat's. "And how's your patient?"

"On the mend. Should be prancing around within the week."

"Good to hear," she said, petting a calico kitten.

Gideon's cap wasn't in place, a rarity. He never went without it for very long. Watching him now, Ireland had to admit the slightly longer dark blond waves looked good despite the effects of the hat. He scratched at his full beard that hung a good three inches off his chin. Beards were never a huge attraction to her, but the way Gideon wore it made all others fade away.

His eyes slowly slid over her body, and her stomach flipped when she remembered him doing exactly that years ago in a more intimate setting. A slow smile crept over his features and sealed her fate. There was something in his gorgeous depths that she couldn't resist.

"You never said how long you'd be here."

Ireland's hand paused above a black kitten's fur. "That's because I'll be coming and going." He didn't bat an eyelash, so she continued, "I have several business meetings before Zavier's wedding that I can't miss."

Gideon plucked a stray bit of straw from his hair and nodded. "Ah, sure."

Carefully, Ireland unloaded the cats from her lap and stood. She brushed off the fur from her purple tank top and escaped the meowing stall. "You're going to go, aren't you?"

He took a step backward and grabbed his small black bag. "Yeah, I better. The best man can't miss the wedding."

Moving to the next stall, Ireland smiled at the newborn chocolate labs. "Oh, then yes, you better make it."

Gideon's steps drew closer and shuffled the dirt. He stood directly behind her, his breath hitting her bare shoulders. "Can I bring a date?"

Whirling around, she tried to keep her jealousy harnessed. She didn't get jealous. Not when it came to guys she wasn't with. At the teasing grin on his face, she realized her failure. "I think that's up to the bride and groom."

"Hmm, I'll check with them, then."

Studying his beard at eye level, she smirked. He'd always been taller than her, a fact she dismissed when they were younger. After spending time around mostly short men while abroad, it was nice to come back to a country-raised guy over her six-foot stature.

Her eyes dipped to his clothes. *Dirty jeans and all.*

She reached out and flicked a speck of dust from his

shoulder. It wasn't noticeable, but she needed to touch him. The solid muscle didn't disappoint. *Gideon has a body that just won't quit. Damn, was he always like this?* She could only imagine what the rest of him looked like. A shot of desire traveled up her spine the longer she maintained his blue gaze.

His eyes briefly dipped to her lips before he spoke.

"I need to head back."

"Right, of course." She stuffed her hands in the back pockets of her jean shorts. "Do you need any help?" she asked as he reached the barn door.

Gideon turned on his heels and shrugged. With the sun behind him, his face was all but obscured save those blue eyes. "I'm doing coops next. You sure you want to get chicken feathers all over you?"

Not bothering to wave at the slumbering pups, Ireland skipped over to him and snagged a hat from one of the wooden pegs. Pulling her hair into a ponytail and then through the back, she nodded. "If I spend one more hour listening to my mom talk about wedding preparations, I'll lose my mind." She smiled. "I'm all yours."

"I wish," he mumbled. Before Ireland could question him, he added, "Let's get a move on. The hens wait for no man or woman." He practically ran toward his truck, tossing his bag in the bed.

Ireland followed at a slower pace, wondering if Gideon was serious about his wish or merely joking. Either way, she wanted to spend more than just the day with the tattooed farmer to find out more. She'd missed him, and they were friends once upon a time.

She caught her bottom lip between her teeth when he bent over to retrieve his keys. *Yeah, totally just friends.*

***

They were halfway to his farm when another car threw dust around the dirt road.

"Wait, that's Krista," Ireland said, placing a hand on his thigh. "I need to go over some wedding details with her."

Gideon pressed on the brake and rolled down his window. The other car did the same. Before he could speak, Ireland climbed over him and popped her head out his window.

"Hey!" The excitement in her voice wasn't lost on him. And neither was the ponytail in his face.

"Hey, what's up?" Krista honked her horn for effect.

"I spoke with Toby this morning, and we have a wedding planner down in Barbados," Ireland began. "There are a few time-sensitive things for the preparations. Do you have a few minutes for a video chat?"

"Yeah, you bet."

"Great." Ireland cleared her throat and looked down at him. Her face turned red, as if she'd just realized their position. "Why don't you take me back to my house and we can talk," she suggested, moving off him.

Gideon immediately missed her warm vanilla scent. "I can turn around," he offered.

The two women exchanged glances. Opening the door, Ireland hopped down. "Thanks, but we really need to get this done." She shut the door and smiled. "Why don't we do something tomorrow?"

"Such as?" He flipped off the radio, already annoyed at losing her to another person. *Just my luck.*

"Well, it's been a while since I was on a farm. I could use a refresher course."

"Oh yeah, that sounds fun," Krista interrupted. "I bet Zavier would like me being around too. We can meet up."

Gideon thought it over, even though he already had his answer. Like he'd ever turn down a chance to be around the beautiful woman currently hanging on the window. "All right. I'm up at six in the morning."

"Whoa, cowboy," Ireland cut in. "I like to sleep in."

"Okay, how about ten?"

"We can work with that," Ireland answered for both of them.

Gideon nodded once, then waited until Ireland climbed into Krista's Honda before letting his foot off the brake. The other car rumbled down the road, but he simply coasted. It was what he did best when it came to Ireland.

A problem he aimed to correct if given a real chance.

***

Typing the last details for the ceremony, Ireland looked up from the keyboard. Krista lounged on the love seat, flipping through bridal magazines. With perfect blonde hair, a shimmering disposition, and rose-tinted glasses about marriage, Krista was a cookie-cutter bride.

For a moment, Ireland just sat and stared. *I wonder if I would've been like that with Gideon.* She shook her head away from those thoughts. *Too far gone for such nonsense.*

"Do you have a gown in mind?" she asked, sending an email to Toby.

Krista sat up quickly and scrambled over to Ireland on the couch. She thrust a thick magazine in Ireland's face. "Yes. Since it's a beach wedding, I was thinking a lighter material. Maybe strapless."

Ireland reviewed the tabbed pages. They were pretty, but not her style. "These are great."

"They are, but I don't think I can get one in time." Krista's face fell. "A few weeks is kind of fast for designer gowns, not to mention alterations."

Remembering a trip to New York City the year before, Ireland grabbed her phone. She found the designer's phone number and sent him a text message. "Well, what if I could get a similar one from a new designer in New York?"

Krista's blue eyes widened. "You think you can? In a few weeks?"

Ireland's phone dinged with a response. *He's in.* She held her phone up. "Yep. We'll go to town to get your measurements, then send them over to Marco. He'll do the adjustments, and then we'll fly out to try it on."

"Oh my God!" Krista hugged her tight. "Thank you so much. You're seriously the best almost sister-in-law ever."

Ireland giggled at the other woman's animated response. Krista truly was an ideal fit for Zavier's quiet nature.

"What's all this ruckus?" Zavier asked, coming down

the stairs and into the living room.

Krista spun around on the couch. "Your sister is hooking me up with a New York dress designer." She leapt into his arms and kissed him.

Once he took a breath, Zavier glanced at Ireland. "Really?" She nodded. "Thanks, sis. You don't know how much this means."

Ireland smirked at the lively blonde. "I think I do." She gathered her laptop. "I'll see you tomorrow."

Neither one heard, but she didn't mind, escaping before they started making out. Ireland's stomach lurched at their connection. What they had was real and raw. It was what she wanted in her own life.

She climbed the stairs and shut the bedroom door, knowing she couldn't have that. *Not unless I have a fairy godmother.*

Grabbing her phone, she dialed Toby, waiting anxiously for him to answer. He was her voice of reason whenever she needed one. And she needed him right then.

"Hello, gorgeous."

"Hey, handsome." She sank into the bed she once thought comfortable. "Did you get my email?"

"Don't I always?" His voice tapered off as if he was reading it for the first time then and there.

"Think we can pull it off?"

He chuckled. "Most assuredly, sweet cheeks. Now, tell me about your day."

"I'd rather discuss my grandmother."

"Speaking of," Toby started, "Mason came by the office

today. Apparently, he wants to chat about a few things."

Ireland thought back to her visit with Mason a month before. "Um, yeah. His attorneys sent over the initial merger agreement. I haven't had a chance to review it yet. Guess he and I will be business partners before the end of the summer. Well, if everything goes as planned."

Toby purred seductively. "And a sexy partner at that. I just wish he was up my alley, if you know what I—"

"Seriously, Tobes?"

"What? He's uber hot. I looked him up today. Other than a few model girlfriends, he's been out of the dating game."

She grabbed her pajamas. "So?"

"So the word on the street is that Mr. Hottie with a smokin' body is looking for a special lady to help him spend all that cash. As in wifey material."

"Mmhmm, and you think I'm that lady?" She changed quickly into her pajamas.

"Well, he did stop by the office. If a hunk like that came after me, I wouldn't leave him waiting."

Ireland paced. "I should tell you something."

Toby chuckled. "I knew it! He's into you, isn't he?"

"Well...." She paused. Toby was a drama fiend, and she was more than willing to make him wait for the reprieve. "It's not exactly how it sounds."

"Pray tell, explain."

"You already know about the merger that would make us a ton of money."

Snoring sounds came across the line. "Boring."

"Hold on, I'm getting to the good stuff." She let out a

breath. "My grandmother suggested we be more than just business partners."

"Dear Lord, I think I'm going to faint."

Ireland plopped into the bed. "You're much too dramatic, you know that, right?"

"Princess, if the tables were reversed, you'd already have my plate set ordered."

"True." She rolled over and stared at the ceiling. "Mason and I discussed it, but we both want to see how our partnership goes first and foremost."

"Hmm, I can't hate him for that, now can I?"

"Nope. Neither of us thought about it until my grandmother mentioned it."

"No! Please no. You're both too beautiful not to like each other."

She winced at the higher pitch of Toby's voice. "Okay, yes, he's good-looking, successful, and probably the best guy I've met in years, but I don't have any feelings for him."

"Grow some. I'll help you."

Ireland let out a loud breath. "It doesn't happen like that."

"I'm going to weep on my pillow tonight."

Snorting, she could picture his pouty face even then. It'd perfectly match his dramatic flair. "You're supposed to be my best friend. You know, the person who doesn't want me to marry someone I don't love."

"It's all so *Princess Diaries 2* meets *The Proposal*. You know, you agree to your relationship just being business then end up falling madly in love." He sighed whimsically.

"Other than those being movie references, that never happens in real life, Toby." She smoothed the quilt. "Love doesn't just fall in your lap."

"Hey, a guy can dream, can't he? Like tonight, I'll be having delicious dreams of what I'd do if both Mason Straight and your yummy Gideon Taggart suddenly switched sides and couldn't resist me."

Ireland groaned. "Eww, Tobes. We talked about this. I don't want to hear your orgy dreams anymore."

"All right, fine. But admit it made you smile."

She couldn't argue with him there. "You win." He giggled. "I'll be back in Barbados soon enough. We'll talk about Mason and all that later."

"Fine," Toby whined. "But I get to be the maid of honor."

Yawning, she grinned. "Yeah, yeah. Talk to you later."

After hanging up, she climbed under the covers. The last thing she wanted to think about was love and relationships. Unfortunately for her, all the dreams she had that night included both.

CHAPTER FOUR

The next morning, Gideon was disappointed when Ireland didn't greet him at the agreed time. He checked his phone, then shrugged at the lack of messages. Waiting around for a woman wasn't something he did anymore. He'd done it once for Ireland and it didn't go as planned. She'd have to search him out if she wanted to see him. A farm didn't work itself, and he was burning daylight the longer he stood and stared at Ireland's closed window.

Zavier and Krista eventually met up with him, but neither tried to explain the younger Leighton's absence. Ireland was her own woman. If she didn't want to spend time with him, he'd get over it. *Just like I got over her leaving.*

Afternoon turned into evening, and Gideon's resolve slowly ate away at him and his sour mood worsened over the day. His Aussies chased each other around the yard, their daily duties completed hours ago. The familiar bell tolled on the Taggart front porch. Craning his neck, he spied his mother clanging it obnoxiously. While he was grateful that dinner was done, his headache doubled at the sound.

This year's crops aren't looking the best. Blaming the Iowa weather would do no good, but the fields were in dire need of rain. He could only afford to run the sprinkler lines for a few hours, thus leaving part of the crop thirsty each day.

Kicking a rock down the dirt road, he spat a line of curses. The bank wouldn't be much help. His credit was maxed out. By the end of the summer, the farm would be entirely the Taggart sons' responsibility. His pops hinted at moving somewhere warm for the winter months, but it didn't become real until they bought a condo in Florida three months ago. The farm was in a family trust, and the deed was in his and Lance's names alone. It was as terrifying as it was exciting.

The time to branch out with his vet clinic still seemed too far off. Gideon wasn't sure if Lance could run the place without him, and he wasn't about to let his brother ruin the family legacy.

He bounded up the front steps and swung open the door. Diesel and Dallas ran to the kitchen, their noisy drinking soon following. His parents were never keen on inside dogs, but they made the exception for his Aussies.

"How'd it go, son?" Walt asked.

Gideon took off his hat and wiped his forehead with his arm. "Animals are on pace. The crops not so much."

His dad set down his glass of iced tea. "The rain will

come," he encouraged.

"Let's hope so." Gideon washed up, then returned to the dining area. A freshly made lasagna sat alongside homemade bread and green beans in the middle of the table. "You made my favorite." He gave his mom a suspicious look. "Why?" Though not unusual, Frances Taggart saved certain meals for special occasions or visitors. A Wednesday in July was neither.

It was then that Gideon noticed only two place settings. Rolling his eyes, he grumbled, "Mom, what did you do?"

"Well, I heard a beautiful lady had an emergency meeting this morning," Frances said with a shy smile.

Gideon held his breath until both parents left the room. It was just like his mom to try to make things right.

He stared at the table, the tasty food beckoning him to sit. He slathered butter on a piece of warm bread. *At least she cooks while she meddles.* It was Frances's best and worst attribute. She'd get too involved in her sons' lives, then cook them something divine to soften the blow. *Well, it isn't going to work this time. I'll eat and then disappear before Ireland arrives.*

Just as he dished lasagna onto his plate, the front door screeched open with a new arrival.

"Hello, Mrs. Taggart, I'm here. Did I miss Gideon?" Ireland's sweet voice called.

Dammit. The sound made his body react more than he liked. It was music to his ears, and deadly if he didn't rein himself in.

After her footsteps echoed in the kitchen, Ireland came

into the room, her hair up in a messy bun with wisps hanging around her neck. It was one of his favorite hairstyles on her. "Hey, you're here."

Gideon hunched over the plate, etiquette be damned. "For now." He shoveled the hot lasagna in his mouth, instantly regretting the act when his tongue screamed at the burning sensation. He reached for the fresh milk, but the pain barely lessened when she came back into view.

"Look, I'm sorry I bailed on you," Ireland began, sitting across from him. "I forgot about the board meeting with my advisors, and Toby needed my approval for a new building."

"Never stopped you before," he said, scooping green beans on his plate. "You'd wake up with the birds in high school."

"When I lived out here, yeah," she shot back with more sass than he expected. "I didn't have a choice." She grabbed the spatula and dug into the main course. "It's been a few years, Tagg. I like my sleep these days."

His cheek twitched at the use of his nickname. She never called him that. Her brother, sure, but not Ireland.

He met her eyes that reminded him of ground cinnamon. She wasn't one to back down when confronted, a fact that both grated and soothed his nerves. "Then maybe I'll drive the tractor by your window every morning until you get back into the routine." He'd meant it to be a joke, but his tone came off rough. Much too rough.

"You wouldn't do that," Ireland said, grabbing a slice of bread.

"Oh, but I would." He held up his glass in salute, then

took a drink.

Gideon quickly finished off his plate, not wanting to give Ireland a chance to talk him out of being mad at her. She'd done it too many times during their relationship. But things were different now. He wouldn't buckle. *Not again.*

After wiping his mouth with a napkin, he stood and pushed in his chair. "Wish I could chat, but I need to do my nightly rounds." He snagged his cap and pulled it on tight. Shuffling of chairs reached his ears, and Ireland rushed after him just as he made it to the door.

"Gideon, wait. I made a pie." She looked up at him hopefully. She was only a few inches shorter than him, and he'd always loved it. Too many girls were a foot or more shorter than him. It wasn't what he craved in a woman. *It definitely made kissing much better.*

"It's your favorite," she added, searching his face. "Peach."

He smirked. "That's your favorite."

A mischievous grin covered her lips. "Right, I thought it sounded familiar. Maybe I'll make yours next time."

Gideon wanted to press his mouth against hers until that damn sassy grin dissolved into something much more sensual. His cock twitched at the thought, but he refrained. Somehow. "There won't be a next time," he said, then pushed at the screen door.

Ireland huffed but followed him nonetheless. She didn't like not getting her way. *Well tough.* He wasn't about to let her off that easy, even if she baked the right pie.

"Please, I'm sorry I screwed it all up. I'm just not used

to—"

"Make it up to me," he suggested, interrupting her. Though she looked awfully cute apologizing, her brows scrunched together and her fingers threaded through her belt loops.

"How?"

Her vanilla scent caught flight on the wind and tickled his nose. "Four-wheeling."

Ireland's face lit up and she slowly nodded. "I think I can manage that."

He whistled, and both Aussies hopped off the front porch and into the back of the truck. "Perfect. I have to run some errands in the morning. You can get all your business shit out of the way so you don't stand me up again." She blushed, but he wasn't done. "Pick you up at four in the afternoon." Climbing into the truck, he added, "And don't forget, you owe me a pie."

Ireland stood on the truck runner and poked her head inside the cab. "You won't let that go, will you?"

Gideon shook his head. "Nah, you know I don't let things I love go easily." He swallowed hard at the two ways his words could've gone. Judging from the look on her face, Ireland took it the way he meant, but didn't want her to.

She chuckled nervously and backed away. "Yeah, sure. You and your food. I forgot how much you loved it."

He put the truck into Reverse. "You have no idea," he said before cranking up a Blake Shelton song on the radio. He didn't want her to know how much he still cared for her. She wasn't ready.

She'll never be ready.

***

The next afternoon, true to his word, Gideon picked Ireland up right on time. Once they drove into the country a little farther, he parked the blue truck on the edge of an empty field.

"Is this the Kissinger place?" Ireland asked.

Gideon grabbed a pair of shades out of his pocket. "Yep. Well, it was. We bought it before planting season." He slid the sunglasses over his eyes, and Ireland immediately missed the mesmerizing blue shade. "It has access to the pond and decent hunting woods. I figured it'll come in handy, and the price was low enough." He scanned the barren land. "I kind of felt bad for Kissinger. With his health deteriorating, it made maintaining all these plots impossible."

Ireland nodded. Her dad told her about the old farmer's health issues that morning at breakfast. She'd assumed her family would buy Kissinger out, but since Gideon already had one piece of land, she doubted her dad would get in the way if he wanted the rest.

Gideon brought out the last set of keys and protective wear. "I assume I don't need to worry about you?"

"No, I'll be fine. Thanks." Ireland's fingers grazed his when the keys exchanged hands. A shock of electricity shot through her body. Iowa needed rain severely if she was letting off static.

He stepped closer. *Then again, maybe it isn't mere static*

between us.

"Great, let's go. You'll be eating my dust." He walked over to his machine and straddled it. The act shouldn't have been sexy, but the tight way his jeans stretched over his ass made her comment disappear. Gideon Taggart was so much hotter than all the men she'd met across the globe.

No, bad Ireland. You broke up for a reason. Let it go.

Gideon revved the throttle, then let it loose, indeed leaving her in his wake.

"Hell no," Ireland said, following him. She brought up the rear, but once the manmade path vanished, so did the neat row of four-wheelers. The bright sun overhead combined with the whipping wind sent her back to all her summers in Iowa. This activity in particular was one of her favorites.

Birds floated high in the sky while rabbits darted out of their way. She could do this for hours, and in fact, they did. Not even the darkening sky above could dampen Ireland's happy demeanor. She didn't think anything could until her four-wheeler got stuck in a rut.

Waving both hands, she got Gideon's attention. He quickly turned around and rolled over to her. "You all right?" he asked, cutting the engine.

Watching him climb off the machine was just as entertaining as the mount. His long legs strode over to her.

"Yeah, but I think I'm stuck," she finished lamely.

Of course he knows you're stuck. You aren't moving.

Ireland crawled off while Gideon inspected the damage. She cursed herself for not watching the terrain. It'd been a few years since she'd been out in the fields, but surely all her fine dining hadn't changed her country roots.

Gideon hunkered down in front of the stalled vehicle and poked around. After a minute, he stood and wiped his hands on his pants. A shimmer of grease only made him appear more rugged. It also caused Ireland's heart to speed up. *He didn't look like this when we were younger.* His eyes met hers and her knees knocked together. *Or did I take him for granted?*

"Front axle is jacked up." He scratched his chin and smirked. "You always had a knack for breaking things."

"Can you fix it?"

"Yeah, for sure, but my winch is on the four-wheeler in my shop." He lifted his head to the clouds. "We don't have enough time to go back and get it either. Hope you're ready for a bit of a shower." A rumble of thunder followed by a streak of lightning reinforced his words.

"We should head home," he suggested.

"Am I walking back?"

Gideon retrieved Ireland's helmet. "You know I'd never leave you."

"Are you driving or me?" she asked, reaching his four-wheeler.

Gideon didn't bother to reply, simply grabbed her by the hips and placed her on the seat. His weight shifted the machine when he climbed in front of her. "You know I like to be in control. Plus I don't want to end up in a ditch."

He cranked the throttle, drowning out her fake gasp of horror. Rain pelted her bare arms, and she was grateful for the helmets. Growing up, they didn't wear any protective coverings, but after Lance spilled out on his dirt bike and spent a week in the hospital, both families changed their tune about safety.

Ireland was glad her four-wheeler broke if it meant she had a moment with Gideon. Despite all they'd gone through over the years, she was drawn to him unlike any other man. It'd always been that way. One thing was certain, Gideon made moving on nearly impossible.

But I have to, don't I? He doesn't want a life abroad.

She didn't want to think about the possibility of another man. Not with him pressed against her.

She peeked over his shoulder. He gripped the handles tightly, easily maneuvering the machine. It was hard to keep her gaze on the path ahead when he was much more tantalizing. Gideon's long fingers held remnants of dirt and displayed years of manual labor. She'd never thought hands could be attractive, but his were. Her eyes slid up his arms, then dipped to his jean-clad legs. From where she sat, everything about Gideon was attractive.

They went over a bump and she tightened her hold around his waist. Even that was solid muscle.

He reached back and patted her thigh. "Don't go falling on your head," he teased. "I'd never forgive myself if anything happened to you."

His warm words sent a spark directly to her gut. "Right," she replied sarcastically. The roar of the storm thundered around them, but she still heard him chuckle.

Gideon snuck a glance behind him. "Sassy as ever. You

didn't change much after all. Good."

Ireland leaned forward to look at his face but couldn't get a word in before sheets of rain fell. They reached the truck and ran through the rain to pile inside the cab.

He cranked on the air as water pelted the windshield. The wiper blades sloshed back and forth while Gideon hummed along to the country song on the radio. Ireland glanced at him, but he didn't look her way again until they pulled into her parents' driveway.

"All right, get inside and warm up before you catch some nasty cold." He unlocked the doors for good measure.

Ireland looked at the house, then back to Gideon. "I'll help you bring the four-wheeler back," she said, not asking.

"Uh, no. It's raining cats and dogs and—"

"And it'll go twice as fast if you have help," she finished, making herself comfortable in the seat.

"Still stubborn, aren't you?" She raised her chin defiantly, and Gideon narrowed his eyes. "All right, fine."

After they picked up the winch from the Taggart farm, the two returned to the plot of farmland. They didn't exchange any words, a fact that perturbed Ireland more than she'd admit. He was never very talkative, but they could always keep a conversation going.

Guess some things do change.

"You're sure about this?" he asked for the second time as they reached the stuck four-wheeler. The next set of events would be messy and wet. *Doesn't sound so bad with Gideon involved.* She bit her tongue to deter any further thoughts down that rabbit hole.

Ireland snatched the hooded sweatshirt from the back seat and pulled it on. It smelled like Gideon, and she couldn't help but inhale deeply, memories flooding her mind at the simple act.

Eventually, the rain outside pulled her out of her Gideon stupor and she flipped the hood over her hair. "I may have millions in the bank, but rain won't melt me." When he didn't budge, she added, "Move your ass, Taggart."

"Okay, you asked for it." He handed her the keys. "You hop on and I'll hook it up to my truck."

They rushed out of the cab's safety. Mud instantly stuck to Ireland's boots, but she trudged through until she reached the abandoned machine. Gideon made quick work of the winch and patted the hood.

"All right, when I give you the thumbs-up, floor it," he hollered from the driver seat.

Ireland started the four-wheeler and waited for her cue. Ironically, she felt completely content, mud-caked and all. Whether it was with Gideon or simply being back in Iowa, she couldn't pin it down to one thing. She'd stayed away too long. *Especially when Gideon looks like a freaking lumberjack model.* She tried to stop her line of thought before it got away from her. Fantasizing about him wouldn't do her any good.

Gideon held up his thumb and she cranked her wrist backward. Mud splattered from the tires, slapping up and landing on her. She laughed at how horrible she must look.

The four-wheeler slowly wiggled free of the rut, a low groan emitting from the front end. Once it was on level ground, Gideon stopped and ran toward her.

"You good?"

Ireland wiped her hands on the front of the sweatshirt, though it didn't help much since that was coated in mud too. "Hell yeah." She grinned. "This reminds me of when we used to go mudding."

Gideon pulled the ramps from the bed of the truck and lined them up on the ground. "Those were some good times." She shivered at the steamy memories, and he paused as if he was also thinking of what they used to do after their adrenaline-pumped high. He coughed, then nodded to the newly rescued vehicle. "I'll drive it up the ramp if you guide me."

It didn't take long to get the four-wheeler into the truck bed. Silently, they strapped it down and then jumped back into the truck. They worked well as a team. Something she'd taken for granted years ago.

"Thanks for your help." He turned on the defroster and rubbed his hands together. "I like this look on you," he said, surveying the muddy damage. "Less preppy millionaire heir, more country girl having a good time."

Pushing back a bit of hair that strayed from her ponytail, Ireland eyed her clothes. "I look like I fell in a mud puddle and wrestled a pig."

Gideon leaned over and wiped off a smudge on her face with his thumb. "I still say you're beautiful."

Ireland's cheeks flushed and she laughed nervously. "Yeah, okay."

"I'm serious, Ireland." He tipped up her chin with his

index finger. His starry blue eyes clashed with hers at the same time a clap of thunder resounded above them. "You are the most beautiful person I've ever met."

She rolled her eyes. "You've never been outside the USA, Gideon. You can't honestly think—"

Gideon's lips covered hers, silencing the rest of her rambling. A million fireflies might as well have burned her stomach from the reaction her body demanded. The earthy scent of rain and dirt mingled together on his soft yet determined lips. Her eyes slid shut automatically, senses on high alert. She expected his beard to scratch her face, but it merely enhanced the possessive kiss.

Gideon drew back until a breath was the only thing between them. His heavy lids opened and his blue gaze glued her to the seat. "I don't need to go anywhere to know how gorgeous you are."

He traced her bottom lip with his thumb, and all Ireland wanted to do was dart her tongue out and taste him again. She was rapidly losing all self-control around him. If she had her way, they'd stay right there in the middle of the field and repeat that kiss until it stopped raining.

"C'mon, your ma will think I kidnapped you." He slid back to the steering wheel and the truck lurched forward a second later.

Ireland sat back in silence, worrying her lips together. The same lips he possessed better than any other man.

It doesn't make sense.

She watched him adjust his ball cap, not once looking at her. Crossing her legs, Ireland couldn't deny the pool of desire now lining her underwear.

Holy hell, what did I just do?

***

It was one of the best kisses of his life.

Gideon wrapped a towel around his waist and sprawled out on the king-sized bed. He'd finished unloading the four-wheeler into the shop before he headed to the house to shower. His parents were watching television when he'd walked through the front door, though he wasn't sure if his dad snoring constituted paying attention to the comedy rerun.

Diesel whined from the floor, bringing Gideon back to the present. The red merle was looking up at the bed with hopeful eyes. Realizing Dallas was growling at the younger dog, Gideon patted the quilt. "Hop up, boy. There's enough room for you." Diesel tentatively jumped but was sure to keep a safe distance from Dallas and his rawhide bone.

Gideon's phone buzzed from the side table. For a brief moment, he thought it was Ireland—no, he *hoped* it was Ireland—on the other end. He let out a huff at the text message from his brother. "She's not gonna contact you," he mumbled, flipping through the channels. The TV's light shone in the dark room, and the sight was lonelier than normal.

What he wouldn't give to have Ireland lounging next to him instead of two drooling dogs. He rubbed Diesel's belly until the dog's leg thumped happily, then glanced to the window. He couldn't see the Leighton house, but he knew it was out there. And Ireland's room was directly across from his, give or take an acre.

He ran both hands over his face. It was a mistake to kiss her. He'd realized it after he'd dropped her off earlier. They'd run their course, but he couldn't resist her lips. Not when she snorted despite the mud on her cheeks and in her hair. He loved her—nothing had changed in that regard for him—but they weren't twenty-two anymore. He didn't know the woman she'd become.

But I sure as hell want to.

He groaned and flopped onto his back. Staring at the ceiling, he remembered how she tasted like cucumbers and mint, the same as the times they'd kissed as teenagers. He used to tease her about the organic lip balm, but he wasn't laughing now. He craved her.

But she didn't want him back. She proved it by leaving right after he'd begged her to stay. She'd begged him right back to go with her. Neither budged on their argument. There'd been a ring in his pocket, but it didn't make an appearance that night. Afterward, he'd been determined to make something of himself. It wasn't for her—or at least that's what he told himself and anyone who questioned his motives. He'd finished vet school and juggled two jobs to stay ahead.

He closed his eyes and listened to the commercial drone in the background. She didn't know any of that, though. Ireland may have been rich, but she was the same self-obsessed princess. He was glad no one had mentioned his success either. If she ever found out, he wanted to be the reason. Plus, if she ever desired him, he wanted her to love him and not any other incentive he provided. Sure, they used to be friends and she loved him back then. But she also left, and he chose to remain in Iowa. Part of him couldn't help but wonder if things would've been different if he'd been finished with vet school instead of only knowing how to farm. He had a second chance with Ireland and he wanted her to fall for the farmer again. It was who he was underneath the DVM degree.

Another buzz from his phone had Gideon pawing at the table. He grunted when it kept vibrating. Expecting another message from Lance, he haphazardly looked at the screen. It was a text from Ireland. His heart pounded and he sat up.

Ireland: You up?

He unlocked the screen, fingers stalling over the keyboard.

Gideon: Yes.

He didn't know what else to say. Talking to ladies came easy for his brother. Him, not so much. Conversations weren't his forte. Ireland was his only steady girlfriend. His success rate plummeted after she left, so his experience was minimal.

Little bubbles popped up on the other end, then disappeared. He held his breath, willing her to respond. He couldn't lose out on a chat with Ireland because he was speechless—er, wordless.

Ireland: We're having a late 4th of July picnic on Saturday at Saylorville Lake. Bring your parents and

Lance too.

The little hope he'd built up withered to ash. "Fuck my life." She only saw him as an ex. "I don't know why I thought it'd be different."

Gideon: Yeah, sure. Ma will talk to yours about what to bring.

Ireland: Great, thanks.

He tossed the phone to the bed and Diesel licked it. "Yeah, that's about as much action as I'll get too."

He quickly shed the towel and grabbed a new set of clothes. It took all his willpower to not march over to the Leighton house and kiss Ireland's lips until they were raw. He shook his head at the idiotic idea. As badly as he wanted that, he doubted she did.

Opting to grab a quick sandwich from the kitchen, he returned to the bedroom with his mouth full. A new message blinked on his phone.

Ireland: And we need to talk about that kiss.

A drop of water fell from his hair and landed on the screen. He wasn't sure which direction to take her statement.

He paused his reply when more bubbles lit up the screen, her next words nearly sending him sprinting across the farmyard.

Ireland: Because it was amazing.

CHAPTER FIVE

The skyline of New York City met Ireland's gaze two days later. It was a sight to behold no matter how many times a person saw it. Next to her, Krista sat with her nose pressed against the private jet's window. Seeing the city through a newbie would be fun.

"You ready for this?"

Krista bobbed her blonde head up and down. Turning toward Ireland, she squealed, "Oh my God, yes. I've never been more excited in my whole life. I mean, it's New York. Every girl dreams of shopping these streets."

Sitting back, Ireland wasn't sure if she'd agree with the broad statement, but New York City wasn't to be missed no matter what shopping preferences one might have.

The plane touched down, and after Krista took plenty of photos at the airport, the two women watched from the ground as they met the skyscrapers on a more personal level.

As usual, the streets were busy, and Ireland was never more grateful to have someone else driving. She loved big cities, but not driving in them.

After thirty minutes of traffic, the car stopped in front of a studio with a large window display of fashionable clothing on mannequins. The driver opened the door, and Ireland smiled at the bustle around them. A person could get lost in a place like this, and she had a time or two. It was mostly lonely in a crowd of faces. Days like today, she loved the smell of hot dog vendors and the sound of street peddlers. It may have been strange to some, but the oddities put her at ease.

Looking over to Krista, Ireland smirked. The shorter woman stood in awe of her surroundings. *I bet I looked the same all those years ago.*

"Marco is waiting," she called, moving to the front door.

Krista hurried over to her. Once inside the shop, the fashion designer met them.

"You look stunning as always." Marco kissed Ireland's cheeks and turned toward Krista. "And you are yummy. A glowing bride-to-be." He waved them toward the fitting area. "I finished this beauty last night." He pulled out a garment bag and unzipped it.

Krista gasped at the masterpiece inside. "Holy crap. It's gorgeous."

Marco pulled it out with a broad smile. "*Grazie, bella.* Now go try it on." He pointed to a woman nearby. "Mia, my sister, will help."

While the bride rushed to undress, Ireland sank into

the plush love seat across from the full panel of mirrors. "You've outdone yourself again, Marco," she said when the Italian man sat beside her.

He pushed his black ringlets out of his eyes. "Ah, it's nothing. I wouldn't be here if not for you." He chuckled. "I'd probably still be working in my father's bakery in Milan, so believe me, I owe you plenty."

Reviewing the shop, Ireland nodded. "Happy I could help."

Marco gently nudged her arm. "And when you need a gown, I will make it *perfetto*. Your body was made for one-of-a-kind clothing."

She grabbed a flute of champagne from the small table in front of them. The conversation needed to veer another direction, so she pointed to the display case filled with jewelry. "Looks like my investment is paying off well too."

Marco crossed one leg over the other. "*Sì*, it is, but if you hadn't taken a chance on me—"

"Then I wouldn't have a sexy Italian friend with connections in baguettes and fashion."

He chuckled, the rich sound easily filling the space. "If I didn't have a boyfriend…."

Ireland shook her head. "Yeah, that's the only thing holding you back."

Marco sipped the champagne and winked. "I swing both ways, *bella*, don't you ever forget." He leaned forward and bopped her nose with his finger. "If the day ever comes when we're both single, get ready for endless nights of pure *Italiano* loving."

Krista came out of the dressing room, silencing Ireland's snarky response.

"Well?"

"You look… wow." Ireland stood, tears creeping to her eyes. "My brother is the luckiest guy alive."

Krista slowly twirled, the lightweight gown ideal for a beach wedding. "I think so too."

"*Sì. Bellisima.*" Marco pulled Krista toward the accessories and jewelry section of the shop, and Ireland finished the champagne in her glass. Weddings were supposed to be happy, but all she felt was the opposite.

Checking her phone, she noticed two missed calls from Toby, one from her grandmother, and another one from Mason. She ignored the latter and focused on the first two. They'd both encouraged her to dive into different pools of investments. Looking at the shop, Ireland was glad she'd met Marco, even if taffeta made her gag.

She flipped through the calendar on her phone. *Plenty of business to do while in town.* Glancing at Krista laughing, she decided work could wait a few minutes. It'd been too long since she'd enjoyed herself with her old college roommate. The meetings could wait. Life couldn't. Today at least, she'd slow down and explore New York City like a first-time visitor.

***

White clouds dotted the horizon, and Gideon raised one hand over his eyes to review the recently mowed field. Normally he wouldn't bother, but it'd been too long since it was last cut.

Once he reached the equipment shed, he hopped off the riding mower and nodded to Lance and Zavier.

"Hey, what's up?"

"Needed a break." Zavier held up a mug of coffee. No matter the temperature, he had to have his hot coffee.

Lance pulled a sack of feed off the truck bed and hauled it to the side of the barn. "And he likes to watch me work."

Gideon rolled up his sleeves and grabbed two more sacks from the back. "Lazy ass."

Zavier chuckled. "Never said I wasn't." He took a drink, then added, "But at least I go for the girl I want."

"What's that supposed to mean?" Gideon continued to unload the truck and glanced between the two men.

"He means Ireland, dumbass," Lance added.

Gideon narrowed his eyes at his older brother, who was covered in sweat. With jet-black hair, piercing blue eyes and a charming personality, the eldest Taggart son was a ladies' man to his core. When Gideon was dating Ireland, Lance went through twenty girls in the same time span.

"What about her?"

"You still interested?" His brother lifted his brows, waiting for an answer.

Setting down the last load from the truck, Gideon leaned against the side of the barn and took off his ball cap. "That was a long time ago."

"Yeah, but she also didn't want to go out with me—"

"When did you ask her out?" Gideon asked, frowning.

Lance smirked. "I didn't. Just wanted to see your reaction."

"Ha-ha, jackass. She'd never go out with you because you're a man whore," Gideon said pointedly. He didn't like the joke at his expense. From their shit-eating grins, he was the only one.

Zavier shifted his weight and drained the rest of his coffee. "And because she still has feelings for you."

"Nah, I'm pretty sure she doesn't." Gideon wiped his hands off on the back of his jeans. The kiss from earlier in the week came to mind and he stared at his dusty boots.

"Huh, then I guess it's a good thing you don't have feelings for her either."

Both Lance and Gideon looked to Zavier. "Why's that?" Lance asked before Gideon could.

"I overheard her phone conversation with her assistant the other day." Zavier scanned the horizon. "They were talking about a guy coming to Iowa to meet her family."

Getting hit in the gut by a wild stallion couldn't match how Gideon felt in that moment. "Who?" He swore under his breath at the raspy sound.

Zavier shrugged and joined Gideon by the barn. "I don't know. From the sounds of it, the guy has money too."

Lance tossed a rag at Gideon's face and the dirty cloth stuck to his beard. "Ooh, competition. I like the sound of that."

Gideon brushed off the rag and shook his head. "I think I'm mature enough to not try that shit. It wouldn't work with Ireland anyway."

"Have you told her about your vet clinic?" Zavier pointed to the small barn on the east end of the farm.

"No, and it doesn't matter."

"It could."

Pushing off the barn, Gideon stalked toward the mower. He needed to get away from his prying best friend and annoying brother. Reaching it, he turned around. "Ireland made her choice six years ago. Even if I manage to convince her I'm the better guy, she'll make the same decision because this isn't her home anymore. We aren't her home." He let out a frustrated sigh. "I'm not her home."

Zavier opened his mouth, and Gideon took that moment to crank on the lawnmower. They meant well, but loving Ireland was too hard after all this time. It physically hurt to even admit he had feelings. His heart pounded against his rib cage and sent jolts of pain up and down his body. The worst part about the entire situation was that he wanted to work through the bullshit with her so they could be together.

I'm an idiot.

He returned to the long grass and started clipping. Making a sharp left turn, he ignored the goofy wave from Zavier and the ridiculous and suggestive dance moves from Lance. He tried to stifle his smile but couldn't. *Always the class clowns.* It was partly why he loved the two so much. Gideon was the serious one of their group, which meant it was up to Zavier and Lance to keep things light.

Finishing the row, he moved on to the next one. Zavier's comment from the recent conversation made him clench his jaw. *Ireland's moving on.* He knew she had, but actually seeing a man with her in his own backyard was bound to be difficult. He told himself he wasn't jealous, which would've been easier to swallow if his pulse hadn't increased at Zavier's statement. In his mind, Ireland would always be his. She was his first, and he'd hoped she'd be his last.

Life's a bitch like that.

He clenched the steering wheel tighter. *If and when some rich guy comes to Iowa for Ireland, I'll accept it.* He nodded once as if to solidify the thought. *And I won't try to compete with him.* Gideon winced at simply letting her go without a fight. *Okay, maybe just a little competition wouldn't be so bad.*

While he didn't want to ruin their shaky friendship, he also wanted to touch her just to see if their connection was the same, different, or better after time apart.

The sun ducked beneath a wave of clouds and he picked up his pace; he had too many chores around the farm and his clinic to get done to loaf around on the mower. Getting his hands dirty would keep his mind off Ireland, and that was the most important thing at the moment.

CHAPTER SIX

Seagulls shrieked overhead on Saturday. Scanning Saylorville Lake, Ireland smiled at the abundance of boats on the waves. Fishing boats and recreational pontoons dotted the water while happy hoots filled the air. It made sense since the humid ninety-degree weather made most Iowans either hide in the air conditioning or hit the local lakes for a reprieve.

"Ireland, come set the table," her mother called from the picnic shelter.

Swiveling her torso away from the beach, Ireland walked through the freshly cut grass and took over the mundane task. Her dad and brother were untangling their fishing lines. *Big shocker there.* Zavier was horrible at fishing—odd for a country boy—and the two caught lines on the first cast.

She unwrapped the paper plates and Krista's laugh met her ears. It was still a little weird to have her around, but their New York shopping spree helped changed the feeling. She looked over and saw Krista and Joanna setting up the dessert table with Fourth of July-themed sweets. Ireland's three-layer cake was over there somewhere, decorated with strawberries, blueberries and white chocolate chips to make a flag. She smiled. It'd taken more time than baking an apple pie from scratch, but it looked damned good. *Let's hope it tastes good too.*

A whiff of soap filled her nostrils. Without looking, she recognized it as Gideon's. It held just enough of a natural scent for the manliness to only be his. While some men bought expensive and fragranced shampoo and body wash, Gideon never had. A distant memory of them showering together drifted across her mind, and tingles ran over her skin.

"Something smells good," his deep voice stated.

Startled out of the past, Ireland lifted her eyes. His gaze was orgasmic. *Yes, orgasmic.* It was how Toby described Gideon's blue eyes when they spoke earlier in the day, and she couldn't agree more. Apparently, her best friend wasn't beyond internet stalking the entire Taggart crew since he also mentioned Lance's bite-worthy ass. "I was thinking the same thing," she replied with a grin.

"So, where do you want this?" He held up a container of potato salad. "Made it myself."

"Wow, impressive." She pointed to the end of the table. "Anywhere down there is fine. Thanks."

Out of the corner of her eye, she saw him carefully place his concoction a few feet away. Ever since he'd kissed her in the truck, she wanted to do it again. She craved it so much that she'd dreamed of him every night since.

Shaking her head, Ireland pushed the notion aside. *I can't kiss him again.* The wedding wouldn't last forever, and then she'd be gone. Getting attached would be stupid.

Plus there's the merger I need to focus on. She chewed her bottom lip. Whatever she felt for Gideon would disperse once she focused back on work and not how incredible those jeans looked on Gideon. *I think.* Gideon didn't share, and he didn't like to fight for attention. He'd made it plenty clear when they were together. It was partly why she was attracted to him. He'd go all caveman when he was jealous, and it was hotter than a day at the Iowa State Fair. He'd constantly be fighting for her attention if they were together again. Her businesses and charities pulled her every direction and made being in one place too long impossible.

"Did you have a good time in New York City?" he asked, breaking into her train of thought.

Ireland smoothed the tablecloth. "Uh, yeah. Krista and I picked up her wedding dress, then hit up a few stores."

Gideon leaned his back against one of the shelter posts. "Sounds fun."

"Shopping is always fun." She glanced toward where Krista and Zavier stood kissing. "She's going to look fabulous."

"I'll bet."

"We ironed out more wedding details on the ride home." She paused and watched him look out toward the lake. He always did prefer a quiet area versus a full fishing spot.

"That's partly why we're having this picnic. I need to go over the final list with everyone."

Ignoring her grandmother's ringtone from her purse, Ireland nodded at her father when he approached. The sooner they were in Barbados, the better. Being in Iowa, around Gideon, tempted her to fall back into the routine they once shared.

"Everybody gather around," Kenny called. Both families returned to the picnic area. "First, enjoy this tasty food. Afterward, Ireland will tell us about the wedding."

Once the two families were properly fed, Ireland stood and passed out the booklets Toby had overnighted. "All right, all the information about the Leighton and Kellogg wedding is in these." She held one up. "Flight information, room keys, and wedding schedules are included. Please review and make sure it all looks correct. As it's a small wedding, my private plane can take everyone who's here today." She pointed to Krista. "Since your folks live in Arkansas, they'll be on a similar flight the same day."

"And when's that again?" Gideon asked.

"Next weekend." She decided not to add the part about it being one of the details in the packet, since he hadn't opened his yet. "And as a special surprise, I've rented out one resort solely for this event for two weeks. I also hired a group of very reputable farmers to keep tabs on the fields and livestock while we're gone."

Joanna and Frances gasped while their husbands exchanged glances.

"That sounds expensive," Zavier commented.

Ireland waved his worry aside. "My treat." She met the eyes of each person present. "I can't ever repay the friendships I have with all of you, so let me give you a dream wedding slash vacation slash honeymoon."

Tears sprang to Frances's eyes. "You're such a sweet girl."

"You're my family. Simple as that." As the last word left Ireland's mouth, her parents and Zavier wrapped her in a giant family hug. It felt good to help others, especially people special to her.

"Okay, I think it's time for dessert," she said, escaping the lovefest.

While the families returned to the table full of goodies, Gideon hung back. "That's really nice of you, Ireland."

She shrugged. "I have the resources and money to make people's lives better. I can't imagine enjoying anything more."

"What else do you spend your money on? I could use a new bass boat," Lance teased.

Krista shrieked, then hurried over to them. "Oh my God, you booked us a cruise! I've always wanted to go on a Caribbean cruise." She wrapped her arms around Ireland's neck. "Thank you so much."

Laughing, Ireland detached her soon-to-be sister's arms. "Don't thank me. Toby found all the extra things and booked them."

"I'm giving Toby the biggest hug when I see him." Krista bit her lip. "He's in Barbados, right?"

"Yep, he's my right-hand guy."

"Perfect. I'm going to bring him something special from Iowa," Krista said, then hurried back to her fiancé.

Ireland smiled. It felt good to help the people she loved. "Well, Toby's actually—"

"So, who's this Toby guy again?" Gideon interrupted, still standing next to her.

"He's my personal assistant."

Gideon crossed his arms over his chest. "Mmhmm, and what exactly does he *assist* you with?"

Ireland held in a smug grin. He looked too cute with his eyes narrowed. "Aw, is somebody jealous?"

He straightened. "No."

Teasing him was much too easy. "That's too bad." She fanned herself dramatically. "He's just my type too."

"So am I."

Ireland laughed and cocked her head to the right. "Who says you're my type? Just because we dated doesn't mean you're my type anymore."

Gideon stepped closer and he lowered his voice. "If your reaction from the kiss the other day—"

"It was just a kiss."

He didn't budge, but his eyes showed her statement wounded him. "Then do it again."

"Wh-what?"

"Kiss me again," he dared.

Ireland's stance wobbled. "Why would I do that?"

Gideon smirked, the act sexier than any other she'd seen on him before. "To prove you like kissing me. Oh, and that I'm still your type, whether or not you want to admit it."

Ireland stared into his eyes, digesting his words at the terrifying truth. She *had* liked kissing him the other day. She'd always liked kissing him. Locking lips with Gideon wasn't a problem. Falling for him was. She couldn't afford to do it again, no matter how badly she wanted to.

He leaned toward her, but only to grab a napkin from the table before the breeze threw it to the grass. She heard her sharp intake of breath and realized she'd hoped he was leaning in to brush his lips to hers.

Gideon chuckled and winked. "Don't fight it, darlin'," he said, then took a seat next to Zavier.

She told herself to look away but couldn't. Her eyes were drawn to him no matter where he went. Gideon was familiar and much too addictive on her lips. The other day wasn't *just* a kiss. It was sheer perfection. She'd sampled plenty of men, but none tasted as sweet as him. They all paled, any comparison illogical and a waste of time. He was the best, hands down. Without even trying, he rattled her brain loose and then put her back together all with that damned mouth of his. It wasn't a coincidence either; he'd been doing it since they were teens.

But I can't.

She lifted her chin and went on the hunt for something chocolate. As easy as succumbing to Gideon once more would be, they both deserved more than constant bickering about her leaving for another trip. She realized then that their issue six years ago was travel. She wanted to see the world and he didn't. Gideon was satisfied with an Iowa lifestyle. Ireland wasn't. Not if she was completely honest.

I'm not about to repeat history. No matter how good a kisser he is.

***

Finally finished folding her clothes, Ireland dialed the only number she knew by heart these days. She put it on speakerphone and studied the neat piles of colors.

"How is my goddess?" Toby answered, his voice chipper as always.

"Ready to be home." She lifted her luggage onto the bed and started packing what she needed for her trip. "I'm getting my bag all set for Monday."

"Well, everything is on schedule for the big day, right down to the bouquets."

"Great, thanks. I don't know how I get anything done without you."

"Me either." Clicking of keys skittered across the line. "The orphanage in Jamaica is ready for the ribbon cutting, by the way."

Ireland nodded, glad the construction was finally complete. Out of all the places where she'd built group homes or orphanages, the ones in the Caribbean meant the most to her.

She looked down at her tanned skin. Though she'd seen pictures of her parents, she still didn't know where the darker pigmentation came from. She didn't mind it one bit. In fact, she rather liked the tan shade all year around.

"When's it set for?"

Toby clicked his mouse. "Looks like a week from tomorrow."

Making the calculations, she figured sneaking away from family mid-wedding festivities wouldn't be so bad. "All right. Please make sure it's all set up. Those kids deserve the best."

"You bet, boss lady."

A lawn mower caught her attention, and she moved to the window. Her brother was riding around with Krista at the helm. They were cute together. A hastily put-together wedding suited them; they were both spur-of-the-moment kind of people.

"Any update on that cute neighbor I cyber-stalked?" Toby asked.

"He kissed me."

"Wait, what? Details."

Ireland shook her head. "Not much to say. We went four-wheeling, then got all muddy and the next thing I know, we're kissing in his truck."

"Oh, girl. I mean, sounds gross but fun. Was he any good?"

She smiled before she could stop it. "Yes, very, very good."

"He'll be at the wedding, right?"

"Yeah."

Toby let out a mockingly sinister laugh. If she had to guess, he was also rubbing his hands together maniacally. "Hmm, maybe I should set up a few dates for you."

"Toby, don't. We dated years ago," she argued.

"There's nothing left."

He harrumphed. "Nothing but sex appeal."

"Tobes."

"If you don't hop on that stallion, some other girl will."

"I've come to grips with that." A loud beep resounded on her end of the call. Checking the screen, she saw a new message from Gideon. "Hey, I need to go. I'll see you in two days."

"Get some!" Toby called before he disconnected.

Ireland opened the message.

Gideon: What's up, buttercup?

She started to respond, then paused. If she started a conversation with Gideon, it could lead to other places. Way too many other places. A little part of her wanted to see if he was the same guy she dated.

Ireland: Just packing for a business trip to Barbados. You?

She didn't have to wait long for a response.

Gideon: Checking soil in the north cornfield.

It didn't sound fun, but neither did packing.

Ireland: Want some company?

Gideon: Sure, meet you between fields.

Giddy for the first time that day, she checked her reflection, then raced down the stairs and out toward the barn. After stealing the keys to her dad's John Deere utility vehicle, she set off toward the Taggart fields. As she neared, she spotted two Australian shepherds running in her direction. Gideon came into view seconds later.

Whoa, he looks tasty. His faithful hat was turned

backward, hair poking out on the sides. The light-wash blue jeans hugged every bit of muscles but looked comfortable enough to work in. They weren't city jeans; the streaks of dirt and frayed holes told her as much. His charcoal gray T-shirt fluttered in the breeze while he watched her park. She didn't mind it, since the wind lifted his shirt and gave her a peek at those delirious abs of his.

"Your pops let you take the UTV, huh?"

Ireland stuffed the keys in one of the front pockets of her shorts overalls. "He doesn't know yet." She laughed. "But I'll bet I'm on dish duty tonight if I get a scratch on it."

Gideon pointed to her shirt barely visible through the overalls. "What's your shirt say?"

She glanced down at the "Farm girls have nice calves" on the front of the faded red tank top and unbuttoned one half of the overalls so he could read the pun.

"I like that one. It fits you." He nodded to her rubber boots. "Even if I can't see your calves."

"Thanks. Zavier bought it for me when he went to town." Pushing past him, Ireland leaned down and patted the red merle's head. "This must be Diesel." The dog licked her face and she giggled.

"Yep, he's my troublemaker." Gideon whistled, and Dallas poked his nose out of the corn row. "I need to get back to it or I won't finish before dinner."

"Right, sorry." Standing, she smiled at the two dogs. "I can play with these cuties later." She fell into step with Gideon. His long strides overwhelmed hers, and she found herself hustling to keep up. It was usually the opposite with

Toby's short legs.

"So, what're you looking for?" she asked when he stooped down and dug a device with two prongs in the ground.

"Moisture levels in the different fields." He read the results on the meter and jotted them down on a small notepad. "Dad used his hands back in the day, but I like to keep up with technology." He waved the tool. "This is faster and more accurate."

They moved farther into the rows of tall cornstalks. "From the looks of it, the rain's been lacking this year."

He knelt and crumbled a clod of soil through his fingers. "Unfortunately, yes. We've had some rain, but not enough to keep the bank from threatening to recall the loan if our harvest isn't profitable." His brows bunched together, and worry lined his blue eyes.

The thought that he could lose the farm made her stomach churn. Gideon was all in when it came to farm life. At least that was how he used to be. She didn't know him these days. He'd pleaded her to stay even after she inherited millions because he needed to stay with the farm. She'd begged him to leave and offered to pay for someone else to run his farm.

She bit her bottom lip. The entire fight flooded back and guilt gnawed at her. *We were naïve at twenty-two.*

"Anything I can do?"

Gideon walked around Dallas, who had decided the middle of the path was the perfect spot to scratch an itch, and shrugged. "Not unless you know a rain dance." He snapped her overall strap. "I thought they stopped making these things."

Ireland hooked her thumbs in the sides. "What? No way. They're back in style."

"Hmm, interesting." He stepped closer and trailed his index finger and thumb along the right strap. "Are they fashionable like this?" he teased, unbuttoning one side. The strap slipped off her shoulder, exposing the right half of her shirt to him.

"Actually, yes." She held her breath when his callused fingers grazed her collarbone.

"That's too bad." Gideon paused just above her breast, then withdrew his hand. She couldn't stop the sigh of displeasure. "I was hoping you'd set a new trend and I was the first to see it." He moved farther down the corn row, leaving her speechless. His touch still burning her body, she quickly followed in hopes of a repeat performance.

"So, uh, do you have a special lady?" The moment the question left her lips, she regretted it. His dating life was none of her business. "For the wedding, of course."

He took another sample, then stood. At four inches taller than her, he resembled a woodsy magazine model, dirt-covered and all. His eyes met hers, and longing shot down her spine and rested in her belly. "Well, there is this one lady."

"Oh, sure." Ireland mentally kicked herself. She shouldn't have asked. Just because they dated years ago and kissed once didn't mean his sights weren't set on someone else. "I'll add a plus one for you."

Gideon chuckled and tossed the moisture-reading device

to the ground. With agonizingly slow movements, his hand dipped into the side of her overalls and under her shirt. She gasped at the intrusion, but once his palm cupped her braless breast, she shuddered with desire. Blue eyes clashed with brown and Ireland swore she was having an out of body experience.

"You really believe I can think of another woman when you consume my mind at all times?" he whispered in her ear. "It's a constant loop, Ireland. Just when I think I've forgotten, you show up out of nowhere and I relive it all again."

Before she could reply, he caught her earlobe between his teeth and pulled. Gripping his shoulders, Ireland gasped. Desire sprinted between her legs as he pinched her nipple and nipped the side of her neck.

"Gideon."

He kissed down her neck. "Yeah, darlin'?" He replaced his fingers with his tongue and she bucked toward him as he grazed her breast with his teeth, tasting, licking, sucking until her knees knocked together. This wasn't the shy Gideon she grew up with. He was a man who knew what he wanted and didn't hide it.

Damn, it's hot too.

Abruptly his mouth left her body and his hands disappeared. Whimpering, she opened her eyes and pouted. "What're you—"

Grabbing her hand, he guided it to his chest. "This is what you do to me, Ireland." His heart beat wildly against her palm. He kissed her hard, the taste of him heady with lust.

"Is it bad that I want you?"

He kissed her bottom lip, then the top one. "Never."

"What if I want you right here?"

"You'll get me." He pulled her flush to him. "All of me."

Her better sense was overwhelmed with what her body wanted, demanded even. "Right now."

Shaking his head, he placed his hand over hers. "Nah. Not yet."

"When?" she whined. Men didn't cut her off when it came to sex. It was usually the other way around. *Plus, it's not like I haven't been with Gideon before.*

He tugged the overalls back in place, then grabbed the back of her neck and kissed her roughly. "You'll know when."

"Please."

He chuckled, eyes dark with need. "I wish it were that easy."

Stupefied, Ireland stood there and watched him walk away, resuming his task like nothing had happened. For a minute, she couldn't move. Her brain was still trying to compute what he'd done. How he'd rejected her, begging be damned.

"Phone's ringing," he called.

Fishing it out of her back pocket, Ireland saw her grandmother's name on the screen. She glanced to Gideon, then back to the phone. "Yeah, I, uh, should take this."

He shrugged and continued on his way as Ireland stumbled in the opposite direction. Gideon kissed the bones out of her legs. Even jelly would've been a better replacement for the quivering appendages.

Her flight back to Barbados couldn't come at a better time. She needed time away from Gideon Taggart; otherwise, she might lose her mind entirely.

She made it to the row opening, and a flash blinded her. She held her breath and prayed it was just the sun's reflection off the UTV. When she glanced around the area, she spotted footprints and another set of tire marks from a dirt bike. "Dammit!" She couldn't decide if she should answer the call or track down the nosy bastard. When her grandmother called again and she didn't see a person in sight, she answered.

"Hey, so I think the paps are on the farm. No guarantees, but you probably won't appreciate the pictures soon to flood the internet."

The fact that the reporters found her only reiterated her necessary return to Barbados.

CHAPTER SEVEN

The beach was exactly what Ireland needed after her time in Iowa. Merely stepping back on Barbados sand was enough to make her momentarily forget why she regretted going home in the first place. Since she was only on the island for two days, she'd finished her duties early so she had most of the second day all to herself.

Sure enough, a slew of photos popped up on gossip websites. They would've been worse if Gideon's face wasn't obscured. Still, the images of her kissing an "unknown Iowa hottie" made her glad for the escape to the tropics.

Gideon called multiple times, as did her brother, parents, and Krista. While she spoke with her family and Krista, she ignored a direct conversation with Gideon. She wasn't sure how to handle the situation. *He's probably not very happy with becoming famous.* When she returned to Iowa, she'd find a way to smooth it over. She sent him a few texts, apologizing for the invasion of privacy. He hadn't replied, so she stopped trying. It was what she did best when it came to Gideon.

Ireland leaned back on the beach towel and watched local children play in the waves. Knowing she did even an ounce of good for the kids in Barbados made her smile. *I have a long way to go still.* New schools were her next project and one she was determined to see through. She couldn't do it in her personal life, but she could follow through with her professional one.

Her phone rang, and she glanced at the text message from Toby, reminding her of their departure time. He truly was the best. No matter where she went, he was right beside her, ready to help. Thinking back over the last day, she was glad the meeting with a food distributor in Jamaica went smoothly. Last night, she'd even managed to reach out to a trusted translator with the Maasai tribe leaders in Africa and planned a trip at the end of the year to check on the project there.

Closing her eyes, she listened to the sounds around her. Several vendors called out to tourists on the beach while childish giggles put her at ease. Sure, she could retreat to her condo and avoid all the noise on the private beach, but she enjoyed her time with these people. They were an extension of her family after living there for four years. Making Barbados her home base was a no-brainer. The climate was perfection—minus hurricane weather, when she'd head to France to visit her grandmother—the people were abundantly friendly, and there was plenty to keep her busy in her downtime. She didn't see herself leaving anytime soon either. Iowa may have been the state she grew up in, but Barbados was where she felt completely at home.

Ireland tipped her head back when a shadow crossed her face, blocking the sun's rays. Top-of-the-line cologne drifted to her, and she recognized the scent before he spoke.

"And here I thought you were a Little Miss Goody-Two-shoes," a man teased, his British accent prevalent. "But no, here you are in an absolutely sinful bikini that clearly says the opposite."

Meeting the espresso-colored eyes of Mason Straight, Ireland's heart thumped faster. Though they were friends, she was worried he might think less of her for being caught with her pants down. *Or almost down.*

She smirked and couldn't help but tease him back. "Mr. Straight, I'm pleased to inform you that not all the rumors of me are true."

Mason plopped down onto the sand beside her, no second thought given to the five-thousand-dollar suit he wore. "Then you aren't a regular Angelina Jolie helping orphaned kids around the world?" He turned toward her. "Or do I have the wrong Ireland Leighton?"

Blushing, she hoped her time in the sun hid the reaction. "Actually, that is true." She held up a finger and added, "And so are the ones about skinny-dipping in the Blue Grotto."

Mason's hearty laughter floated through the palm trees around them. "Your grandmother said you had spirit. I like that in a partner." He glanced over to the blue waves. "Among other things, such as your grace with the paps. I'd have slugged one long ago if I didn't hire bodyguards."

"I should get some of those." It was then that she noticed three well-built men surrounding them at a distance. "How did you meet my grandmother again?"

"Funny story, that. I met her years ago when I visited the French countryside. I got lost while horseback riding and ended up in her backyard. She handed me a cuppa when I was astride my mare, and the rest is history. Our tastes are similar, so we joined in a select few business ventures." He brushed sand from his pants. "She's the one who suggested we might get along."

A piece of hair fell out of Ireland's braid and into her face. Even though they'd met six months prior, they became friends quickly. The endless teasing was just one facet of their platonic friendship. "And now that you've gotten to know me?"

Mason reached over and tucked the hair behind her ear. "Well, I dare say I owe your grandmother a rather large thank-you."

She smiled and couldn't help but compare Mason to the man she'd left in Iowa two days before. It was wrong, but this refined Brit beside her made Gideon seem like a country hillbilly. "Now that you've found me, what will you do?"

A dashing grin crossed his tan features. "First, invite you to lunch. I'm famished, and you are much too skinny. Second, I'll woo you to become the face of my current charities because you have a heart of gold. Plus, you're much prettier than I am."

Ireland rolled her eyes. The gods themselves couldn't

have created a better physique. Mason's body extended longer than her own by a good five inches, and a stubbled yet prominent jaw and straight nose only accented his high cheekbones and manicured face. He was the polar opposite of Gideon. *And just my type.*

He stood and helped her to her feet, towering over her and instantly making him that much more attractive to her. "Then third, I'm going to enchant you until you realize what a catch I am and agree to go on a date with me."

Sliding on her sunglasses, Ireland tilted her head to the right. "Cocky, British, and a millionaire. Hmm, not my type." She moved up the beach. "Thanks for the offer, though."

Mason grabbed her hand and gently pulled her back toward him. She gasped when he pushed up the designer shades and intently gazed into her eyes. "I do like a challenge, Ireland. If a confident man of wealth isn't your cup of tea, then I won't stop until I find out what is so I can win you over."

She smirked and bopped him on the nose with her index finger. "Aw, too bad. I like coffee, sorry."

He outright laughed, small crinkles lining the corner of his eyes. "How very American of you. Well, I suppose alternative methods will need to be used to convert you."

"And what might those be?"

"I've heard a certain style of courting has worked wonders. I'm not French by birth, but I am fond of the kiss they're known for." He leaned closer and gently kissed her cheek. There wasn't anything passionate about the embrace, and Ireland reminded herself for the umpteenth time that they were friends and almost business partners. *Nothing more.* The paparazzi had caught wind of their friendship and hadn't left them alone ever since. Of course, her grandmother wanted them to be romantically involved, but it never felt right for either of them. They had a good thing going in their friendship. The next plausible act was to join businesses not bloodlines.

"Do you think they're buying that we're merely chatting about the weather?" he asked.

She looked over to the street and saw the familiar flash of cameras and nodded slightly. "Yes."

"Good. I want to keep this merger under wraps for as long as possible." Mason chuckled and his dark eyes searched hers.

Ireland parted her lips to give a smart remark, but Toby's voice interrupted her.

"Oh my God, the two of you are stupidly adorable."

Mason glanced to the shorter man. "Hello, Toby. Your timing is impeccable."

Toby grinned wider than the time she caught him making out with her masseuse. "So I've been told."

One of the stocky bodyguards walked over and whispered to Mason. He looked at his phone, then turned back to Ireland. "I'm sorry, but I need to take a rain check on our lunch date." He kissed the top of her hand. "I promise to make up for it."

"I'll remember that."

Mason took a step toward the street. "Good, then I'll

be in your thoughts until I see you again." He leaned in to kiss her cheek. "I'll be in Iowa the day after tomorrow. I think this will be good. I've wondered about the family of the infamous Ireland. If things go well, you can meet my motley crew in England. My mum is dying to meet you." He frowned. "On second thought, maybe you shouldn't meet my family. They'll think we're engaged."

"Whatever you want sounds good to me."

"Perfect. I look forward to seeing your childhood farm." He paused. "You may think it's odd, but I like to get to know my potential business partners before I sign on the dotted line. Friendship is one thing, but when money mingles, I'm extra cautious."

She glanced to the waves. "I completely understand. It's not a bad idea. Why didn't I think of it before?"

He leaned in to whisper, "Because you're still new at this. Stick with me, I'll show you the way."

The click of cameras was closer now, and she held in a groan. Mason wasn't wrong there. Her grandmother helped as did the board of trustees when it came to how to handle large business deals, but it was daunting. This was her first multimillion-dollar merger where Ireland's ass was solely on the line. She wouldn't mess it up no matter what.

"Ireland, I do hate when you frown," Mason commented. "Are you all right?"

She forced a smile. "Yeah, just thinking."

"About Iowa? Because I'll be my charming self. Don't worry."

"I'm not worried about you."

He tapped his chin. "You're worried about the guy you kissed, aren't you? I did see those racy photos. Naughty, Ireland." Mason clucked his tongue then chuckled. "I suspect he'll be jealous when I arrive. You haven't told anyone who I am, have you?"

"Not exactly. I mentioned to my parents that a business partner was coming to town, though. And I'm sure Gideon will be jealous when you arrive."

His smile broadened. "Should I pretend that I'm your beau so Gideon finally makes that ultimate move on you? You know, the bended knee one. I'm quite positive you've already done the one between the sheets."

She laughed so hard she snorted. Thanks to their close friendship, he was more than aware of her history with Gideon. The fact that he was willing to help Gideon along was sweet. Unnecessary, but sweet. She and Gideon couldn't have a future.

"No. But don't be surprised if people think that. I'll clear it up if they do."

Vying the two against each other wasn't what she ever had in mind. Mason was a friend. Gideon was the man she wanted but couldn't have.

"You know I don't care about any of the gossip, right, Ireland?" He held her hands in his and squeezed. "We're on the cusp of making a ginormous merger that will benefit both our businesses plus give you free time to work on your charities."

"I know, but I almost feel like I should warn him."

Mason shrugged. "Well, I know I'm rather good looking,

but I'm focused on business. And a little friendship here and there." He glanced at his watch. "Now I need to go, but first, I propose we give these trolls something to sell,"

"Such as?"

His lips hovered slightly above hers, close but not touching. "I wouldn't be opposed to kissing you."

Outright laughing, she playfully slapped his chest. "Tempting, but I can't."

"That dreadful old boyfriend again?" He sighed when she nodded but remained a mere breath away from catching her lips beneath his.

"Yep. I don't know why, but I can't let him go yet."

"Pity."

"Holy mother, if you get any closer, I swear I'll get pregnant." Toby's voice broke them apart.

Mason nodded toward Toby. "Delightful to see you as always. Keep tabs on her for me, will you?"

"Oh yes, of course," Toby agreed.

Ireland fanned the back of her neck, suddenly aware of the sun's rays. "See you in two days."

Mason winked, then climbed into the luxury SUV waiting on the street. Only then did the paparazzi disperse, leaving Ireland alone with Toby.

Toby tugged on her wrist excitedly. "Girl, why didn't you tell me you and Mason Straight had moved on from friendship?"

Ireland started toward her car and was grateful the driver was already in place. Suddenly, she needed a cold shower. "Because we haven't, Tobes."

"Uh-huh, sure. He's your grandmother's number one pick for you." Toby jogged after her, panting slightly. "Even if he wasn't, Mason Straight doesn't go around spending personal time with business partners. Ever."

"We're friends, Toby."

"Uh-huh, sure. Whatever you say." He licked his lips suggestively. "I hear wedding bells covered in diamonds even now. Hell, we could probably fit in a double wedding if you wanted."

Ireland tossed her towel in the back seat and climbed in after smiling at the driver. "I think you need to get your hearing checked. The only wedding bells are for my brother and Krista."

Toby slid into the seat beside her and rolled down his window. "Mark my words."

He kept rambling on about the millionaire, but Ireland stopped listening. Her business arrangement with Mason was strategic and necessary. She wasn't a mogul in the board room. She preferred to be out helping people and animals. Their merger would give her that opportunity.

She watched the scenery pass out the window. She'd never allow anyone to control her life. It was the main point of contention with her grandmother who wanted to do exactly that. Over the years, Ireland found a way to be happy. Part of that hinged on her business success. There was still one part missing, though. She didn't think a man was the answer, but after spending time with Gideon, she realized she may have been wrong.

Ireland thought back to the recent time spent with Mason

and her grandmother's suggestion that they marry.

Ever since learning about the struggle her biological parents had when they fell in love, Ireland hadn't been keen on finding a husband. Naturally, that was directly after her breakup with Gideon and she truly didn't want to think about moving on. Her mother had never been accepted by the Bourgeois family, which led to the couple running away to the Caribbean. If things had gone differently, her life wouldn't have started out in such a tragic way.

She studied the heirloom piece on her right ring finger. The Victorian-style ring with a dark purple gem in the middle was meant for her mother, but by the time her father's family accepted her, they were both gone and it was too late.

"Miss Leighton, you're home," the driver announced, opening the back door.

Looking up from her hand, she smiled. "Thanks, Jimmy. Toby and I will see you in the morning."

Taking the front steps two at a time, she looked up. Her condo wasn't the most expensive, but with no close neighbors and a gorgeous view of the ocean, it was a dream come true. Someday she'd inherit the estate in France, but for now she'd enjoy the beauty of Barbados.

Her packed bag by the door gave her pause.

Until tomorrow, when I return to Iowa. She bit her bottom lip. *And to Gideon.*

CHAPTER EIGHT

Gideon sat on the front porch and watched the dogs play in the yard. It always made him smile to watch them bite and chase each other until dirt spiraled in the air.

His phone lit up with a new message. Glancing at it, he grunted and swiped the dating app off the screen. He didn't want some random girl who liked country living. Zavier had downloaded the app and made him a profile one night, but Gideon hadn't given it much thought. He'd tried the dating scene, found it wasn't for him. Different girls every night, pretending to give a shit about their hobbies, and spending money he didn't have weren't his idea of a good time. He wanted Ireland, and that was a pipe dream.

"You can't have her," he reminded himself again. It was a common occurrence for him since their interaction in the cornfield and subsequent photos on the internet. His one saving grace was that the paparazzi hadn't gotten his name or even tried to follow him. All it'd take was a little research, but Gideon didn't think the press cared much for accuracy. They wanted a story, and an heiress stooping down the social ladder to kiss a farmer was exactly that.

Ireland was due back from Barbados any time now. He'd be the first person she talked to if he had any say. She'd apologized via text message, but that wasn't enough for him. He needed to discuss the photos with her.

She's different. She may swear her money hadn't changed her, but it had. The girl who used to wear ball caps and sing off-key in his truck was a distant memory. He'd never get a second chance because he was still in love with that version of Ireland Leighton. He barely knew this new Ireland, but some part of his heart wouldn't let him give up, obscure and racy photos be damned. He'd liked kissing her in the field. *Glad that's all we did.* He didn't want to think of the ramifications if they'd stripped to skivvies with the cameras nearby to snap shots.

He squinted at an oncoming taxi. Gravel flew up behind the yellow sedan as it whizzed by his house.

Ireland. She's back. His stomach jumped at the thought. She'd only been gone a few days, but he'd missed her.

Damn, don't do that, Tagg. He shook his head. *Don't get attached.* This wasn't like the time she went to Spain for a semester abroad. Her main residence was overseas these days. Any visit with Ireland had an expiration. Getting involved was stupid, but also too easy for him.

Whistling, he stood and both Aussies ran to his heels. "You want to go see who's here?

Dallas whined beside him and sniffed the air. Patting the dog's head, Gideon nodded. "All right, nosy, let's go."

By the time he made it to the Leighton farmhouse, the taxi driver was already halfway down the drive. Ireland's laughter filled the night air, and he held his breath. Reaching the porch, he quietly peered in the screened door. She was hugging a man shorter than her. He was well-dressed, but Gideon couldn't see beyond the guy's backside.

"I'm glad you came with me," Ireland said, looping her arm through the man's.

"Please, you can't live without me long. You'd miss me too much," the guy responded, pecking her cheek.

Gideon told himself not to freak out. He had zero claim on Ireland, after all. The ring box in his jeans pocket begged to differ, but he shoved that thought aside. It'd been there for six years. It could wait until Ireland was prepared to see it.

If she's ever ready.

"Let's go upstairs, and I'll show you what I have for the invitations," Ireland said, nearing the stairs.

"Stairs? How perfect. Then I get to stare at your tight arse all the way to the top," the guy responded, his British accent grating on Gideon's ears. Even Diesel and Dallas growled low at the sound.

Ireland snorted and the two disappeared.

Gideon waited until he couldn't hear them anymore before running his hand over his face. He didn't know what he'd just heard, but he needed to step up his game. He wasn't the greatest with words, but he'd be damned if Ireland wouldn't listen to him at least once before she vanished on another flight.

Gideon rubbed his hands down the front of his jeans. He actually thought kissing her would make a difference. He should've known better. Ireland Leighton didn't fall for flowery words or grand acts. It was one of the things he loved about her, and it made it even more difficult for him. He wasn't the cute neighbor boy who snuck her out of the house anymore. She needed something different now, and he didn't know what it was.

Walking along the road, he pulled out his phone and eyed the dating app. "It'd be so much easier if I didn't love her." He shoved the device back into his pocket and picked up his pace. Falling into bed sounded like the best plan for the remainder of the night. He'd deal with Ireland and her mystery guest with the morning light.

Too bad for him, that thought kept him up all night.

***

"So this is what a farm is." Toby scanned the Leighton land and tapped his finger on his chin. He sniffed the air. "Ugh, it smells."

"You grew up in London, Tobes. This is nothing." Ireland grabbed a pail of feed and opened the barn door. "Help me feed the horses."

Toby scrunched his nose at her but followed nonetheless. "I can't believe you're doing chores. You're the heir to a fortune, Ireland."

"Yeah, but I'm in Iowa today." She scooped the grain into the stall for the first mare. "Apparently, people around here think I'm some kind of princess and can't do manual labor."

"Doll, have you looked at yourself lately? You *are* a princess."

Ireland glanced at her clothes first. Blue jeans from the farm fleet store up the road and an orange hunting T-shirt with the silhouette of two deer met her gaze. The rubber boots with white stenciled horses were brand-new, but held specks of dust from their morning activities. "What's wrong with my clothes? They're very farm-y."

Trailing behind, he cleared his throat. "Okay yes, your clothes fit in, but uh, have you seen your jewelry?"

Her hands quickly fingered the studs in her ears. The pear-shaped one-carat diamonds definitely didn't belong in a horse barn. "Oh, yeah."

"And that pretty sapphire on your finger doesn't exactly scream 'country.'" He patted her back. "I still love you, though, princess."

Clenching her hand around the bucket handle, Ireland moved down the line. She didn't want to admit Toby was right, but he was, 100 percent.

The horses whinnied their impatience and she picked up her pace. After feeding them, she'd show Toby how to brush them down. If they had enough time, she'd even take him for a ride.

"Hey, Ireland, what do you get when you pair a brooding tattooed farmer and an heiress trying to prove she's not a princess?" Toby asked from his spot near the barn door.

Turning, she frowned. "What're you talking about?"

"Ha! Yes, that face. You're too good at this game." He skipped toward her. "Gideon's on his way."

"Shit." She eyed the grain in her bucket. It was only half empty. "I need you to finish this while I talk to him."

Toby squirmed away from the extended pail. "Uh, no. Have you met me? I don't do manual labor unless it includes a man."

"Please." She stuck out her bottom lip.

"Ugh, you and that damn puppy dog face." He carefully grabbed the dirty bucket with two fingers. "This is so gross."

"I'll make it up to you, I swear." She grinned at Toby's attempts to feed the horses. Every time he neared a stall, he let out a little yelp when the horse poked its head out. It would've been funny to get on film.

"Ireland, we need to talk."

Gideon's harsh tone should've made her cringe, but it sent her heart thudding faster instead. She gathered her hair into a bun at the base of her neck and braced herself for his wrath.

"Sure, of course." She nodded toward her friend. "Have you met Toby? He's my assistant and has been helping with all the wedding preparation."

He looked toward the shorter man and his posture seemed to relax a little. "He's Toby?"

"Yep, and the best friend a girl could ask for."

A smirk covered his face, but he quickly hid it. "Good to know."

She wanted to question Gideon's reaction, but from the way he looked at her, she opted against it. "So, what's up?"

Gideon stood in front of her for a minute with his hands on his hips. He couldn't look more like a farmer if he tried. The forest-green shirt with the 4H logo left nothing to the imagination for his muscles, paired with dark-wash jeans with hems covered in mud. She could stare at him all day every day.

He took off his hat and flung it behind him. "'What's up?' That's what you have to say to me after my entire life is broadcast on the internet?"

"I see your temper is under control as usual." She moved toward the horse supplies in search of a brush.

"Oh no. Don't go changing the subject." He was hot on her heels. "You want to know how many phone calls I got the day those pictures hit the web? A lot, Ireland. My clients even called me. I was recognizable to people around here. I'm sure you don't care about that, but I do. I have to live here after you leave again."

Finding what she needed in a drawer, she closed it and spun around. "I care, Gideon, and I'm sorry. I didn't think the paps followed me to the farm, and I definitely didn't think they'd catch us making out in a cornfield."

The anger slowly drained from his gaze. He took a step backward and pinched the bridge of his nose. "I know." He let out a breath and nodded to Toby. "Should he be unsupervised?"

Ireland looked around Gideon and watched Toby sing a show tune to one of the older horses. Oddly enough, it worked to move the mare away from the door. "Probably not, but I'm nearby in case things go awry."

Moving past him, she grinned when Toby started adding moves to his performance. *He keeps things lively, that's for certain.*

"Tagg, the Winn's prize-winning Labrador went into labor and the pups are stuck," Lance yelled from the entrance.

Three sets of eyes swung to the sweat-covered Taggart.

"And I'll take one of those under my Christmas tree too," Toby said under his breath.

"All right, on my way." Gideon squeezed Ireland's hand. "I need to go, but we're not done here."

"Sure, you know where to find me."

Gideon retrieved his cap and tucked it in his back pocket. "Today, at least."

Ireland crossed her arms over her chest, but he didn't stick around long enough to see her reaction. He jogged out of the barn, and the familiar sound of his truck kicked up gravel on the way down the drive.

"Wow, Dr. Doolittle sure is hot," Toby sighed, plopping the empty pail on the floor. "I wish I had a tattooed farmer drooling over me."

Nudging Toby with her elbow, Ireland picked up the bucket and handed him a brush. "Yeah, yeah. It's time to brush the horses."

Toby's eyes widened and he shook his head. "No way."

"Come on, city boy, let's see if I can remember how to do it."

She linked her arm with his and started toward her favorite mare. If she could figure out a way to not discuss the paparazzi with Gideon, the churning in her stomach would go away.

Yeah, right.

***

Gideon held up the last black Lab puppy and grinned. He didn't want to hold the cutie longer than necessary, but seeing the little one yawn made him remember why he went to vet school. Placing the puppy alongside his brothers and sisters, he gave the mama a scratch behind the ears before he stood.

"She'll be all right," he told the anxious couple standing at the doorway. "I'll check back in a few days to make sure."

"Thank you so much. She normally births fine, but the ungodly sounds had us worried," Mrs. Winn said.

"It happens now and then. I'm glad I was around to help." He took off his gloves and washed his hands before he gathered his black bag. Latching the baby gate behind him, Gideon handed a business card to her husband. "Let me know if you need anything. In a few weeks, I'll come out to give them shots."

He slipped out the side door after Mr. Winn handed him a wad of cash. This was the type of payment he preferred; then he could stockpile it until he had enough to put a down payment on a clinic off the Taggart lands.

Taking a deep breath, he noticed the sun starting to dip

over the horizon. He headed toward his truck, happy for the first time that day. Using his veterinarian skills on the farm was one thing, but making town visits boosted his confidence since he ran off word-of-mouth referrals. He didn't know who suggested him to the well-off couple, but he'd be damned if he'd refuse such work.

His phone beeped in his pocket and he hopped in his truck before checking it. Nothing unusual caught his attention, so he tossed it on the dashboard and made his way home.

Driving with one arm on the steering wheel, Gideon thought back to that afternoon. Ireland fit right in with the animals, her tender touch putting them at ease. Unfortunately, that also included him—one touch from her and his anger nearly dissolved.

Another notification rang from his phone. After he turned down the dirt road to his house, he pulled off to the side and read the text from his cousin. She tended to be obsessed with Ireland both before and after she became rich. He opened the website article and choked. *And they found my name. Great.* He gripped the phone harder and read the rest of the blog. It didn't hurt him, but it sure as hell wasn't flattering to be the heiress's latest conquest.

After he finished reading, he sat in silence. It was too late to pull the photos off the internet. Everything associated with Ireland went viral. *Maybe I'll get some more business out of it.* He tried to chuckle, but it sounded forced to his own ears.

He pulled back onto the road. His conversation with Ireland would take longer than he initially anticipated. He shook his head. He didn't give a damn about the photos, if he was completely honest. What he cared about was Ireland. If she felt even an iota of the connection he did, he'd agree to a photo shoot for as many pictures as the photographers wanted.

Parking his truck in the grass outside the Leightons' main barn, Gideon scanned the area for Ireland. He spotted Toby near the garden, knowing she wouldn't be far off. Reaching the large area, he watched Ireland stoop down to pick banana peppers from the plants.

"Hey, not to be a perv, but why does your family have so many cucumbers?" Toby asked, holding up a large one.

Ireland giggled and playfully smacked her friend's leg. "For pickles. Is your mind ever out of the gutter?"

Toby struck a shocked pose. "As if."

Gideon would've stayed there longer, but his phone rang, giving away his location.

"Hey, farmer, want to help?" Toby asked, waving the cucumber.

"Yeah, I think I'll pass." He smirked. "But I do need to steal Ireland for a few minutes."

Ireland tentatively looked up and nodded. "Sure. Toby, why don't you work on the carrots. I think they're ready." She brushed off her hands. "How're the puppies?"

"Great." He opened the garden gate. "All seven of them."

"Aw, I bet they're adorable." She closed the gate and started walking toward the open yard.

He nodded. "They are."

Grass whipped Ireland's boots, the sound filling his ears.

From her appearance, she was trying to fit in. He didn't want to break it to her that she'd never fit in again. Not in Iowa.

"About the pictures…."

"They found my name," he filled in quickly.

"Shit." She stopped walking and faced him. "I'm so sorry."

"Well, it'll either be great for business, or I'll want to become a hermit after it's over." He looked toward the Taggart farm. Lance was working on one of the tractors. *Better double-check his work later.*

"Do you regret it?"

Her question caught him off guard. Gideon watched her bite her thumbnail when he didn't respond right away.

Shaking his head, he reached over and pushed up her sunglasses. Nutmeg-brown eyes stared hesitantly up at him and his heart reacted. *Fuck, those eyes do it every time.*

"I could never regret kissing you, Ireland. It'd be wrong on too many levels." He lightly traced his knuckles across her cheek.

"Well, I'm glad we both agree."

She grinned, and he told himself to keep his distance. Ireland wasn't his girlfriend. She had her own life and her own relationships, ones he didn't know about. Getting involved with her would only end in tragedy on his side.

"Damn, they're back." She pointed toward the road.

Gideon followed her gaze and saw the news van. "Wow, they really don't let go of a story, do they?"

"Not when I'm involved." She patted her hair and

frowned. "Sorry about all this."

"If it means you stick around, I'll deal with them."

Ireland leaned up and kissed his cheek. "Thanks, but I'll handle them. If I don't, they'll camp out in the bushes and watch you brush your teeth." She undid her ponytail and put on lip balm, clearly ready for her celebrity status.

"Hey, you're gorgeous, you know that, right?" he said, snaking an arm around her waist and pulling her back to him. Dark pink flushed her cheeks. He'd never get sick of seeing her blush.

"I should go take care of that." She nodded toward the group of reporters searching for her. Already, Zavier was outside talking to them. They'd see Gideon and Ireland soon enough.

"All right, but first...." He bent his head and captured her lips beneath his. She tasted sweeter than the honey lip balm, and he tilted her head up for a better angle. Her fingers slipped around his neck, tugging until his body collided with hers. He didn't ever want to imagine anyone else touching her. If all he had to do to be with Ireland was let a few photographers snap away, he'd readily let them have their way.

Ireland whimpered when he broke the kiss, and the sound ripped through his body. He couldn't let that be the last sound he heard from her. Overtaking her mouth once more, his hands traced her back until they rested on her ass. *Two handfuls, just like I remember.* She moaned but didn't stop kissing him. His mind buzzed with longing to tear off her clothes and lay her down in the clover.

"Ireland, Gideon, you have company," Toby singsonged.

Breaking free, he glanced at Ireland's lips, now red and plump. He swallowed at the sight and let out a breath. "I'll see you tomorrow."

She nodded, eyes still hazy. "Yeah, sure."

Smirking, Gideon patted her ass and walked in the opposite direction. Once he was out of earshot, he looked over his shoulder. Sure enough, five reporters surrounded Ireland and Toby.

Only she wasn't paying attention to them. She was staring at him.

CHAPTER NINE

"Ireland, wake up." Toby shook her shoulder.

"Bugger off, Toby," she said in a mock British accent and rolled over.

He exaggerated a gasp but didn't give up trying to wake her. "No, seriously, you need to wake your arse up. Now."

Coming to grips with the fact that he wouldn't leave her alone until she pried her eyes open, Ireland sat up. "What is so freaking important that you wake me up at—" She glanced at the clock on the wall. "—six in the morning. God, are you crazy?"

Instead of answering, he thrust a tablet in her face. Her eyes widened at the photos on the gossip site. "They took the bait. Hook, line, and sinker. That's what Americans say, right?"

Ireland grabbed the iPad and scrolled through the article. Most of the page was filled with photos of her and Mason on the beach the other day. She grimaced at the close-ups of them. The shots from the day before of her and Gideon were far off and fuzzy. The headline hinting at a battle for the heiress made her groan. There was also a nice comparison between her kisses with Gideon and her near kiss with Mason.

If they only knew.

"Ugh. I hate paparazzi sometimes."

Toby swiped the tablet back. "I think it's hot. Can you imagine the kind of press you'll get today?" He shook his head. "A lot. And those stuffy businessmen who didn't want to sign with Bourgeois Investments will change their minds immediately. It's amazing how slapping Mason's name on something helps."

"Great. I'm going back to bed." She flopped down to the pillow and pulled the blanket over her face. Her little chat with the reporters the other day helped keep them at a distance. She'd had to promise exclusives, but they were worth it if they left Gideon alone.

"Uh, Ireland, I don't think that's going to happen anytime soon." Toby poked her side.

"Ow!" She sat up and scowled. "What're you—"

The buzzing sound from outside interrupted the rest of her question. Following the noise, she and Toby pressed their noses against the bedroom window. Her eyes widened, and she pulled up the double pane.

A helicopter slowly descended from the sky and landed on the empty field to the south of the house. Mason dismounted from the shiny chopper with his bag in tow, his thick hair tossing in the wind caused by the blades.

Once clear of the helicopter, he waved at the pilot. She watched in slow motion as the breeze whipped across his shirt until it was tight enough to see his six-pack abs. He trudged toward the farmhouse, searching the windows. When he spotted her, his white teeth shone in a broad smile.

"Girl, if you don't suck his—" The rest of Toby's lewd statement was drowned out when she popped her head out the window as the helicopter lifted off.

"Now let's see. I'm rather rusty at all things romantic, but this does resemble either Rapunzel or Romeo." Mason jested, reaching the house. He dropped his bag and glanced at the hydrangea bush directly below her window. "I don't think that'll be much help getting to you. Do you have a door by chance?"

Ireland pushed back her hair that was sure to be a mangled mess. "Around the front."

Mason tucked his sunglasses in his breast pocket. "Perfect, but for the sake of Shakespeare, I'm going to scale this wall and hope you see how diligent I am when it comes to my businesses and friends."

"You wouldn't?" She gasped when he shed his jacket.

Toby sighed like a lovestruck teenager. "He's so romantic."

"Not the word I was thinking." Ireland rolled her eyes and backed off the bed and looked under it. Finding the fire ladder, she tossed it down the side of the house. It nearly reached the bottom. "There. I don't need my soon-to-be business partner cracking his neck."

Mason tugged on the ladder. "Touché."

He started climbing, his muscular arms easily scaling the side of the house.

"What the living hell?" a new voice questioned from the lawn.

Ireland peeked around Mason and burst out laughing at her brother's expression. His hair was disarrayed, and he only had boxers and rubber boots on. "Uh, um… good morning."

"Good morning? I wake up to a freaking helicopter outside, then see some dude climbing an emergency ladder to my sister's window. It's not a good morning."

Mason reached the top of the ladder and slid through the window, then poked his head back outside and waved. "My apologies. You must be Zavier."

Zavier crossed his arms over his chest and squinted at them. "Wait, I know you. You're Mason Straight, right? The man who revolutionized wine in France and Italy."

"In the flesh." He smiled. "Though, I wouldn't say revolutionized."

Nodding, Zavier glanced at his sister with a perplexed expression. "I think you have some explaining to do, little sis."

Ireland looked to Mason, then Toby. "You're probably right."

Zavier pointed to the kitchen and nodded. "I know I'm right. You're making breakfast." He jogged toward the front of the house, and within seconds the screen door slammed shut.

The trio sat back on the bed. "So, I take it you haven't told your family about anything?" Mason asked.

"Not so much."

"Wonderful." He leaned over and patted her shoulder. "Well, I'll let you get dressed."

Thirty minutes later, Ireland flipped pancakes while she listened to Toby and Mason discuss the business trends in Europe. She was grateful her parents and Zavier hadn't made an appearance yet, wanting to make everything perfect when she introduced them to Mason.

The bacon sizzled on the stovetop, and she flipped the slices over as the front door squeaked open. "Z, you here?"

"Shit!" she yelped, though whether from the bacon grease or Gideon's voice, she didn't know.

"You okay?" Gideon came into the kitchen and noticed her wrist, now red from the hot grease. "Here, let's get some water on it." He led her over to the sink and turned on the faucet.

Ireland stared up at Gideon while he washed off her hands. The tenderness in his touch was like every other time. *Then he hasn't seen Mason yet.* She winced at the pain, still trying to decipher which one caused it.

"There. Slap a bandage on it and you'll be fine." He smiled beneath his beard. If smiles could melt underwear off, his would every time. "Anything else hurt?"

"No. Thanks." She slowly shook her head.

He stepped back and grabbed the tongs to flip the bacon. "Good. I, uh, saw a chopper over here this morning and wanted to see if Zavier knew anything about it." His eyes grazed her body. "Or you, maybe."

Ireland wiped off her hands. "Actually I do. It was a friend of mine."

"A friend?" His brows rose.

"Yeah, he's my business partner."

"Ireland, you have to tell Toby that he can't possibly buy land in Iceland." Mason walked into the kitchen area and paused. "Oh, hello."

Gideon's body instantly tensed at the intrusion. He turned his head toward the newcomer, and Ireland wished she could vanish.

Mason glanced between the two of them, then stuck out his hand. "I'm Mason Straight."

"Gideon Taggart."

The two shook hands, and Mason looked to Ireland. "*The* Gideon Taggart?"

"Yeah." She stopped herself from fleeing the room when Mason walked over to stand beside her.

"Lovely to meet the farmer who's made international news just by kissing this gorgeous lady."

Gideon's eyes drifted to Ireland and then Mason before he turned around and focused on the bacon and pancakes. "I never wanted the publicity."

Ireland held in a groan. He was pissed and he didn't even know the whole story yet.

God, I want to disappear.

"Ireland, what kind of picture is this?" she heard her mom call out, coming into the kitchen. Her father and brother were hot on Joanna's heels. Suddenly the space was entirely too small.

"Who's this?" her dad asked.

"Mason." Zavier filled in, stealing a piece of bacon.

"Mason?" Joanna's eyes widened and she held up her tablet. "Mason Straight?"

"Yeah, he's my friend and business—"

Joanna didn't slow down. "I thought he was in France. And why are people talking about Gideon online? They're comparing both men like it's some sick game."

A pancake soared through the air and landed on the floor instead of Zavier's plate. She watched Gideon's face darken as he tossed the spatula to the counter to investigate Joanna's words.

The four of them crowded around the tablet while Ireland and Mason stood at the opposite end of the kitchen. After a good thirty seconds, eight eyes were suddenly on the duo. Gideon's were pissed. Very pissed.

Her dad took a step toward them, pausing her interaction with Gideon. "Kenny Leighton."

Mason shook his hand. "Pleased to meet you."

"And the commotion I heard this morning, was that you?"

Mason chuckled. "Actually yes. My chum dropped me off a bit early. I apologize for the inconvenience, but—" He looked down at Ireland and smiled. "—I couldn't wait to meet this lady's family. She's told me all about you."

A slow smile crossed Kenny's face. "In that case, I'll take an extra nap later to make up for it."

Ireland sighed in relief. Her dad could be extremely

protective, but it seemed Mason had passed the initial test. She met her mom's eyes and saw tears in them. "Mom? Are you okay?"

"Oh, honey, I'm fine. I'm just so happy for you." Joanna wrapped them both in a hug. "I can already tell he's a keeper."

"Oh my God, Mom, he's not my—" She stopped herself there when her mom kept carrying on.

Once Joanna detached, Ireland watched her brother. He remained intent on the breakfast preparations, which wasn't unusual, but his silence was. "Zavier, get over here and meet your sister's… Ireland, is he your boyfriend?"

Ireland's throat clogged and her mind blanked.

"Actually no. Just friends and partners," Mason stepped in to say.

"Oh sure, honey." Joanna winked at Ireland then waved at her son. "Zavier, did you greet Mason?"

Zavier went to the refrigerator and pulled out a package of sausages. It was only after he put them in a pan that he spoke. "We met. Jury's still out."

Joanna chuckled at Zavier's statement. "Don't mind him. He didn't like any of Ireland's boyfriends."

"Oh my God, Mom, for the last time, he's not—"

"That's because she only had one I cared to meet, and he was the best," Zavier mumbled over the sizzling pork.

"Well, well, well, a sausage fest to start the morning? Yes, please," Toby said, entering the room. He met Ireland's eyes and nodded once. No ESP needed; he knew exactly what she needed with one glance. "Come on, Mama and

Papa Leighton, we have so much to discuss about Barbados. I'll give you the skinny on the best beaches." He led them out of the room, and Ireland was more than aware she'd pay for his distraction later.

Silence simmered among the breakfast meats on the griddle. She watched Gideon stare at Mason, who seemed oblivious to the act. *At least intros are out of the way.* She shifted her weight. No one was speaking, which made it more awkward.

Zavier opened the refrigerator. "Ireland, will you go grab some eggs from the coop? We're almost out." He eyed Mason and Gideon. "And since we have extra guests, I think we'll need more."

"Sure, no problem." She grabbed the basket for egg collecting. "Be nice," she felt compelled to say before she moved to the back door. She didn't chance looking over her shoulder, but if she had to guess, each man inside gave her an annoyed glance.

It was still early when she stepped off the porch. Dew drenched the grass, though not for much longer if the humidity in the air was any indicator. She trekked toward the chicken coops and inside the first one. The scent of poultry made her gag when she was younger, and she noticed her nose hadn't evolved. Hens clucked all around her, voicing their displeasure at the disturbance.

"Sorry, girls. Just need a few eggs."

Chickens huddled around on the floor and she carefully stepped over them. She went for the empty boxes first, finding eggs in each one. It was too easy to fall back into the farm routine. She knew exactly what to do to make the chickens move around enough to snatch their prized possessions to add to her basket. *This is kind of fun.*

When she moved to the second coop, Ireland felt a smile tug her cheeks. All she needed were overalls, braids, and braces and she'd be the teenager with normal farm chores again.

"When were you going to tell me about your millionaire boyfriend?"

Startled at the low voice, Ireland dropped the egg in her hand. It splattered on the ground and she shrieked. "Stop scaring me, geez."

Gideon put his hands on his hips. "Stop hiding things from me."

"Good point." She moved to the next box but came up empty.

"Ireland."

Ignoring him, she finished off the row. Naturally, he positioned himself so she couldn't get around him without physically moving him, which would be impossible.

"I need to finish this coop."

He shook his head. "Not until you tell me why you lied."

Her eyes flashed. "I didn't lie."

"You also didn't tell me about the damn millionaire you're obviously in love with."

"First off, I'm not in love with him. Far from it." She chuckled at the notion. "We're friends and business partners."

Gideon laughed, though it wasn't his usual cheerful one.

This sound made her spine tingle. "Right, well whatever you want to call it, he likes you, and you like him. The end."

Ireland set down the nearly full basket and glared at him. With a white T-shirt, his tanned forearms stood out even more in the dim lighting. His dirty jeans and matching boots almost blended into their setting. "Mason and I have an understanding—"

He squinted. "Wait, so an open relationship? Seriously, Ireland?"

"Um, I never said that."

He cursed. "I don't get it. You could have any man, yet you go for the playboy and agree to a relationship where you're always going to be hurt by him."

"It's not like that. You don't understand at all." She was officially fed up with him. He clearly wasn't going to listen, even if she explained everything about her merger with Mason. Gideon was jealous and talking to him right now would just be ignored.

Gideon gripped her shoulders, forcing her eyes to meet his. "Then make me understand, Ireland. Because from where I'm standing, you're throwing away the best parts of you to be with somebody rich."

She swallowed at the emotions quickly rising to her eyes. "Damn, you're just as jealous as ever."

"How could you kiss me and then kiss him days later?" The blue in his eyes darkened. "Was I just a fill-in for him?"

Ireland reached up and traced the side of his face. "No. Listen, I didn't kiss him. We flirted, yes. It was dumb but we're just friends. Plus, I don't want to kiss him." She searched his eyes. "And you aren't a fill-in, Gideon." She let out a breath, scared to finish the thought. Her brain told her not to, but her heart urged her forward. "There is no fill-in for you."

The moment the words left her lips, Gideon was there, kissing them into oblivion. She tightly gripped the front of his shirt, afraid she might tear it apart. Feathers fluttered around them, but the only thing she could focus on was the way Gideon's lips felt against her own. She gasped when his hands roamed down her back and cupped her ass. He lifted her off the coop floor, and she wrapped her legs around his waist.

If she could make them vanish to somewhere more private, she would. All she'd wanted since the moment she saw him was to be completely his again in every possible way.

His hot breath clashed with the side of her neck and he nibbled up to her jaw. "Then don't be with him."

His words were the cold water she needed. Ireland's eyes flew open and she wiggled free. Heaving to catch her breath, she stared at Gideon. His lips were bruised from her touch, and his shirt was wrinkled from where she'd grasped it. "I'm not. But I have to for business."

"Why?"

Ireland ran her fingers along her lips. "Because he can help me."

"Is it because he has money because—"

"No, it's…." She stopped herself there. Part of the reason

to join their businesses was due to money. She couldn't lie about that. "It's complicated, Gideon. His connections are exactly what I need for my future." His face fell at her words, so she quickly added, "And it's not because I want him." She reached up and smoothed back his wild hair. "It's because it's what's best for me."

"He doesn't seem like a guy who's just here to close a deal, Ireland. I only just met the guy, but I see the way he looks at you."

She ran her hand against his chest. "Believe me, I'm nowhere near ready to fall in love again. Mason knows that." Ireland ached to tell Gideon the rest of her tale. It'd be so easy to spill her secret about still being half in love with him, but her father's voice called across the yard.

"Ireland, are you laying the eggs yourself? Come on, girl, we're hungry."

Reaching down, she gathered the basket full of eggs and headed to the exit. "I'm sorry, Gideon. I need to go."

"Wait." He caught her hand. "Is there any chance for us?"

As much as she wanted to give him hope, she wouldn't. Gideon deserved a woman who wasn't tangled up with mergers and millionaires.

She shook her head. "No."

***

Gideon didn't want to stay for breakfast, but he couldn't say no to Kenny and Joanna, since they were a second set of parents to him. Every bite he ate was tasteless, though. He didn't feel anything except envy and anger the entire time he sat across from Ireland. Not once did she look over to him. Of course, that could've been because she was withholding information from him.

It wasn't hard to decipher. She was a horrible liar. Always had been, always would be. She couldn't make eye contact when she lied. It was her tell, and one he never forgot.

He finished his cup of coffee and was grateful the conversation focused on the newest guest. The shorter Brit didn't worry him. The tall, good-looking, rich one did. Mason was obviously entranced by Ireland. *Well, join the crowd, buddy.* The guy made every effort to touch her, even if just briefly, though Gideon would do the same if the roles were reversed.

He stood and took his dishes to the kitchen. Setting them in the sink, he gripped the edge of the counter and took a deep breath at the snort Ireland let out.

"Don't worry about this rich dude. Like she said, he's here to get to know his new business partner," Zavier encouraged, pushing Gideon out of the way so he could fill the dishwasher.

A sneaking feeling came over Gideon and he pulled out his smartphone. Typing in a vague search on the internet, he grunted. "According to a bunch of gossip blogs and social media, she and Mr. Millionaire have been sighted together for the last few months."

Zavier stopped his dish duty and wiped his hands on the back of his jeans. "Let me see that." He grabbed the phone and scrolled the pages with his thumb. His brows furrowed together the longer he stared at the screen. "So what? She said they were friends. Friends hang out, Tagg. You're being stupid."

"Yeah, maybe you're right."

He slid the phone back into his pocket and walked to the doorway. From his viewpoint, Ireland looked perfectly content being Mason's arm candy. He'd stopped frequenting any articles about Ireland after the first year she'd been gone—most of it hurt to see, and he wasn't even sure if the facts were true—but the same couldn't be said now. She admitted her relationship with Mason was professional, but he still didn't like it. Any guy with a brain would want Ireland as more than a friend or business partner.

"I'm heading to town."

"To talk to the bank?"

Gideon nodded, his stomach rolling at the thought. "Yeah. Hopefully they'll extend the loan a little longer."

"When are you going to tell your folks you want to be a vet and not a farmhand?"

He rubbed the back of his neck. "I can't yet. It's not the time."

Zavier scrubbed a pan. "It'll never be the time, Tagg. If you don't act on your dream, you'll wake up fifty years from now and regret it."

Gideon knew his friend meant the words more than one way. "I'll think on it some more." He decided the back exit was the best way to escape without being questioned.

Quietly, he made his way to the door and paused long

enough to see Mason lean over and kiss Ireland's cheek. He swore his blood cooled to arctic temperatures at the sight. Ireland may not have been his, but she wasn't Mason's either. Giving up wasn't in the cards. Not when there was a possibility that Ireland could change her mind. After all, she was a terrible liar, and the last one she'd told him stood out the most before she retreated to the house.

He may not have millions in the bank like Mason Straight, but Gideon had something better for the heiress.

He had love.

CHAPTER TEN

Following Mason's dramatic arrival, they'd spent most of the day with her family. Naturally, her dad gave him the grand tour of the farm and talked his ear off about livestock. Mason took it all in stride. She was surprised when he even managed to give sound advice about the next planting season. Either Mason was great at making things up on the fly, or he actually did research about Iowa and crops before arriving. She went with the latter when Mason pointed out Iowa's native bird in the brush near the chicken coops.

After the never-ending tour, she was glad her dad went and helped her mom get dinner ready. She could use some time off after being with them the entire day.

She watched Zavier greet Krista with a long kiss.

"They're adorably in love," Mason stated from beside her on the straw bale.

She pulled a handful of straw out and picked at it. "Yeah.

She's good for him, I think."

"So, how am I doing?"

Ireland looked over. He'd changed out of his expensive clothes, though she was positive the jeans and T-shirt he wore were brand new and overly pricey. "You're doing great."

He squeezed her knee. "Good. Maybe I've earned some brownie points, and you'll decide to throw in your California vineyard in the merger documents tonight, yeah?"

She tossed straw at him and laughed when it stuck in his dark hair. "We'll see."

"Hey, Mason, want to get your hands dirty?" Zavier asked, an ax over one shoulder. Krista clung to his free hand, a lovestruck expression in her eyes.

Mason looked over to her. "Well, what do you think? Should I try and impress your brother with my bulging muscles?"

"Do you even know how to split wood?"

"Madam, you wound me with your doubt." He plunged a pretend knife in his heart, then stood. "Lead the way, Zavier."

Still wary of the outcome, Ireland followed Zavier, Krista, and Mason toward the pile of uncut wood. She choked on her spit when she saw Lance and Gideon already there, shirtless. *Of course they are.* She managed to cover up her surprise with a laugh when she spotted Toby sitting cross-legged on a pile of logs.

"I always knew you liked wood," she teased, coming up behind him.

Toby chuckled and lifted his shades. "Ooh, and you brought me more eye candy. Thank you, princess." He frowned slightly. "Too bad none of them are gay."

Ireland pulled Toby toward a more comfortable spot, a stack of circular hay bales for the south fields. Once they were situated, she stretched out on her stomach on the large bale. Krista wasn't far away on her own hay bale. They were the perfect height to see and hear all the action.

"Right, so, how do we do this?" Mason asked, picking up a spare ax.

Lance chuckled and grabbed a large piece of wood, placed it on the chopping block and swung his ax over his shoulder. The sharp sound of split wood echoed in the fields. He tossed the wood pieces to the pile nearby and nodded to Mason. "Like that, rich boy."

Mason looked to Ireland, then back to the three men. "All right, seems simple enough."

Zavier tore off his shirt—resulting in Krista whistling—before he chopped his chunk of tree into two slices. "It's easy, really." He nudged Gideon as if giving him the okay to show off as well.

Ireland rolled her eyes at the juvenile act. She'd seen it plenty of times, but just between the three of them. Having a new person around made her anxious for the outcome.

Gideon turned away from her and she noticed the artwork on his back. Her throat dried at the primitive yet compelling tribal tattoo running down his spine. A few other tattoos stood out on his ribs, but she couldn't tell what they were from the distance. She settled her chin into her hand

and tried not to think about tracing all his tattoos with her fingers. Or tongue.

"Mm, he's tasty," Toby said dreamily.

She didn't have time to respond before Gideon lifted his ax and brought it down on the wood. It cracked into even pieces, and he tossed them aside as if they were as light as twigs.

Ireland caught Mason's eyes and he winked. *Dear God, don't do something stupid.* She sat up when he handed his ax to Lance.

"You know, I never grew up on a farm," he started, pulling his shirt off. "But I did spend several summers with my uncle in Scotland. He was one woodsy bastard who also taught me a lot of tricks for surviving in the wilderness alone."

Toby tapped on Ireland's thigh when Mason's naked chest came into view. "I know, I know!" she whispered at the chiseled features.

"You could wash clothes on those damn abs."

Ireland giggled at Toby all but drooling next to her. "Or lick for days."

Toby nodded in agreement. "Yeah, put a little salt on those abs, the tequila in his belly button and the lime on his—"

Mason turned around and Toby lost all his words. The front of Mason Straight was gorgeous, but the backside was even better.

"Please make him gay," Toby prayed, hands clasped together as he looked up at the sky.

"I don't think that's how it works."

Toby snorted. "You never know. I believe in miracles."

She chuckled, then focused on Mason. With fluid movements, he grabbed the ax and two chunks of wood.

After stacking the wood on opposite sides of him, he nodded to Gideon. "Mind if I borrow yours?"

Gideon eyed him oddly but handed over his ax.

They all watched in amazement as he easily brought down both axes and chopped the pieces of wood into four slices at once.

"Holy fuck, that's hot," Toby said a little too loud.

Mason beamed her direction as the women and Toby clapped enthusiastically. He bowed and turned back to the men. "And that is how we do it in the United Kingdom, gentlemen."

Ireland noticed Gideon's jaw clench tight. It shouldn't have been humorous, but it was nonetheless. Without asking, she guessed one of them thought this stunt would embarrass Mason. Well, the joke was on them since Mason blew them all out of the water with his finesse.

Zavier grinned. "Impressive. Very impressive" He glanced over to his sister and nodded once.

"Well, he passed Z's test," she said quietly to Toby.

"Mason will pass everyone's test, Ireland. He's the perfect guy no matter how you look at it."

Sitting back, Ireland decided to watch it all unfold.

Toby wasn't wrong. Mason blew by any challenge given to him, though it shouldn't have come as a shock. Since knowing him, Ireland learned Mason didn't do something unless he was certain he'd come out victorious. He clearly wanted her to sign the merger documents, but there was a little part of her that held back.

But if the gleam in Gideon's eyes was any indicator, chopping wood wasn't the only test of manliness and resilience Mason was sure to endure during his short stay at the Leighton farm.

***

Gideon chucked his hat across the room and leaned over the exam table. Thankfully he didn't have any patients staying the night or they would've gotten quite the show. He wasn't one to make a scene, but he never wanted to do it more than that afternoon.

Mason was more than a millionaire. The guy crumpled any British stereotype Gideon knew of and made three Iowa boys look like… well, boys. It'd been Zavier's idea to try their hand at splitting firewood. It would've worked too, if Mason hadn't been raised by woodsmen.

He stared at the posters on the wall of the makeshift clinic. The guy even got the upper hand when it came to what Gideon did best. When they checked on a horse, Mason took over completely and dug out a nail from the mare's shoe. Afterward, he watched the millionaire soothe a spooked stallion—thanks to Toby—and even rescue a kitten from falling out of the barn loft.

If that didn't make Gideon feel inadequate, then pitching hay made it worse. The large stack of hay in the Leighton barn wasn't going to move itself, and since he was officially competing for Ireland, he'd suggested they do it by hand instead of forklift.

Yeah, because that worked well. He picked hay out of his beard and crumpled it in his hand.

He didn't get why the women and Toby fawned over Mason. He had muscles, but none that compared to Gideon's. The Englishman had a fancy accent, but Gideon had kickass tattoos. That had to count for something, right? So what if he didn't have millions? He was just as good if not better than Mason.

Gideon rested his forehead on the cool metal table to steady his breathing. The hot sun did a number on him, but not as much as when Ireland paid more attention to Mason than him. That was why he failed at dating—the only thing he cared about was what Ireland thought. If the day had taught him anything, it was that he was at a loss no matter what direction he went. She'd made it clear she wouldn't change her mind. Well, he was equally as stubborn as her.

Glancing around the small area, he blew a noisy raspberry. If he could work there all day every day, he'd be happy.

He rolled his shoulders back, the muscles straining painfully.

Mostly happy.

His cell phone rang, and he recognized it as Mrs. Baughman. Her border collie suffered from terrible allergies, the black-and-white dog one of his most frequent clients.

Right now, he'd see what good he could do to help

someone who'd appreciate his efforts. When it came to Ireland, he wasn't so sure.

CHAPTER ELEVEN

Twilight tapered off to darkness by the time Ireland reached the makeshift dock at Miller Pond. After a day filled with stacking hay bales, hoeing the gardens, and mucking out stalls, she thought for sure Mason would run for the nearest airport and hightail it to international waters. He didn't, which pissed Gideon off—at least that's what it looked like to Ireland when she watched him stalk back to his farm for a late dinner.

Even after all that, the Taggart sons invited the Leightons and guests for one of their childhood outings. Ireland stared at her phone and wondered why the hell she convinced Toby and Mason to visit the pond at that time of night. Already, mosquitos swarmed her not-so-quiet partner in crime, Toby. Mason didn't seem to mind the insects.

"Remind me again what we're doing at a stinky pond at ten at night?" Toby asked, scanning the area with the flashlight app on his phone. He looked far out of his element for a man who supposedly grew up near a lake.

"It's called gigging," Ireland replied, holding up a camping lantern. "I haven't been in years."

"Good God, I think I just caught Zika virus!" Toby yelled, swatting at his arms. He took out the bug repellent and sprayed the air around him. "I'm officially dying. Are you happy?"

Giggling, Ireland shook her head and exchanged a humored glance with Mason. "We're in Iowa, Tobes. No Zika and no dying. Stop being dramatic."

Toby shot her a droll glance. "Doll, I love you, but I'm going to kill you for dragging me out here like this."

"Oh no you don't. You said you wanted to see what I did in Iowa as a kid and—"

"There you are." Gideon's voice cut through the night sky and startled the trio. His tall silhouette was accompanied by two other shadows. "I thought you guys might've bailed on me."

Ireland grinned at him, then to Zavier and Krista once they came into view. "And miss out on you jumping around like frogs? Hell to the no." She glanced around. "Wait, where's Lance? I thought he was coming too."

"He had a date." Gideon crossed his arms and stared at Mason. "You ready for this?"

Mason eyed Gideon from head to toe, then wrapped his arm around Ireland's waist. "I'm always up for something new and exciting."

For a moment, neither man moved. "Great. Me too."

The tension in the air choked her. Both men were speaking in underlying tones, and she wished they'd get it over with already. She'd been very clear with Gideon, but apparently not enough to make it stick.

Her eyes swung back to her ex. He wore tall waders with an old T-shirt, and his damned hat as usual. She rolled her eyes. *Why does he even need it at night?*

He caught her staring and grinned.

"Not to be a downer, but I don't hear any frogs," Toby pointed out.

Zavier clicked on his headlight. "Not yet. Stick with me, city boy. I'll show you all the good spots."

"God, this is so American and redneck," Toby complained when Zavier handed him an ice cooler.

"Yep, sure is." Zavier shot a wry grin to Ireland, then grabbed his gig. "There's not much to do around here, so we think up new ways to get in trouble."

"Plus frog legs are delicious," Gideon added.

Toby made a face, but Ireland held up her net. "You won't know until you try it. Z's recipe is pure perfection."

"Let's just get this over with so I can soak in a tub." Toby shivered. "I can feel slimy critters everywhere." He took a step and grimaced.

"You come with me and Krista," Zavier suggested. "We'll show you the ropes. Who knows? Maybe you'll like it."

"Not likely." Toby frowned.

"How are there frogs big enough in Iowa to eat?" Mason asked.

Zavier jutted his chin up. "We stock this pond, and the Millers let us hunt it."

"Bloody hell, you really are bored." Toby shrieked and jumped. "I swear to God, something just bit my arse!"

"C'mon," Zavier laughed, leading Toby away from the spot.

Toby kept complaining as he followed Zavier and Krista around to the north side of the quiet pond.

"Guess the two of you are with me," Gideon said, voice a bit disgruntled when he looked at Mason. He took off before she could respond.

They walked in silence, shining flashlights on the shallow shores every now and then.

"Toby seems nice," Gideon said once they were far enough away from the other three. He made it a point to ignore Mason, not that she expected anything else.

Ireland batted at a spider web. She may have grown up on a farm, but they were still creepy as hell. "Yeah, Toby's great. He's been my travel buddy since day one."

"Nice." He moved closer to the bank.

"Do you travel much?" Mason asked, joining the conversation.

Gideon cleared his throat. "Nah. Not a lot of time when you're running a farm."

Mason lifted his brows to Ireland at the curt reply. She mouthed, "Sorry" right before Gideon spoke to her again.

"Shine the light to the left. I heard splashes."

Cursing her lack of focus, Ireland aimed her flashlight at the top of the water. They waited in silence for what seemed like an hour. Finally, Gideon sprang into action, his spear-like gig in hand. Croaking, splashing, and grunting met her ears while he went under after the frogs. It came as no surprise when he emerged from the water with both hands full. His broad smile was well worth the smell of the muck covering the rest of him.

"Three big ones." He grabbed his Styrofoam icebox and tossed them inside. "Want to take a turn?"

A spark of excitement filled her stomach. "Yes!" She shoved him out of the way and scoured the murky water. Bubbles popped up here and there, the sounds of Iowa at night coming awake the longer they stayed outside. The croaking frogs overwhelmed the crickets, and Ireland smirked over at Gideon. He smelled like a swamp after the first round, but she had to admit, he looked handsome despite the dip.

Toby screamed from the other end of the pond and they exchanged a glance. "I'm gonna go out on a limb and say your friend isn't a fan of getting dirty."

Ireland shook her head and hopped over a fallen log. "Um, no. Toby thinks most things are too dirty." She scanned the area with her light. "Ironically, not when we were in Europe. He made me do some crazy shit over there."

"Like what?"

She noticed Mason lagged behind them, intent on finding his own frog. Thinking back over her travels, she realized there were too many to sort through, but she settled on one in Italy. "Well, this one time we were in Rome, Toby and I were flirting with these guys."

"Great start," he grunted.

Ignoring him, she continued. "And he convinced me to enroll in the gladiator school." She smiled. "I have to admit it was fun, even if I dropped the shield on my pinky toe and broke it. He ended up taking both our dates back to his hotel room." Heat flooded her cheeks. "Let's just say the walls between our rooms weren't very thick, and evidently both of them were very into Toby."

She glanced over her shoulder and noticed Mason was staring into the water with his light. Deciding he could catch up with them, she picked up her feet so she didn't lose Gideon.

"Your pal is a little wild." Gideon wiped his brow with his forearm. His face was barely visible by the old lantern light, but she could see he wasn't a fan of the last part of the story. He pushed a tree branch out of her way. "Do you like, uh, that sort of thing? Two guys." He scratched his neck. "Or girls, maybe?"

Ireland burst out laughing at the delicate way of asking. It was too cute, and she held her sides while snorting. "No, definitely not." He looked a tad too relieved until she added, "But maybe I should try it. Toby said it was fun, after all."

The blood in Gideon's face all but drained and he coughed. "Um, well, then—"

"I'm kidding." She punched his arm. "I don't swing both ways. And I don't think I could handle more than one guy at a time." Heat flooded her face at the thought. As delightful as Gideon had been the other day, there was no way she could take another guy at the same time. She shivered, her mind rerunning the way Gideon's tongue, lips, and fingers knew her so intimately.

"Glad to hear it," he replied with a small smile. "I sure wouldn't want to handle more than one woman at a time, but I'm old-fashioned."

Ireland's ankle turned in the mud, but Gideon caught her before she stumbled headfirst into the water.

"And I'm also possessive like that." His arm tightened around her waist. "I wouldn't be able to watch another man touch what's mine." His eyes dipped to her lips. "I'd be too jealous."

Swallowing hard, she considered closing the minimal distance between their faces. If he kissed her, she wouldn't deny him. But she shouldn't encourage his affection. Not after already feeling her heart shift his direction when she first saw him. She would leave after Zavier's wedding and once again, Gideon wouldn't go with her.

Gideon leaned in, his nose brushing hers. The kiss was coming; she just knew it. Her body buzzed with anticipation. Briefly their lips met, but he drew back. "We better get back to it if we want a snack later." He pulled away completely and pulled her out of the knee-deep mud.

Disappointed, Ireland watched him trudge through the water and snatch two more bullfrogs. He held them up, grinning from ear to ear. They'd have food later, that was for certain.

She wasn't so sure about her feelings for Gideon. The longer she stayed in Iowa, the more she felt herself slipping back into the farm girl who fell for the boy next door.

Mason's voice caught up with her and she felt instant shame. She'd been too worried about Gideon that she completely forgot that the entire reason Mason was visiting was to see if they'd make good partners. Well, she was failing miserably in that department.

The tall Brit held up a frog when he reached her. "This is incredible! I completely understand why you'd like doing this. It's an adrenaline high." He pulled her toward the pond. "Come on, let's see how many more we can get."

***

Gideon battered the dozen frog legs and added oil to the frying pan. Their frog hunt only lasted thirty minutes before Toby complained about his manicure. Subsequently, the short man also fell into the marsh, making everyone but him burst out laughing. The only bad part about his unexpected swan dive was that he knocked over the containers that held their catch.

Now, an hour later, he dug out a bag of frozen frog legs and got to work. Zavier moseyed around the Leighton kitchen while Toby and Ireland showered the muck away. He had to hand it to Ireland—she didn't shy away from the fun, and even flopped in once to get a frog.

"Damn, Tagg, you reek," Zavier said, holding his nose.

Gideon lifted his shirt and sniffed. His friend wasn't wrong. "Hey, you were the one to suggest Miller's. That place smells bad even without the frogs."

Zavier shrugged and handed him a plate. "True, but you

wanted to go frog gigging, and it's the best spot around here."

"Good point." The oil sizzled in the pan, and Gideon carefully placed the meat inside. The noise intensified, as did the rumble in his belly. "I guess we're both to blame."

"Plus you wouldn't have set this up to make Mr. Millionaire feel inadequate for my little sis, now would you?"

Gideon didn't answer. It was the truth, but he wouldn't admit it.

"Ha! I knew it. You've been acting like a caveman all day, trying to show him up, haven't you?"

"Maybe."

"No maybes, Tagg. You still love her, huh?"

Adding more oil, Gideon nodded. "Yeah."

"And she brought the perfect husband material home. Man, that's got to be rough." He patted Gideon's shoulder. "I'm sorry."

"It is what it is."

From the corner of his eye, Gideon saw Zavier pull off his shirt and walk toward the downstairs bathroom. "I'm going to hop in the shower really quick before Krista finishes up in there." He wiggled his eyebrows. "Save me a few, yeah?" Zavier called, disappearing around the corner.

With Zavier gone, Gideon grabbed a pair of tongs and focused on his task. He couldn't help but think of how beautiful Ireland looked after she caught a frog. Naturally, she was always gorgeous, but seeing her in the element that he knew her best gave his heart a jump. He'd wanted to hate her after she left. For a while he did, but no matter what he tried, the best he did was push down his feelings. *And they never went away.* Having Mason along with them only made it worse. Seeing another man flourish at the same activities he and Ireland used to do hit too close to his heart.

An exotic scent wafted past the fishiness of the frogs, and he felt Ireland's presence before he saw her. She was a cloud of everything he desired. It was too easy for him to get lost in her eyes, her smile, her touch and never want to find the way out.

"All clean?" he asked, not breaking contact with the pan.

"I am." Bare feet padded on the linoleum flooring. Soon her dark red toenails were within his sight. "Ugh, I'm going to throw you in next. You smell horrible."

He looked up in time to see her nose all scrunched up. The smallest acts were cute on her, a fact he'd long loved. "Gladly." He flipped the frog legs. "But not until these are golden brown."

Ireland poked her head around his left arm and gazed at the concoction. "Mm, they smell incredible." She smiled up at him. "Though I'm pretty sure Toby will barf after one taste."

Gideon held up one of the legs. "Shred it off and tell him it's chicken." He waved it at her. "Maybe he won't notice the difference."

"I can try, but Toby is a snob when it comes to new food." Ireland shuffled to the cabinets and grabbed plates. Gideon couldn't tear his gaze away from the short blue pajama bottoms and matching tank top. She wasn't wearing a bra, and his dick twitched within seconds of seeing her bounce up and down to get a cup from the top shelf.

Spinning, Ireland caught him ogling. She offered him a shy grin but didn't say anything.

Gideon immediately returned to the pan spitting oil at him. A well-deserved speck of hot oil smacked his cheek. *What the hell are you doing? She told you she didn't want you.* His mind traveled to the other day when she'd begged him to screw her in the corn row. *Well, not exactly.*

He tried to reason with himself until he lost all control of what he was doing.

"You're burning them," Ireland advised, grabbing the pan's handle and pulling it off the stovetop.

Gideon huffed at the nearly blackened frog legs. "Dammit. Sorry, I was lost in thought."

Scrutinizing the food, she poked at the legs with a fork, then nodded once as if they passed her test and were still edible. "No worries. Just adds extra character, right?"

She called up the stairs to Toby and Mason and knocked on the door for Zavier, but no one rushed to the kitchen. Returning to the wooden table, she pulled out a chair and sat. "Might as well eat it while it's hot."

Gideon divvied up the frog legs onto plates, brought two of them to the table, and handed one to her. He sat opposite Ireland and they both dug into the Southern cuisine.

"These are so good," she mumbled between bites.

He chewed longer than normal to keep from leaning over and wiping the side of her mouth with his hand. "You miss a lot when you travel the world."

Ireland grabbed a napkin and dabbed her face. "Home cooking at its finest. I've missed it, if I'm being honest. Some of the food I had overseas was disgusting."

"I can only imagine." His phone chirped, and he pulled it out of his pocket.

"Need to take that?"

"Nah, I'm fine." He swiped left on the screen, then tossed it on the table. Ireland peeked his way, and he held in a smile. *At least she's somewhat interested.*

They ate in silence until his phone beeped again. Ireland glanced over but didn't comment. He'd bide his time. She was curious, and he'd wait. He may not give a damn about the person on the other end of the phone chat, but Ireland did. It was enough for him, even if he'd have to use a little white lie.

"About what happened in the cornfield and then the field near the garden," she began, lowering her voice.

Gideon met her wary gaze. "What about it?"

"Er, uh, well, it was nice," she stammered. "But…."

His jaw clenched instinctively. *Nice.* That was the word she'd use to describe it. "Mmhmm." His phone went off once more, and that time he picked it up. "Sorry, it's this dumb farmer dating site Zavier set up for me. He thinks it'll get me a wife or something."

Ireland's brown eyes flicked from his face to the phone and then back again. "Oh, sure. I guess I didn't realize you were actively looking for a, um, wife."

His pulse accelerated. Ireland all riled up was adorable. She twisted her hands in the hem of her tank top and acted cool, but she most assuredly was not calm and collected. *Shit, if I'd known she'd react like this, I would've turned on the app when she first arrived.*

He wiped his beard with a napkin. "I like to keep my options open," he said casually.

Ireland snorted, then picked at the last frog leg on her plate. "Then I should assume what happened between us was just old feelings, right?"

He shook his head. She wasn't dumb, but sometimes she was dense. While some of his old feelings may have been in play, they didn't control his actions. He sure as hell knew they didn't control hers.

Standing, he stacked the plates together and placed them in the sink, then rested his hands on the edge of the counter. "Ireland, you live in Barbados, you like traveling the world, and you have some weird shit going on with the rich British guy currently in your shower."

"Who Toby may or may not be secretly filming," Ireland added, laughing.

He paused at her joke and veered back to the serious. "I always thought you'd come home." Turning around, he ran a hand through his dirty hair. "Now that you have, I don't know what to do with you."

"What do you mean?" Her brows knit together as she stood.

Gideon's eyes slowly slid over her. "I mean one minute, I want to kiss you because you're that same girl I fell in love with. And then the next, I remember why you left and how I'll never be who you want. I go insane around you, Ireland.

Especially when that Mason guy is near you. Hell, it doesn't matter who the guy is if I'm honest."

"Gideon—" she started, touching his forearm.

He pulled away and backed out the rear door. "I need to shower. Catch you later, darlin'."

He didn't give her the opportunity to call after him. He needed space and fast. If Ireland couldn't see how connected they still were, she never would.

CHAPTER TWELVE

Two rings and Fiona answered the call, her rich French accent sending a smile to Ireland's lips. She'd made it a necessity to learn the language of her ancestors when she'd first learned her parentage.

"*Bonjour*, Grandmother. How are you today?"

"Oh quite fine, my girl. Though I am disappointed you haven't visited me lately."

Ireland walked through the garden farthest from the house and ran her hands over the tomato plants. It was just like her mom to maintain the gardens so pristinely. "Sorry, I've been busy."

"Is your brother all set for the wedding?"

"Yes, I think so." She shielded her eyes and saw Zavier working on a tractor in the other end of the yard. "He seems happy."

"And why wouldn't he be? He's getting married." Fiona

cleared her throat. "Just as I hope you will be soon."

"Grandmother—"

"I'm on borrowed time, Ireland. For too many years, I didn't know you. I don't want the same to be said about my great-grandchildren."

Picking a green bean from a plant, Ireland placed it in the bucket already brimming with fresh vegetables. "Mason's here."

Ireland could practically hear Fiona's smile. "Good, good. He's quite the catch. I think the two of you are ideal together. I wouldn't have suggested the merger if I thought differently."

"Well, he is very business savvy and charming."

Fiona chuckled. "Yes, he is."

"I'm not there yet. I don't know if mixing friendship and business is the greatest idea." She paused and hoped her mom wasn't torturing Mason too much in the kitchen while she was on her call. "Is there anything you know about him that I wouldn't?" She had to ask. She and Mason never had much time to discuss casual things, since they usually spoke about business even when they were out and about as friends.

"Well, as you know, Mason's family is well-off in England. They own several manors and thrive in business ventures. He works closely with his father, who's grooming him to take over the family accounts someday."

"It's just as I thought. He's a trust fund baby." Ireland grabbed an empty bucket and started down the row of squash.

"Somewhat, but he also branched off with his own factory, which led to numerous holdings across the globe." Fiona took a breath, and Ireland heard rattling china in the background. Tea outside in the garden, if she had to take a guess. "Mason knows hard work, as do you. He became a millionaire on his own back. His family money has yet to hit his accounts. He doesn't speak of it often, so I'm not surprised he hasn't told you. Truly, he is a good person and will make a fine partner."

Ireland squatted to pick up the zucchini. All in all, Mason wasn't bad. The few articles she'd read weren't damning. He had a stint of playboy philandering in college, but that was over fifteen years ago. The news now focused on his limited dating life and his lewd business affairs. He seemed to have learned from the publicity and chose to privatize his personal life. She couldn't ask for more from a partner.

"Ireland, are you still there?"

"Yes, sorry. I've spoken to Mason about everything including your secret matchmaking agenda, but I don't feel anything for him."

"Ireland—"

"I know, I know. You want us together and all that, but there's just something holding me back."

The line was silent for a long minute before her grandmother spoke. "I'd never force anything on you, my dear. If you decide that Mason isn't a suitable husband, then I will support you. But I do hope you'll agree to the merger."

"Thanks, that means a lot. On the flip side, we'll finish up the logistics of the business agreement before the end of the summer."

Fiona sighed, relief prevalent on the other end. "Thank you. Oh, but please seriously consider Mason. He's a catch for any young lady. Plus, think of all the adorable babies you'd have. I can picture them now."

Ireland chuckled, but the thought quickly became real. Marrying anyone meant kids of her own. While she wanted a few, she was also scared history may repeat and something would happen to her and her husband. She didn't remember being an orphaned child, but she witnessed plenty of them over the last six years. It wasn't a fate she'd wish on anyone.

"I need to finish up out here. I'll talk to you later." She hung up and sank onto the ground.

Her gaze drifted over to the Taggart farm. *I wonder if he's thought about kids.* She rested her arms on her knees and closed her eyes. *I'm overthinking everything. Just relax.*

She swallowed hard. Her relationship with Gideon was strained because of their past heartbreak. *Perhaps, Grandmother is right, and a marriage without love is a better idea.* It didn't sound good, but it'd be easier.

Standing, she brushed off her shorts. *And easier sounds better than getting your heart ripped out again.*

***

Taking off his gloves, Gideon shut off the engine and cupped his hand to his ear. His brother was yelling something across the yard, but he couldn't hear with the tractor running.

"Dinner in fifteen," Lance said, jogging over to him.

"I'm not done."

Lance shrugged. "Mom invited the Leightons and guests. You don't want to miss it."

Gritting his teeth, he pulled the key and hopped down. "I'm guessing no time for a shower either?"

"Nah, but it's not like Ireland's going to be going gaga over you anyway." His brother chuckled. "She has a British guy to stare at instead."

"Keep it up, Lance, and see what that gets you." He smirked. "Don't forget, I'm the one who has the lion share of the farm. Don't piss me off."

"Psh, but it's so easy." Lance punched his arm and ran in the other direction. "And fun."

Ignoring him, Gideon strode toward the farmhouse. He had enough time to splash water on his face and change before the Leightons arrived.

Rounding the cornstalks, he grunted at the UTV and truck in his parents' driveway.

Or not.

Seeing his only option to clean up now was the barn, he steered in that direction, stopping to pet the pair of sheep he was taking care of while the farmer was away before continuing toward the water faucet in the back. It wasn't the best and hadn't seen the light of day in over thirty years, but it'd get the job done.

His back ached after hauling firewood to the main house. If that'd been the entire day, it would've been bearable. But it was his turn to spray the fields for insects, so he'd lugged the giant water jug from the broken tractor to the running one. A massage and long soak in the tub would do him well.

But we have company.

Tearing off his shirt, he tossed it toward the empty stall where he and Lance kept spare clothes. It'd started in high school when they wanted to sneak out for a party, but the duo continued the extra stash for occasions such as these. Lance mostly used it for when he had ladies over and didn't feel like dragging them to the house for a romp.

He splashed water on his chest and winced at the cold temperature. *Brr. We should get a water heater in here.* Grabbing a clean rag, he scrubbed the grime from his face first. As long as his showing skin was clean, he could get the rest later.

The row of Lance's colognes on the shelf caught his eye. *Probably need to use some of that too.*

Kicking off his boots next, Gideon unbuttoned his jeans and rifled through the clothes in the stall. Finding his size, he pulled on the fresh pair.

"Gideon, your mom sent me out to…." Ireland fell silent when she peered through the stall window. He silently applauded the strapless yellow sundress. She was magnificent in anything, but dresses made her long legs even more heavenly.

A crass finish to her statement tempted him, but he bit his tongue. "Dinner ready?"

"Uh-huh." Her eyes dipped to his unbuckled jeans, then slowly up his sculpted stomach and chest. They lingered on his tattoos and he smirked.

"Like what you see?" he teased, and she backed up.

"Sorry, I just hadn't seen the tattoos up close."

Gideon grabbed her hand and pressed it against his ink. "Feel for yourself. I don't mind."

She let out a shaky breath and traced the tattoo on his arm. Keeping his breathing steady was difficult when she leaned down to inspect the artwork. Her hair brushed against his arm, the soft tresses beautiful torture.

"Can I see the one on your back too?"

Instead of answering, he turned. That one was his favorite. Other guys had elaborate tattoos, but he had his own style. The tribal marks up and down his spine were all his.

"This is incredible. Who designed it?" Ireland's fingers ran up and down his spine, her breath warm on his skin.

"I did."

Ireland walked back around and shook her head. "Wow, it's amazing."

"Thanks, I think." He scanned the area for a clean shirt. From the looks of it, he needed to do laundry.

"I should get back."

"Yeah, wouldn't want your millionaire to get anxious." He found a shirt and tugged it over his head.

"Stop it, okay? Mason and I aren't together. He's my friend, not that my grandmother doesn't want more," she mumbled and reached down and zipped up his jeans.

"Whoa there," he said, but she didn't stop. Her fingers flew over the top button and he held back the primal reaction.

"I'm here for Z. Mason's here because our merger closes soon and it's better to keep enemies close and all that." She pulled his buckle through the loop.

"He's your enemy now?" She frowned and he placed a hand over hers on his buckle. "All right, we'll stop talking about him. What about me? Do I fit in your little plan at all?"

Confusion flashed across her face, but she replaced it with frustration. "Of course you do, but not in the way you want."

"Bummer. I was really looking forward to you taking my belt off, not putting it on."

Ireland rubbed her lips together, eyes darting to where her hand still rested.

"All you have to do is give me a shot, darlin'. There's something between us and it isn't old. At least not for me. You know I won't let you down." He brushed her hair behind her shoulders, giving his eyes plenty to feast on thanks to his position. "I never left you unhappy, did I?"

"N-no."

He cupped the back of her neck and lifted her gaze to him. "Or unsatisfied?"

A spark of lust lit in her brown eyes. "Never."

"I won't start now."

A breath of uncertainty hung in the air between them, but in one split second, Ireland pressed him against the stall door and kissed him hard. Her fingers delved beneath his shirt, and she moaned at the hard muscles there. Gideon grabbed her ass and lifted her off the floor, adoring the way she clung to him. He couldn't kiss her fast enough, and he sure as hell hated the amount of clothes between them.

Ireland wiggled free and both hands went to work on the buckle she recently tightened. By the time she freed his jeans and shoved them down his thighs, her chest heaved against him.

Willing himself to take things slow, Gideon snuck his hands under her skirt and shuddered at the thong he felt. His body took over from there. He wasn't going to resist the urge to take her every way to Sunday.

The clanging sound of the Taggart meal bell split the air.

"We need to go to dinner," he managed, breaking away from her lips.

Ireland caught her breath and fixed her dress. "Um, yeah, good idea." She looked at him as if weighing her options before she hustled out of the barn.

Gideon glanced to the pants around his ankles and shook his head. "The one time I actually need a cold shower...."

***

"Everything go all right in the barn?" Frances asked when Ireland swung open the screen door.

Startled at the question, Ireland nodded. "Yep, Gideon's on his way."

Frances waved from the kitchen. "Perfect. I knew you were the right lady to reel him in."

You have no idea.

She pulled back the chair between Toby and Mason. They were her new buffer. She couldn't be around Gideon without wanting to jump his bones. It shouldn't have been that way, but the more time she spent in Iowa, the more she wanted him. He was her past, and one she knew would thrill her just like he used to.

It's fatal attraction. Get over it, Ireland.

She turned her head toward Mason, but saw he was in a deep discussion with Walt about a new way to expedite global deliveries.

She rolled her eyes and turned to Toby.

He winked. "Anything nasty happen in the barn?"

"Well—"

"Oh my God." He lowered his voice. "What did my good little girl do now?"

"Nothing. I mean, I probably would've done something—"

"Or someone—"

"If the bell hadn't disturbed us."

Toby took a sip of his iced tea. "Girl, you're playing with fire."

"I know, but it feels so good."

He spat out his tea. "Oh my, I need all the nasty details, you little minx."

Ireland leaned over when her mother glanced to them. "Shut it, Tobes. I don't exactly want my family to know I still have feelings for him."

"Girl, you'd have to be dense to not see you both still find each other extremely shag-worthy. In any case, hop on the farmer and ride him until sunrise."

The screen door screeched shut and she glanced over to see Gideon enter. "I can't. I need to have self-control. He wants more, and I can't give that to him."

They watched Gideon interact with the Leightons and then his family before he sat across the table and chatted with Krista.

Toby tapped her leg. "Maybe you can. You both grew up, Ireland. Maybe he'll leave Iowa this time. You never know." He added sugar to his tea. "From the blush on your cheeks, I'd say he's a sex god."

"And you're done." She poked his side and was thankful when Walt started to say grace. The rest of the evening would be plenty uncomfortable—mostly because she sat across from Gideon and wanted to rip his clothes to shreds.

CHAPTER THIRTEEN

"Zavier, what's wrong?" Ireland asked, walking into the barn. Her brother looked up from the mare, his features weary. When she saw which horse he was hunkered over, she instantly panicked. "What happened to Ella?" She was Ireland's horse, or was before she'd left. Ella was her 4H horse and a prize winner at the state fair.

"Been up all night." He shook his head. "It's the colt. He's stuck in mama really good."

Panic spread through Ireland's veins. Over the years, she'd seen her fair share of animal births and deaths, but this was different. This was the mare she'd raised herself at the beginning of her senior year. "Is there anything I can do to help?" She sank into the bedding and stroked the horse's snout. Ella whinnied and thrashed.

Rolling back on his heels to stand, Zavier grabbed a rag and wiped off his hands. "Afraid not." He nodded toward the entrance. "Tagg should be here anytime."

No matter how many times she'd thought of him, Ireland couldn't get the nerve to text him. Toby scolded her prolifically after her failure to pick up where the barn rendezvous left off.

"Where're your friends?" Zavier asked, glancing at the house.

"Mason had to run to town, and Toby's on a call with some investors from Prague." She eyed the barn. "It's not exactly Toby's scene. Mine anymore either."

"Maybe yes, maybe no. Don't sell yourself short. There's plenty of good shit you can do around Iowa too, you know."

She softly patted Ella's neck. "I know. I have this connection with the Caribbean and—"

"I get it, but your parents are dead, sis. I'm sorry. They're not going to wash on shore one day."

She nodded sadly. "You're right, but I like being there. Makes me feel like I know them a little better."

"And that's why you opened the orphanages, right?"

Sitting up, she locked eyes with her brother. "How did you know?"

Zavier opened the stall door and lowered his voice. "I didn't. Tagg told me."

She moved closer but didn't get a word in before another person joined them.

"And here I thought you could do something without me, Z," Gideon jibed, walking into the barn.

"And not take advantage of the doctor next door? Yeah right." Zavier patted Gideon's back, then walked to the exit.

"I'll check up on you later. I'm meeting Krista for lunch."

"Wait, you're a doctor? As in actual doctor?" Ireland watched Gideon set his black bag down. She couldn't help but be enamored by his soothing demeanor the moment he walked in. He had a way with animals that rivaled even Zavier. Her heart thudded in her ears when Gideon laid a hand on Ella's head and whispered something to her. He was magical. Ella instantly stilled, her breathing not as labored as moments earlier.

"You're amazing."

Gideon unzipped the bag and grabbed what looked like a full body poncho. "Just me being me, Ireland."

"Did you really finish vet school? I just figured you help out neighbors and such with your skills."

He eyed her and pulled on the long latex glove and plastic covering over his clothes. "This next part isn't fun. Better watch yourself."

"Please, I grew up on a farm. I'm fine," she defended, though her confidence waned when Gideon's entire arm disappeared.

"Holy hell, what's he doing to the poor creature?" Toby asked, coming into the barn.

"You sure have great timing," Ireland teased, seeing his ashen face.

"I can't. No-nope." Toby coughed and retreated to the house.

"The colt didn't flip, so he's in the wrong position," Gideon advised, pulling his arm free.

Ireland clenched her hands. "Can you help?"

"Yeah, but we need to get Ella on her feet. The problem should correct itself once she walks around for a few minutes."

"And if not?" she asked, dreading the answer.

"Then she'll need a C-section and I can't help with that." He pulled out a sugar cube and stuck it under Ella's mouth, enticing her to stand. "Not here at least."

Amazed at how quickly he got the horse up, Ireland held out hope. "We can do this."

"We?"

"Well yeah." She patted Ella's nose. "I'm sticking around until the end."

Gideon studied her for a long second, then reached down and retrieved a stethoscope. "Uh-huh. Too bad that's all you stick around for."

Ireland snapped her attention to him. "Seriously?" She narrowed her eyes when he put the stethoscope in place on the horse's swollen belly and held up his hand like he couldn't hear.

"Both hearts sound strong, but she needs to give birth soon." He looped the listening device around his neck. "From what Z told me, she's been at it a while."

"Are you going to answer my question?"

He dug out another pair of gloves, then checked the foal again. "Ah, good. He turned. Should be ready any time now."

Thoroughly frustrated now, Ireland crossed her arms. "Gideon."

He tossed the dirty gloves to the corner. "Yeah, Ireland?"

He perched both fists on his hips and lowered his head to meet her gaze.

Damn. He's sexy even when he's upset. How could I forget that? Oh right, because I'm an idiot, obviously.

The tone of his voice paired with the brooding expression set off butterflies in her stomach. Angry shouldn't have been attractive, but on Gideon it was.

"Uh… um." She broke eye contact. His blue eyes were too intense. They bored into her soul, beckoning her to him.

"How long's your new guy sticking around?" he asked, changing the direction of their conversation.

"Mason and I leave tomorrow for France."

He scratched his beard. "Oh. Are you coming back?"

"Yes." She saw his lips straighten, so she added, "But Mason's not. He's leaving from the country house to London for a few business trips."

"All right."

Ireland wanted to tell him more, but she didn't know if she should. If she opened her heart to Gideon, he might break it again. She rubbed her lips together. *As much as I'd like to.*

"Should I expect more tabloids from the two of you about a wedding?"

Shoving her hands in her pockets, she glanced around the stall. There was no way around the conversation until she noticed Ella. "Gideon, the colt's coming!"

Gideon swung his gaze to the horse and grabbed a stack of blankets. "Get the disinfectant from my bag," he ordered, stooping down to guide the slippery foal from its mother's womb.

Scrambling, she grabbed the bottle and returned in time to see the baby horse come into the world. "He's beautiful," she murmured, taking it all in. It wasn't pretty and was plenty messy, but this was life. She smiled up at Gideon, and her heart fluttered when he returned with a bright smile of his own. *Life with Gideon.*

"Hell yeah. He's a keeper." He cleaned Ella up, a smile never leaving his face. "I know one when I see it."

She met his gaze and immediately had to look away. He wasn't talking about livestock anymore. Turning back to watch the horses, she noticed Gideon had disappeared. Running water met her ears and time seemed to slow while she watched the mother and baby.

She couldn't deny how happy Gideon looked simply helping out one of the farm animals. The brown-and-white colt snorted and rolled up to its chest. His curious brown eyes studied the warm stall as Ella nuzzled her baby.

Ireland's eyes welled with tears. *Maybe being a mom isn't such a bad idea.*

Suddenly Gideon was beside her, hugging her against his chest. "Are you all right? You don't cry."

She nodded, closing her eyes and burrowing her face in his shirt. Even after a day of hard work, Gideon smelled as good as freshly laundered clothes. She inhaled deeply and snuggled closer. "You smell good," she said against his toned chest.

His laugh rumbled through her ear. It sounded even better close up. "Never heard that one after being in the sun all day, but I'll take it. I didn't know sweat and dirt could smell good."

Ireland tilted her chin up. "It does on you."

Gideon cupped her face and closed the distance to her lips but didn't make contact. The intensity of his gaze froze her body to him. "Do you really think your life abroad is better than a farm in Iowa?"

"Yes, there's so much good I can—"

His chuckle sounded forlorn. "Even if you have a man who loves you in Iowa? There's plenty of good you can do here, darlin'."

Immediately her breathing quickened. He couldn't possibly be saying what she thought. *Surely, he doesn't love, love me anymore. Does he?* What they had six years ago didn't happen twice. She didn't deserve to have a love like his twice. Not when he deserved someone who would be by his side every single day.

She cleared her throat. "I can't do my job here, man or no man. It's too important."

For a split second, he almost called her bluff. She saw it in his eyes. She could never lie to him. Instead, he gave her the reaction she deserved. "Mm, yes, I forgot. Your fancy trust fund job is more important than mine." Gideon kissed her forehead and dropped his hands to his sides. "That pride of yours really gets in the way, princess." He moved away and snatched his black veterinary bag. Pausing at the stall door, he licked his lips. "And to answer your question, yes, I went to vet school, and yes, I'm a veterinarian and a farmer. Not that you give a shit." He shook his head and straightened his cap before walking out of her sight.

Damn, I screwed that up. An unsteady feeling flowed through her body. *I'm not a snob. Am I?*

She swiveled her eyes to Ella and her newborn colt. The recent events flashed in her mind. Watching Gideon work and helping him bring life into the world gave her a surge of accomplishment that she couldn't compare to her other ventures.

Maybe he's right.

She let out a harsh breath. If she ever admitted it, she'd have to face the possibilities that Gideon wasn't far off on his statement. Deep down, she knew it was more than a chance.

Ireland watched the foal for another few minutes, all the while hashing out what the hell she was going to do with herself once she was back in Barbados and away from the man who challenged her in more ways than one.

CHAPTER FOURTEEN

"Grandmother, are you here?" Ireland smiled at the man who dropped off her bags before stepping farther into the castle. "Hello? Anyone home?"

"Yes, yes, I'm here. Stop yelling like an uncivilized banshee." Fiona stepped out of a room to the left of the entrance. She looked stunning as usual in an elegant burgundy gown. "I wasn't sure if you'd make it before dinner."

Ireland carefully hugged the shorter woman. "I caught the red-eye." She yawned. "And I could use a nap, honestly."

Fiona linked her arm with Ireland's. "Of course. Your gown is upstairs in your room. Guests will arrive in three hours. Please be downstairs by then."

Ireland barely remembered climbing the long staircase or falling into the comfortable bed. When she woke two hours later, she yawned at the familiar form hovering over her bed.

"There's our sleeping beauty," Mason said with a smirk. He sank onto the bed beside her and tucked his hands behind his head. "Have a nice rest?"

Curling toward his body garbed in an expensive designer tuxedo, she shook her head. "I need more. Can we just pretend I went to this thing?"

He chuckled. "I'm afraid not. We're meeting several investors for the vineyards we jointly own. Plus I think your grandmother wants to show you off a bit."

"More like show you off."

"Show us both off as a partnership."

He was right. For the limited time she'd known him, there weren't too many times that he wasn't right. "How long do I need to act hospitably before I sneak off to the kitchen and eat all the pastries?"

Mason pulled her up to a sitting position, then crossed the room. He brought over a dark purple dress for her review. "I don't know, but what I do know is that you're going to look fabulous in this. So get your fine arse up and get dressed." He laid the masterpiece on the bed and walked to the door.

Twenty minutes later, Ireland's hair was perfectly plaited at the base of her neck and her scoop-neck gown showed off just the right amount of cleavage. She carefully made her way down the stairs and to the waiting guests below. Her grandmother was easily spotted near the entrance, greeting those who entered.

The whole dinner party soiree still caught Ireland off guard. It was nothing like the ones she had in Iowa with her family. These were extravagant and more expensive than she cared to admit. With a string quartet in the corner of the dining room, the ambiance was eclectic to her once-sheltered life.

"Absolutely breathtaking," Mason complimented at the base of the steps. He tucked her arm in his and led her around the room. "Let me introduce you to the owners of the vineyard neighboring ours in Italy."

Ireland smiled, nodded, and performed as she should, according to her grandmother. She learned plenty about the vineyard differences in France and Italy, though from the sounds of it, they were both spectacular. She made a mental note to visit both plots in the upcoming year. The more she knew about her businesses, the better apt she was at handling them.

"So, tell me more about this Gideon fellow," Mason said, leading her outside to the veranda lit up with twinkling lights. The stars overhead only added to the allure.

Ireland sipped her white wine. "What's there to say? We dated, and we broke up."

Mason took away her empty glass. "Yes, I gathered as much. But I thought there might be more. Given the way he acts around you, I thought maybe you had leftover feelings for him."

It was foolish to lie. This man didn't care either way. Theirs was a business agreement; the more honesty between them, the better they'd be.

"If I'm being truthful, I do have feelings for him." She slipped off her heeled shoes and sighed. "Walking around all night in four-inch heels should be outlawed."

Mason chuckled and picked up the discarded shoes. "They're wasted when you can't see them." He pointed to her floor-length gown. "Next time wear slippers. I won't tell."

She grinned. He was the best she could ask for, minus the love connection. Ireland could easily fall in lust with him. He had the body made for it.

A waiter came by with drinks and she grabbed a glass of wine.

Mason took off his jacket and draped it around Ireland's bare shoulders. "I can't pretend to know all the logistics involved, but I think you should give Gideon a chance."

She sat on a bench. "You and Toby both."

"Honestly, Ireland, if I had a second chance with someone I loved, I wouldn't waste it. There's clearly something between the two of you. I think you'd agree with me that you'd rather sort it out than wonder what could've been."

Ireland noticed his brown eyes darkened further as if he regretted losing out on true love once. While she wanted to ask him about it, the time didn't seem appropriate. "I agree. I just don't know if he'll want to leave Iowa."

"Well, you can't demand something of someone if you aren't willing to do the same."

"Shit, I don't like you sometimes," she teased. "You're too insightful."

"Yes, a horrid trait, let me tell you." Mason joined her. "I say put all your feelings out there and screw Gideon until the cows come in." He smirked. "Pun intended."

"I mean, you don't have to convince me…."

"But if the two of you don't work out and you find yourself wanting a more refined man like myself, just know, I won't allow any external affairs."

Ireland licked her lips at the sudden serious tone. They'd never spoken of anything other than friendship and flirtations. She was suddenly very aware that Mason liked her in more than a business sense. "And if we were together, what about you?"

He fingered the barrette in her hair. "I'm a very understanding man, Ireland, but I'm also a very possessive one. If you're mine, you are wholly mine and no one else's. In return, I am completely and irrevocably yours. No affairs, no lovers, no accidental drunk hookups. That much I can promise you. The moment we're engaged, no one else matters but you and me. What do you say to that?"

The severity of his words hit Ireland hard. He might have seemed flippant about his love life, but in actuality, Mason was the most sincere person she'd ever met. He didn't mince words or promise things he couldn't deliver.

"I say you're perfect in every way." She smiled and kissed his cheek lightly. "I'll let you know if we ever need to agree to those terms."

Mason nodded once. "Good. Now, am I still on probationary status, or should we sign those merger papers?"

She held out her hand. "Well, there are a few changes my attorneys are making."

"I wouldn't expect anything less than perfection." His eyes scanned the dark sky. "Oh, and hopefully this conversation doesn't affect our friendship. I don't want that to change even if you end up married to your tattooed farmer."

Tears bit at Ireland's eyes. How any woman could resist Mason was beyond her. She wasn't even in love with him, but a part of her wanted to be, at least a little bit.

"We'll always be friends, don't worry." She patted Mason's hand. Her stomach jumped at the thought of Gideon. She ran for years against her connection with Gideon. It was time to face her past and hope they had a future.

CHAPTER FIFTEEN

"Mr. Taggart, the bank can't allow the loan to go another year without payment."

Gideon gripped the arms of the chair a little tighter. "I've been making payments," he argued, but the bank manager held up his hand.

"Significant payments, Mr. Taggart. I'm sorry, but this is a place of business, not a charity." The man handed him a business card. "Tell your father hello for me. We always got along well."

Standing, Gideon ignored the offered card and hustled out of the private office. He didn't bother to smile at the cute receptionist on the way out. This meeting was bound to go poorly. He and Lance were behind on their loans, way behind, and no matter what they did, they couldn't bail out.

Getting in his truck, he slapped the steering wheel and cursed. Running the farm was all he'd wanted to do since he was a child. He never realized how expensive it was until he finished vet school and his dad handed over the reins little by little. Student loans and farm loans didn't go together well. His brother wasn't much help either, since Lance had zero interest in the financial side of things.

A new message blinked on his phone. Grabbing it, he reviewed the text from Zavier and clenched his jaw.

Zavier: Why's your brother pawing Ireland?

Gideon: Because he's a dick. Be home soon.

Throwing the truck in gear, he grabbed his ball cap from the empty passenger seat and pulled it on. Lance tended to flirt no matter if Gideon liked the girl or not. It was an annoying habit of his. The jerk had even texted him the other day to see if he'd mind if Ireland went out with him to a local band concert. Well, Gideon did mind, and he was about to show his brother how much. *Lance is just trying to rile me up.* After Mason showed up, it wasn't hard to do, and his brother took things a little too far. Well, he was done with playing.

Thirty minutes later, he climbed out of the truck and slammed the door. Lance's fancy car sat in the Leightons' driveway. Squinting, he frowned. He'd never kill a man, especially not his brother, but the way Lance was leaning toward Ireland made him second-guess the unforgivable sin.

Diesel whined beside him as he walked to the nearby ATV. Hopping on it, he cranked the engine and started toward the Leightons'. *I need to check on the new foal anyway.*

Both dogs ran beside the ATV and barked as they

neared the barn. He slowed down in time to see Lance lean over and kiss Ireland's cheek. His eyelids slid shut and he clenched his hands tighter on the handlebar. Dallas licked his knuckles, forcing his eyes open again. Seeing Ireland so close to another man made him physically ill, but he couldn't pry his gaze away either. The only salvation he found was when Ireland pulled away. It should've calmed him, but no such luck.

Glancing at his two Aussies, he nodded toward the house. Dallas and Diesel barked, then leapt into action. The dogs sprinted to the porch, a blur of red, black, and gray. Both jumped on Lance and Ireland, interrupting the moment. He gave it a few seconds before he headed their direction. It was probably petty and immature, but if he couldn't have Ireland, neither could his brother.

He arrived at the edge of the driveway and shut off the engine. Dismounting, he ignored Lance's smug grin. "There they are." He crouched down and grabbed both dogs' collars. "Hope they didn't get in too much trouble. They tend to do whatever they want."

"Like another person we know," Lance mumbled, wiping dog slobber from his shirt.

Gideon stood and smirked when Lance tried to straighten his posture to be the taller of them. It wasn't happening tonight, or any night since he was seventeen.

"What're you up to?"

He looked between the two of them. Ireland's face didn't give anything away, whereas Lance preened from his spot. Suddenly Gideon didn't want to hear about whatever happened while he was getting shut down by a banker.

Lance looped an arm around her waist. "Nothing much." He kissed Ireland's cheek and flashed Gideon a smile. "I'll see you at breakfast, bro."

Playfully slugging Gideon's arm, Lance brushed by him and climbed into his car. After a quick wave, he sped down the road. Crickets chirped all around, the sound soothing Gideon's nerves. The dogs were now sprawled out on the lawn, tongues hanging out.

He swung his gaze around the yard, lightning bugs starting to light up the dusk. Resting his eyes on Ireland, he was surprised at the glower on her pretty face. He'd seen that look before when they were a couple. The outcome was never good.

"All right, it's getting late. I better check on the new horse." He moved toward the ATV. For a second, he didn't hear Ireland's shoes behind him. The silence didn't last long.

"Oh no you don't. Get back here."

Turning, he shook his head. She stood with her hands on her hips in the middle of the front yard. Her hair flowed from her recent movement, and her tall shadow drifted along the grass, but it was her determined eyes that sent a spark up his spine. *God, she's gorgeous.* He didn't miss their fights, but he'd loved the way they used to make up afterward. Angry sex with Ireland was too good to pass up at any time.

"I think I'll take a rain check." He tipped his cap, turned on his toes, and whistled for the dogs.

"Gideon Lewis Taggart, stop your ass right now!"

That got his attention. Furious Ireland was a sight to behold.

Bracing himself, he spun in her direction in time to feel a searing slap to his face. Stunned, he rubbed his cheek.

"What the—"

"What were you thinking?" she growled, toe-to-toe with him.

"What? The dogs? It was harmless. Plus, Lance is my brother and—"

"Not the dogs." She closed her eyes and opened them again. "Lance told me about what happened after I left."

The blood drained from his face. He might just kill his brother after all. "Aw, shit."

"Yeah." She jutted her chin up at him. "Explain."

Afraid she might stalk back to the house, Gideon grabbed her wrists. The soft flesh burned into his callused fingers, a perfect contrast. "I drank." She yanked but couldn't free her arms. "Okay, I did more than that. I got stupid wasted."

"Why?"

"Seriously, Ireland?" He pulled her closer until he smelled her sweet breath. Her cinnamon-colored eyes held hints of confusion and pain, two things he never wanted to see there. "Because I loved you and you smashed my heart into a million pieces when you left." He brushed back her hair, loving the natural wave it held.

"I asked you to come with me, remember? You broke my heart too. Plus that's not a good reason to try to get on a plane while holding a bottle of tequila."

He winced. So his big brother had spilled all those

details too. *Great.*

"No. It was dumb. I was dumb." He wrapped a tendril of hair around his index finger. "But I wanted to find you and convince you to come home. To me."

Ireland rubbed her lips together and searched his face. Her voice softened. "Gideon—"

"I know, I know. You needed to figure out who you are, and traveling was a big part of that." He cupped the base of her neck. "Did you figure it out yet? Have you found yourself?"

"Well...."

Gideon chuckled softly. "Because I don't need to jump on a plane or see a tropical sunrise to know who I am. Hell, I don't need to go anywhere to know who you are. Who you've always been." He leaned down and kissed her parted lips. Just when he thought his heart couldn't break anymore, the fault lines started cracking. "You're the love of my life and you don't want me. I wish I could've accepted that a long time ago. It would've helped."

He dropped his hold and Ireland let out a small sigh. Taking a step backward, he ran a hand over his beard. She looked too cute with cut-off jean shorts, a green tank top, and old farm boots. "I'm done trying, Ireland. I'll play nice hereon in, but I can't spend time with you. Not unless you actually want all of me."

She took a step toward him. "Gideon, please, just let me—"

"No." He climbed on the four-wheeler and started it. "I gave you enough chances, Ireland. I'm done."

"I know about the farm," she called out before he shifted the gears.

"Damn Lance and his big mouth," he mumbled. "It's not your concern."

"But it could be." Reaching the ATV, she placed a hand on his. "You're having trouble this season. Let me help."

The magnitude of her words slapped him harder than her hand. Money solved her problems. They wouldn't solve his. "Mind your own damn business, Ireland," he growled, gripping the handlebars.

Her eyes darkened. "You are my business."

"Right, of course I am." Gideon grabbed her chin with one hand. "Why do you care about me and my farm? Because we were neighbors growing up? Maybe because we dated?"

She tried to look away, but he held her in place. "Because I'm sorry. I can't put the genie back in the bottle, Gideon, but I am sorry I left the way I did. Let me try to make it right. I'll get your farm back on its feet—"

"And then you'll leave." He dropped his hold. "Super."

Ireland folded her arms over her chest. "Yes, but not like that. If you shut up and let me talk to you—"

Shifting the ATV into first gear, he shook his head. "Keep your money, Ireland. I don't need you."

He revved the engine and escaped before she could continue the conversation. He was done. Thoroughly and completely done with her. Nothing he did was enough. Well, that was fine with him. She didn't care enough to get to know him, so he wouldn't care enough to do the same.

From now on, Ireland would just be a place near the United Kingdom and not the woman who'd frayed his heart. Twice.

***

The roosters crowed from their coops, waking Ireland earlier than she'd have liked. Rolling onto her stomach, she grabbed her phone and checked the notifications. Most were from her grandmother and investors. *Ugh, I'm getting behind on stuff.* She face-planted into the pillow and tried not to think of her chat with Gideon the night before. He'd been adamant that he was done playing nice and she hadn't even had a chance to talk to him yet.

Stubborn as ever.

Her phone started buzzing. Recognizing it as a video chat, she answered without looking. "Good morning, Grandmother. I think I'll head home soon. Maybe visit you before I head to Barbados. I think I've had enough Iowa time."

"Well, I'm not your grandmother, but yes, please do come back to Barbados so I can see your adorable bedhead in person."

Eyes widening, Ireland met the gaze of a very amused Mason. "Shit." She reached her hand up to her head, but it was no use. It stuck up in every direction imaginable and frizzed like crazy. "Um, can I call you back when—"

"Absolutely not. I like this side of you." His grin wasn't forced. In fact, it was sweet. "I already knew you were beautiful. Now I know you don't need makeup to be elegant."

Blushing, she sat up. "Thanks. So, any special reason for my wake-up call?"

Mason held up a cup of tea. "I reviewed the proposal for the hospital in Uganda."

"How'd you…?" She stopped herself there. "Toby, right?"

He smirked. "Yes, that guy is passionate about all things Ireland related."

Shaking her head, Ireland couldn't disagree. Her best friend was pushy, but only in her best interests—most of the time.

"Anyway, I'd like to contribute however you need."

"Wow, really? That'd be fantastic." She pushed back her hair and grabbed the laptop on the bedside table. "I can email you a list of doctors I'm trying to get to donate time to help train the locals if you want."

Mason took a taste of tea. "I do have a chum from university who's on the medical board for Johns Hopkins. I'll give him a ring."

Ireland quickly logged into the database Toby created for her projects and sent the information to Mason. "Perfect. Thanks."

"Of course. Giving back is just as important as making the money."

"I agree." She toyed with the ring on her finger. The more she talked to Mason, the more she liked him. He wasn't pompous like other well-off men she'd met. He was unique in that way.

"Now that business is settled, let's chat about when you're going to teach me how to get my hair to stick up like that."

Ireland snorted, then slapped her hands over her mouth. To her relief, instead of looking down his nose at her, he laughed heartily.

"I dare say that is the cutest sound I've ever heard you make. I thought so last time I heard it, and every new time just makes it that much better."

She lifted her brow. "Really?"

"Ireland, so far, my thirty-six years haven't been very successful when it came to women. Then I met you and it all changed."

He's good. Damned good. She had a feeling he hadn't even begun to try either.

"I know for a fact that I'm not being too forward with you, but if you're ever uncomfortable, please tell me." Mason paused when one of his staff members walked by. "Because I tend to over flirt when I think a woman is even remotely interested in me."

Sitting cross-legged, Ireland fought back a yawn. "Well, that explains a lot."

Mason scratched his chin, then signed something on his table before the paper disappeared with a short woman. "You haven't the foggiest."

Joanna called up the stairs and Ireland sighed. "I better go down there or Zavier will eat all the food."

"Enjoy being a farm girl." He winked. "I look forward

to seeing you soon."

Nodding, she hung up. He wasn't who she wanted, but the one she did would need a little convincing.

CHAPTER SIXTEEN

"All packed and ready to go?" Toby asked, opening the window curtains.

Ireland grunted and slung an arm over her eyes. "You're the devil."

"Give me your soul," he teased, jumping up and down on the bed. "Hurry up, our flight is in a few hours."

Knowing she had a phone conference and video chat to fit in before takeoff, Ireland rolled over and rubbed her eyes. She stretched her arms over her head and tried to forget the conversation she'd had with Gideon the other night. She couldn't. He'd been so adamant that she didn't care about him. He was dead wrong, but she would bide her time. They had another week in Barbados yet and she had a feeling they could work out their issues by then. *If he ever lets me talk to him.*

"So, did you get any Tagg action?" Toby asked, handing

her a cup of coffee. "I saw the two of you getting cuddly in the driveway the other night."

Ireland took a sip of the brew and shrugged. "Nope, no action."

Toby perched on the bed beside her and batted his short black lashes. "Aw, so you didn't get Tagged?"

Try as she might, she couldn't help but smirk at his pun. "Cute, Tobes. Real cute."

He hugged her tight. "I know. Now move it. Your meeting is less than an hour away, and we need to do something with your hair." He scrunched his nose. "And makeup." He tilted his head to the side when she stood. "Oh God, and clothes."

Laughing outright, Ireland finished her coffee and let Toby do his worst. Every now and then, he'd choose her outfits and help with her hair. Forty minutes later, she cracked open her laptop and started her day. Business never slept—at least that's what her grandmother said.

After successfully closing a deal with a manufacturer in Beijing, Ireland glanced around the bedroom and saw her suitcases ready to go. Voices carried from downstairs, letting her know the family was excited to get the show on the road. She shut down her computer, then iPad. Her phone kept buzzing with new emails, but she'd let Toby check them when they were in the air.

For now, she'd bid farewell to her Iowa home. She'd come back, but not because she missed the cornfields. She wouldn't give up her family just because they lived on different continents. Staying away too long was a mistake, she realized that right after arriving.

The Taggart farmhouse caught her eye. She wasn't giving up on Gideon either. They had a misunderstanding and for once in her life, she was going to stop running from her problems and face them instead.

"You ready, Ireland?" her mom called up the stairs.

Patting the bedframe, she swallowed hard and looked out her window. Gideon's farmhouse could be seen in the distance. "Yep. Be down in a minute."

One last nod and she grabbed her suitcases. "Ready or not."

***

The private plane taxied and then plateaued before Gideon was ready. He'd never been on a plane like Ireland's before. It was his first time on a private plane period. Knowing his bank account, it'd be the one and only time too.

Looking around the cabin, he noticed his dad was already snoozing, while his mom chatted with Zavier. Other than being Zavier's best friend and best man, Gideon didn't know why his family was getting a free vacation out of the wedding.

He peeked around Krista's Texas-sized bun of hair and caught a glimpse of Ireland. She sat in a swivel chair with Toby beside her at the front of the plane. From the looks of it, that was their usual spot. A table sat between them, and she typed furiously on her laptop while talking to Toby at the same time. If he had to guess, they were working on a business deal of some sorts.

"No, I said no petunias! Who has petunias at a wedding? That's ludicrous. I said peonies! Are you on another planet, or is your connection bad?" Toby's accented voice screeched.

Or wedding details.

He grinned when the short man stood and paced the small area. Eventually he'd be caught staring, but he couldn't help it. Ireland looked too pretty with her white capris, royal blue blouse, and heeled sandals. Her hair was curled slightly and looked like she'd just tousled it a few times after waking up. A hint of makeup on her face only enhanced her natural beauty. But it was her damn pink lips that made dropping his gaze impossible. He knew from personal experience that they tasted as good as they looked.

"Take a picture, it'd last longer," Zavier teased from across the aisle.

Clearing his throat, Gideon sat back in the comfortable chair. "Whatever, Z."

Zavier shrugged, and Gideon opened a magazine, grateful his friend didn't push the conversation. The last thing he needed was to talk about Ireland. With that in mind, he closed the window shade and let the hum of the plane lull him to sleep.

Nearly twelve hours later, the engines shut off and he sat up in his seat. "Are we here?"

His mom patted his hand, walking up the aisle. "Yes, dear. Let's go see what paradise looks like."

He rolled his eyes at her excitement and waited until he was the last person aboard. After gathering his bag from the overhead bin, he nodded at the pilot and flight attendant before ducking his head and breathing in the Caribbean air. Though the sun had set long ago, a warm glow filled the sky. The airport was brightly lit, but it was the city in the distance that made his breath catch.

"You never forget your first time in Barbados," the flight attendant said from behind him.

"I believe that." Gideon nodded and slowly climbed down the stairs. His family was way ahead of him, but he didn't care. This was the first and probably only time he'd leave the country. *Well, except for that one time....* He shook his head, thankful his idiotic brother hadn't told Ireland everything he'd done as a twenty-two-year-old. It was better if she didn't know.

"Let's go, Tagg. You're holding up the cars," Zavier yelled, waving his arms.

Picking up his pace, Gideon caught up in time to see two SUVs at the private entrance to the airport. The Leightons were already secured in the first one, while his family was in the second. He handed his luggage to the driver at the rear of the vehicle before climbing in beside his brother.

"No wonder she doesn't want to leave Barbados, it's gorgeous," he muttered. The car crept forward, and the caravan quickly wove through the streets of Barbados.

He pushed Lance's head off his shoulder when the other man started to nod off. Eventually, he gave up altogether once Lance started snoring. He couldn't dare shut his eyes after sleeping on the plane most of the trip.

Finally, the SUVs pulled into a private drive surrounded

by shady palm trees on both sides, stopping outside a white house.

"Home sweet home for the next week," the driver said in a thick accent.

Opening the door, Gideon's jaw dropped at the sight. From the outside, the house looked big enough to fit a hundred people at least. All the doors and windows were open, giving the area a smooth flow from outside to inside living. A lap pool sat to the right of the entrance, but he had a feeling there was another one behind the house.

"Your luggage should be in your rooms before you are," Ireland said, coming into view as the group assembled in the courtyard. "Enjoy, relax, and soak up the Caribbean. You'll love it." She smiled, then turned on her heels.

"Your room assignments were in the folder Ireland gave you, but the staff is very accommodating if you forgot," Toby included, following his boss toward the bar.

The families didn't wait to be told again. Krista had the entire third floor for her family arriving the next day, the Leightons had the first, and the Taggarts had the second.

"Guess they didn't want us getting rowdy," Zavier said with a grin. He kissed Krista hard, then raced down the marble flooring to his room.

While his family disappeared to the elevator, Gideon stayed behind and took in the elegance of the house. Buying this place out for the week would've cost a fortune.

"There're a few villas in the back too," Ireland pointed out.

He swung his gaze from the fully stocked rum bar. "Is

that where you'll stay?"

She slipped off her sandals and held them in one hand. "Yep. I practically live in hotels when I'm not home, so I thought it'd be nice to stay at one of the villas." She patted the marble countertop. "Plus this is one of Mason's pet projects I'll be taking over soon." Her lips curved up in a different type of smile, one Gideon was sure he didn't like. "If you'd rather stay in one, just let Toby know."

"Right, sure." He watched her follow a path through the backyard, which was a waterpark and luxury pad in its own. Once the sun returned, he'd explore his surroundings more. For tonight, he was content watching Ireland's backside sway out of sight.

Pulling off his ball cap, he tucked it in his back pocket. While on the island, he might as well blend in. He'd hang it up and keep it in his room until he got back on a plane to Iowa.

He checked his phone and saw the service disconnected thanks to his transatlantic hop. Shrugging, he made a mental note to check out that dating app later. Paradise, weddings, and being so close to Ireland would surely send him over the edge.

***

Digging her toes into the warm sand, Ireland watched the waves lightly lap the shoreline in front of her. The sunset was like all the others in Barbados, breathtaking and gorgeous. She'd never get sick of them.

Krista's mom's laughter drifted to the beach and Ireland smiled. *Their flight got in early. Good.*

She craned her neck and caught sight of Krista as she hopped on Zavier's back. The three families surrounded the large pool outside, Lance and his mom dangling their toes in the tepid water. She couldn't see around all the trees, but she was positive Gideon was among the happy troop.

"Why're you all the way out here instead of with your family?"

Ireland turned toward the voice and saw Mason's tall silhouette near her. "I was just asking myself that same question."

Mason hugged her lightly. "I don't blame you. When I go home sometimes, I get weighed down by my family drama and just need to escape." His mocha eyes met hers. "No, I don't blame you at all for needing alone time."

"I wasn't sure if you were around this week."

Mason meshed his fingers together. "I'll be in and out of the island on business, but I'll be sure to pop in now and again so you don't forget to sign the merger papers." He glanced down and smirked at her. "Because that'd be disappointing."

Ireland rolled her eyes, then heard a rustling in the trees nearby. Casually, she peeked over and saw the familiar gleam of a camera lens. "Looks like we're not alone tonight."

"I thought I saw somebody snooping around."

Thinking back, Ireland couldn't recall seeing any paparazzi around earlier through the day. "It seems like they only snoop when you're with me." She quirked an eyebrow.

"Any idea why?"

Mason let out a forced chuckle. "It could be because of our relationship. Two millionaires in one place sells better photos."

"Hmm, I guess that could be it." Laughter drifted from the main house, and she suddenly wanted to go back to the haven of her family. The paparazzi stayed away from her in Iowa after her little chat and bribe. The reporters here were different, pushier and less considerate of privacy.

Mason turned to face her, obscuring her view of the blue ocean. "I have an idea that will make them leave."

"Like what?"

Mason handed her a pair of black framed glasses. "Like these. They won't get a decent picture while we're wearing them."

"Really? Genius. I knew I liked you for a reason." She slipped them on and giggled when the photographer frowned. "Think it worked?"

"Definitely." Mason gazed over her head. "And there goes the photographer. It pays to know little things like this for instance. The glasses completely obscure your face from the lens. Well, it makes your face look like a shining light on the camera. It's quite fascinating honestly."

"Who gave you this idea?"

He quirked his brow. "My security detail. They like to watch out for me even when I sneak off."

She traced the frames with her fingers. "I think I'll keep this pair if you don't mind."

"Not at all. Happy to help." He held out his arm. "How

about we go see how your parents are enjoying Barbados so far? I'm sure their first day was quite the experience."

Seeing the brightly decorated patio ahead, Ireland did her best to calm the rumbling in her heart. Spending time with Mason was fun in a business way, but she missed Gideon's touch more than she thought possible.

She smiled at her family as they arrived, and her eyes caught Gideon's. She didn't want anyone more than the man across from her. The difficult part would be convincing him.

***

A calm breeze filtered over the beach umbrellas outside Ireland's window. Birds chirped happily in the trees nearby, and the crash of the surf made her smile.

Normally she stayed in her condo, but since her family would be there for a few days, she opted for something closer. *That reminds me, I need to call Mason about the closing in San Juan,* she thought, looking through the break of trees to the ocean.

Ireland took a deep breath and tried to focus on the upcoming wedding. It didn't come as a surprise that Mason sent over several security guards just in case the paparazzi didn't follow him to Prague two days before. No shimmer of lenses met her though, so she guessed the guards did the trick.

Pulling on a lightweight robe, she opened the sliding door and leaned against the cool siding. With only a handful of days until Zavier and Krista's wedding, time seemed to slow. Everything was set for the beachside nuptials, and she hoped it'd go off without a hitch.

She'd spent the entire first day back catching up on her business ventures with Toby while her family toured St. James. Last night, they'd come back from the shops with tourist trinkets and stories to tell, but she couldn't focus on any of that when Gideon sat alone by the lap pool. He looked morose yet serene. She couldn't figure any of it out when Gideon Taggart was involved. One minute he was professing his undying affection, and then the next he wanted nothing to do with her. She was glad work kept her busy. Being around him too long would only cause regret.

"Couldn't sleep?" a voice asked, cutting into her thoughts. She looked over to see a shirtless Gideon in her doorway. With just athletic shorts on, he looked too good to be real. She'd never regret ogling either. He was too delicious to give just a passing glance. His blue eyes appeared several shades of tired, but they were glorious nevertheless.

Ireland held up her cup of coffee. "Nah. Too much to do today." She offered him a small smile. "What about you?"

Gideon stole the cup and took a sip. He shook his head, keeping his eyes trained on the sandy beach in the distance. "Too much on my mind."

"I understand that." She waved at a passing gardener. Somehow, when Gideon was around, the stress slipped away. The stock market meeting in an hour didn't seem so urgent when his bearded face came into view.

"What're the big plans for the wedding party?"

"Snorkeling after breakfast, beach bum after lunch, then the rehearsal dinner." She retrieved the coffee and drank the rest.

"Are you coming with us?" he asked, eyes on the horizon.

"No, I'm actually heading to a new restaurant in Bridgetown to meet Mason for lunch."

"Sounds busy."

She chuckled. "My life is constantly busy. It was nice to go with the flow in Iowa."

"Until you dragged us to Barbados."

She lightly pushed his shoulder. "For good reason. It isn't every day your brother and college roommate get married in the Caribbean."

Gideon toyed with his beard. "No, I guess not." His hands traveled through his hair, tempting her to do the same. "But I never thought I'd be anywhere like this with you unless…." He stopped, and Ireland focused on him completely.

"Unless what?"

Glancing down at her, he let out a sigh. "Unless we were on our honeymoon."

"Gideon—"

"It's fine." He smiled, but it didn't reach his eyes. "This is how we're supposed to be."

A knock on the door shattered the rest of their conversation. Walking through the villa, Ireland swung open the front door to see Toby. "Hey."

Toby rushed into the room, arms flying this way and that. "And good morning to you." He eyed her outfit. "You look delicious, darling. I can't imagine why that farm boy hasn't made ardent love to you yet. I mean, you are a goddess. Mason sure as hell thinks so. He looks at you like he's ready to rip your clothes off and just have his nasty way with you. Though, now that I think of it, he's probably a perfect gentleman in the sack. How boring. I haven't a clue why the man is dragging his feet."

Ireland opened her mouth to speak, but he couldn't be stopped. "The caterer complained about the meal choice for tonight, but I told her to shove it. She's from some fancy-dancy restaurant in France. I don't know why I ever agreed to give her a chance in St. James." He went to the coffeepot, sniffed the contents, then poured it down the drain. "God, what shit is this? We'll get new coffees on the way to the office." He grabbed her purse and pushed her to the exit. "Let's go."

"Er, well—"

"What?"

"Tobes, this is a robe."

Toby paused and held her at arm's length. His eyes grazed her body and he propped his fist on his hip. "Oh yeah it is. We wouldn't want Mason to see you all unwrapped, now would we?" He set off toward her bedroom, talking to himself.

"That guy is everywhere," Gideon said, suddenly in the room.

She put a hand over her heart. She'd completely forgotten he was at the back door. "Yeah, Toby is my constant shadow. It's part of why I love him so much."

Toby reappeared with a day dress. "Honestly, one of these times, Mason's just going to bend you over and—"

"Toby! Oh my God." Ireland waved a hand to her face, feeling warm. She eyed Gideon's surprised face and instantly wished she could disappear. "Sorry. He has no filter."

Gideon's eyes fixed on her scarce coverings as if he'd just figured it out himself. She only slept in panties when she was somewhere warm. It appeared Gideon had noticed.

Their eyes met, and Ireland bit her bottom lip. If she could make Toby vanish from the room, she would. Gideon's starry blue gaze told her everything he couldn't say.

"Have fun today. We'll see you later." He nodded at Toby, then turned around and left.

"Did I interrupt something?" Toby asked after a moment.

Ireland snatched the hanger from him. "Unfortunately, not. Every time I try to talk to him, something pops up." She sighed. "Come on. We better go."

CHAPTER SEVENTEEN

Never in his life did Gideon think he'd enjoy sailing. Their charter catamaran held their entire wedding group, minus Ireland, and set off toward the best snorkeling on the island. Well, that's what the captain said, but from where Gideon sat, he couldn't disagree. The ocean's deep blue color overwhelmed him on every side as they skimmed the waves.

Checking over his shoulder, he spotted their guide for the afternoon. She was in a white bikini and couldn't look better if she tried. He shoved away any romantic thoughts; he couldn't dwell on them with Ireland on some outing with Mason.

Gideon had done an internet search on Mason the day they met. The man was far from penniless. He owned his own island in Fiji, and his net worth teetered toward the billions. And all without his parents' money. Even though Ireland swore there wasn't anything other than friendship and business going on between them, Gideon didn't like the way Mason acted around her. Ireland was a treasure, and he wasn't the only man to realize it.

He inhaled and closed his eyes. The bright summer sun felt so much better in Barbados, though he did miss his dogs. *They'd love it,* he thought, opening his eyes to see fish jump in the distance.

The catamaran slowed, and the captain shut off the engine.

"All right, it's time to swim with the fishes!" the guide, Marbella, said with a grin.

He didn't need any more incentives. After donning his gear, Gideon didn't come back up to the surface until their boat was ready to head to the mainland again. During his time under the water, he opted to swim closer to Marbella. Despite the snorkeling, he felt a kinship with the cute woman. One completely platonic, but fun nonetheless.

The fish swarmed their party and he swore he'd never forget what he saw under the waves that day. Vibrant coral grew rampant and the native groups of fish kept a smile on his face. Marbella showed him all the best spots to see the schools, and they even ran across a sea turtle who became more than fond of Gideon's swim trunks. All in all, the morning went swimmingly—pun intended. He couldn't think of any reason for it to change either. The one regret he felt was when he saw Zavier and Krista cuddling on the ride back, whispering and smiling as if the rest of the group wasn't with them.

Reaching the docks, he picked up the rear of the group.

The three families chatted, complained about sunburn, and laughed, but he didn't join in. He couldn't when he saw Ireland and Mason at the end of the trail.

"Great," he mumbled, kicking at a loose board.

"Everything okay?" Marbella asked, her accent addictive. Bright green eyes stood out against her dark skin, and he doubted she ever had a man turn down any of her requests.

"No, but I'll be fine."

Marbella nudged his side. "Oh come on, tell me. I've heard a lot. Plus, I had to save you from that sea turtle. Twice, remember? You owe me."

"Ah yes, the overly friendly turtle." He paused and pulled off his shades. "See that girl at the top of the hill?" Marbella carefully looked, then nodded. "She's my ex, and that guy is a millionaire."

"Ouch. I'd be all over her too, she's gorgeous." Marbella laughed when he grimaced. "You still love her, then?"

Gideon started walking again and nodded. "Yep. I don't think I'll ever stop."

"And let me guess, you aren't a millionaire?"

"Nope. Not even close."

"Well, does she get jealous easily?"

He shrugged. "Six years ago, yeah, but now? No clue."

"Look, I know we met three hours ago, but you seem like a cool guy and I'll do you a solid." She reached up and wrapped her arms around his neck.

"What're you doing?"

She grinned and said, "Don't worry, I'm more inclined

to hit on your ex than you," before pressing her body against his in a tight hug.

Gideon managed to hug her back and nearly yelped when she reached around and pinched his ass.

Pulling back, he coughed. "Okay, that was unexpected."

Marbella peeked over her shoulder. "But it did the trick." Following her gaze, he saw Ireland's arms across her chest and her lips in a straight line.

"Thanks, I think."

Taking the left trail to the marina, Marbella waved. "Let me know if you need more help. I'm all for stealing from millionaires." She winked, then ran down the wobbly boards.

Gideon finally reached the parking lot, meeting Ireland's gaze before he slipped on his sunglasses. She'd always had a bit of a temper, but he could've sworn he saw smoke leave her ears a moment ago. If he weren't so preoccupied with the wedding details, he just might chance a visit to her lonely villa.

***

Furious. It was the only way she could describe how she felt after seeing Gideon with the bikini-clad beach bunny. And there was no reason why she should feel jealous, but she did.

She managed to put on a straight face when Mason looked her way after Gideon passed, but she couldn't hold back her annoyance once they parted ways. *The jerk did it on purpose.* She let out a huff and tried to focus on the positives in her life.

With the rehearsal dinner in the larger of the two dining rooms, she checked in with the caterer before running back to the villa to change. After going over accounts with Toby that morning and bartering over her vineyard in California with Mason, Ireland was more than ready to slip into sandals and a comfortable outfit.

She'd had to make up an excuse to run without Mason thinking he was the cause. She needed space and copious amounts of rum. Seeing Gideon with someone else churned the remnants of her stomach into a sour concoction. It was childish, but she hated seeing another woman—a gorgeous woman, at that—all but groping him.

I need to tell him how I feel.

She watched from the door as her family sat down for the rehearsal meal. Afterward, they'd head over to the beach for a quick run-through of the ceremony. Krista waved at her before returning to the shrimp cocktail in her hand.

Confident the meal was in full swing, Ireland turned on her heels. There was plenty of time to change and then hurry back for dessert. She'd earned some after the day she'd endured.

"That asshat just goes around hugging everyone," she fumed, slamming the door to the villa. Housekeeping had come and gone, and new towels lay on her bed in a heart shape. She didn't get jealous with any man except Gideon. Her European boyfriends could dance the night away with cute girls and she didn't bat an eyelash, but when Gideon even smiled in another woman's direction, Ireland couldn't handle it. She also couldn't look away.

Kicking off her shoes, she struggled with the zipper on her dress. Toby had helped that morning. *Damn things are my downfall.* She was high and mighty until it came to zippers. Reaching back, she grazed it with her fingernails, then huffed in disgust when she couldn't grab it.

She found her phone and thought about calling Toby, but remembered he was out on a date. Rustling from outside caught her ears and she glanced out the back door. Beach supplies in tow, Gideon was entering the villa beside hers. Weighing the pros and cons of staying in the tight dress or facing him, she eventually gave up and walked on the hand-placed stones until she knocked on Gideon's door.

When he didn't answer right away, she chewed on her bottom lip. *Maybe the boat girl is in there with him. Shit, this was a horrible idea. Why don't I just stick with things I know, like charity and travel?*

She turned and took a step away just as the door opened. "Ireland?"

Spinning around, she clasped her hands together. "Hey, Gideon. I didn't know you were staying in a villa."

Gideon rested an arm on the door handle. His shirtless attire was clearly a commonality in Barbados, not that she minded one bit. "My dad snores." He shrugged. "Plus I'd rather be closer to the ocean. I like the way it sounds."

"Yeah, me too. I mean the ocean thing. My dad doesn't snore." She winced at how awkward she sounded. "Okay, well, I'll see you at dinner."

"Did you need something?" He nodded to her dress. "I like that one, by the way."

Ireland glanced down at the latest fashion from France. "Thanks. It makes breathing difficult since it's really tight."

His left eye twitched. "I noticed."

"Right." She pushed her hair to one shoulder. "I, um, couldn't get the zipper."

A slow smile crossed his face. "You and your short arms," he teased. "Always disproportioned to your long legs."

"Can you help, please?" She turned around, presenting the faulty zipper.

"Since you asked so nicely." Gideon closed the distance between them. His large hands gripped her hips and she inhaled sharply as they slowly traveled up her back to the zipper. She closed her eyes as she heard the familiar sound and felt the rush of fresh air on her bare skin.

"There. All done," he said, his voice barely above a whisper.

"Th-thanks." When she didn't move, his fingers slipped beneath the straps of her bra and slid them down her shoulders. His rough hands traced along her spine and stopped at the same place as the zipper.

"Did you have a good time with your millionaire boyfriend?" he whispered while he placed delicate kisses on the back of her neck.

Ireland's eyes flicked open. "Mason isn't...." She stopped herself there. Gideon was being overly jealous, and it sent a shot of hope to her soul.

"I really don't care about him, but I do know this." He pulled her flush to him. "He wants to touch your soft skin like I am right now."

Breathing felt like a foreign concept with Gideon near her.

"He wants to kiss your neck until he makes goose bumps scatter along your body." Gideon's words caused the bumps to spread long before his lips grazed her shoulder blade.

She gasped when his fingers snaked under the hem of her dress and crept toward the lacy thong beneath. His breath hitched when he felt the underwear and tugged ever so slightly.

"And he sure as hell wants to rip these off you with his teeth." He slid up her dress and cupped her ass. "Just like I do."

"Then why don't you?" she asked when he released his hold on her.

Gideon chuckled and slowly spun her to face him. Lust shimmered in his blue eyes, a sight she never wanted to see diminished. "Because if I have you once, I'll want more. More of you, more of us. And I can't afford that."

"But what if I want more?"

He toyed with his beard, not once looking away from her. "If you want more, Ireland, you have to say it. I can't read your mind."

Gideon wanted more. She couldn't help but want it too. She'd craved him every night for six years. No man could replace the way he made her feel. Life without him wasn't as fun. He was what she'd been missing.

Reaching out, she traced the deep V on his stomach that led below his dark blue shorts. "I want you, Gideon."

A lopsided smile crossed his face. "See, now that wasn't so hard, was it?"

"Well, if you're going to be an ass—"

Gideon pulled her to him and caught her lips beneath his before she could finish her sentence. Tangling her fingers in his hair, she kissed him back. He tasted like pineapple with a hint of salt from the ocean, and she realized then that he hadn't showered since snorkeling. She gasped when Gideon wrapped his arms around her waist and grabbed her ass, moving her closer still. Moaning at the hard planes of his body against hers, her legs weakened when his tongue invaded her mouth. The once cool breeze dissipated the longer Gideon consumed her mouth with his firm one.

Tugging lightly on his hair, she felt her body catch fire when he kissed her deeper. His long and thick erection nearly burst through his shorts. She could only imagine what it'd be like without the barrier between them.

"If you keep this up, we'll give everyone a bit of a show," he rasped, pulling away slightly.

Suddenly remembering where they were, Ireland reeled back and glanced around the cove of villas. Since theirs were toward the back, the only things around them were trees and the beach. The likelihood of a nosy family member checking in on them was more than possible.

"We should—"

"Go inside." He kissed her fast. "Unless…."

She held back a laugh at his pained expression. "Gideon

Taggart, if you don't take me inside this minute, I'll never speak to you again." She barely had time to breathe before he hoisted her off the ground and stepped into the small hut.

Her breath caught in her throat when he pushed her against the heavy front door. "We can't have that, now can we?" He pulled down her dress and cupped her breast, making her moan his name when he flicked her nipple with his tongue. He smiled and nuzzled her neck. "Because I can't stand a single damn day without hearing your voice."

Ireland wrapped her legs around his waist and he walked toward the bedroom. "You might regret saying that."

Gideon chuckled, the tone sending shivers along her spine. "I could never regret a moment of a life with you."

"Fuck, Gideon," she breathed, biting his earlobe.

"That is the plan, yes."

Once her head hit the mattress, all notions of desertion left her. Her head spun in the best way the more his lips caressed her skin.

Gideon abruptly stopped, and she huffed in annoyance. "What the hell are you doing?" she asked, sitting up on the four-poster bed. "The point is to be closer, not farther away."

He moved back another step, his chest heaving and eyes glazed with passion. The lone lamp on the dresser flickered as he slowly returned to the bed. "Oh, believe me, I don't ever want to be out of your arms, but…." He ran a finger down her legs, shivers immediately spreading over her skin. "But I don't want to rush this." He pulled her dress completely off and let out a slow breath. "Because you're worth the wait."

His lips kissed up one leg and down the other while his left hand snuck under the sole piece of clothing left on her, his fingers and mouth drawing closer to her apex simultaneously. Her stomach dropped the closer he got, knowing what his beautiful mouth and hands could do to her. He'd tease her mercilessly all night if he could, but she wanted all of him. Ireland craved his complete touch nearly as much as the man himself.

Squirming, she reached for him. "Please," she begged when his finger slid in and out of her slowly.

"How can I say no to you?" He kissed her right hip, then the left before catching the thong between his teeth and pulling it down her thighs. "I really want to tear these apart, but I'll leave that for another day."

His eyes slowly reviewed her naked body. Finally, his gaze rested on her face. "You're every guy's dream, Ireland. You know that, right?"

Heat crept up from her toes and she sat up. Tracing the divots of his abs, she leaned forward and kissed down his muscular chest. She didn't want to hurry, but at the same time, she desperately needed him. Her fingers popped open his buttons and the satisfying *zip* followed next until his shorts were pooled on the floor. The heat radiating from his black boxer briefs surprised her. She'd been with him before, but it was different this time. The connection between them was new somehow. New and overpowering her common sense.

Reaching one hand over his toned ass, she smiled at his sharp hiss. His hips reacted, jolting toward her. With her right hand, Ireland gripped the velvety thickness of his long cock. She'd never forget how full he felt between her fingers. Her mouth watered at the sight of him. Gideon Taggart was beautiful. She licked her lips and pumped her hand over him, loving the way he hardened further.

"Are you absolutely sure?" His words were hoarse and wary.

Instead of answering, Ireland licked the tip of him. The thick member bobbed appreciatively. Glancing up to him, she grinned. "Oh yes."

Before he could move one muscle of his toned body, she swallowed his length in one swift move, his groan echoing in her ears. Paying special attention to his sensitivity, she sucked him until his hips reacted each time he slid down her throat.

Gideon's fingers threaded through her long hair, pulling ever so gently. When she increased the pressure with her tongue, he pulled out fast. "Oh no you don't." He wrapped a fist in her hair and kissed her before she could pout. And she wanted to badly, but the way his tongue collided with hers was well worth the interruption.

Drawing back, Gideon carefully pushed a hand over her breast until she was on her back. Adrenaline surged in her veins when he peppered kisses down her neck, then captured a nipple between his teeth and bit down. Ireland reached for him, but Gideon grabbed both her wrists and pinned them above her head. Stretched out completely, she writhed beneath him as his tongue explored both nipples, kneading the breasts with his free hand. The desire flooding between her legs heightened at the telling sound of a condom wrapper. Meeting his blue gaze, Ireland slid the protection in place.

"Next time, I'm going to make you come three times before I even get my dick out," he promised, pulling her to his lap and kissing the corner of her mouth. "But right now I need you."

In one move he grabbed her hips and impaled her. Ireland's mouth dropped open at the familiar sensation of Gideon and she gripped his shoulders tightly. He felt bigger, better after six years.

"Damn, darlin', you're perfect." He lifted her up and then slammed her back down on him.

She arched forward until only the tip was inside her. Grinning at him, she pushed back his disheveled hair. "Only for you."

Gideon cupped her face and planted a slow and sensual kiss to her lips. "Is that right?"

Ireland nodded slightly. The men she'd slept with had never fit her the way Gideon did every time he touched her. She swore all her underwear were no good after a day spent within his embrace. In the last six years, sex was quick, and foreplay was minimal. This was different. *Sex with Gideon was always different.* He'd been her first, and she thought other men would be just as good. She was dead wrong.

Gideon sucked on her right nipple as she slowly sheathed him again and again. This pace, this position hit her just right when she moved and her orgasm crashed down on her, Gideon swallowing the breathless moans from her lips.

"You're so gorgeous when you come, Ireland. I could watch you forever and always be surprised at the sounds you make."

Ireland held back a response. She had no words that would do justice, so she tangled her tongue with his, showing him her reply instead.

Repositioning them, Gideon lifted both her legs to his shoulders. He easily slid into her wet core, burying deep. For one long second he stayed there, never breaking eye contact with her, and then he pulled out and jutted into her. Faster and faster he pummeled her until the sound of their bodies together was drowned out by Ireland's moans. She didn't even try to be quiet, calling out his name, begging him to never stop.

Another orgasm was on the cusp, but she needed more. As if reading her mind, Gideon positioned himself closer and slammed into her over and over. The dam broke free and she came violently, uttering his name the whole time. By the time she could see clearly again, Ireland watched his brow wrinkle. He was holding back. His muscles glistened with sweat, but he didn't relent.

"Come for me, Gideon."

He shook his head and thrust again. "Not until you do one more time," he managed. "Three, darlin'. That's the magic number. Gotta have three."

The headboard squeaked from their movements, and Ireland wasn't sure if she could handle one more. "I can't."

She paused when his thumb flicked between her legs. Oh, but she could. Already the warm sensation ravaged her.

Between his fingers and cock, Ireland was certain she'd pass out from pleasure. Her back arched the faster he rubbed, and she opened her mouth to scream. Gideon's lips were there to encompass the desire and she felt his hips buck as he spent himself.

Ireland ran her fingers up his spine, his breaths labored against her neck. "Why three?"

Gideon met her eyes and she was speechless. He didn't bother to hide his affections. He never had. Smoothing her hair, he brushed his mouth to her chin. "You're a smart girl. You'll figure it out."

She couldn't form a sentence if she tried. He chuckled and hopped off the bed long enough to dispose of the condom and turn off the lamp.

Crawling into bed with her, Gideon tucked Ireland in his embrace. They weren't going to make it to the rehearsal dinner—his grip told her as much.

One thing Ireland couldn't deny, she didn't want to leave his bed. Ever. And that thought scared her to her core.

CHAPTER EIGHTEEN

The alluring scent of warm vanilla woke Gideon the next morning, his eyes slowly adjusting to the room bathed in the tropical sunrise. Without looking at the clock on the bedside table, he could tell it was early. It was a curse in its own. After living on a farm his entire life, sleeping in wasn't a common occurrence.

Except this morning, someone else was in bed with him.

Turning over, he couldn't keep from smiling. *Now, this is something I could get used to.*

He propped up on his elbow and studied Ireland's sleeping features. Her hair and makeup were a mess—not that he cared—and there was the most adorable pink to her cheeks and lips that beckoned him closer. Carefully, he traced her mouth with his index finger. The memory of the sounds she made washed over him in waves. Touching her would only make things worse, but he didn't give a damn.

She was all he'd dreamed about for six years, and there she was in his bed again. It seemed too perfect to be real.

His stomach grumbled noisily. *Farmer's gut.* He couldn't escape it, pretty lady in bed with him or not.

Ireland sighed and snuggled deeper into the pillow, her lips parted ever so slightly. She'd earned plenty of sleep after the night they shared. Remarkable was the only word he could imagine describing her with. She was just as incredible as he remembered.

The sheets hung loose around her waist but dipped since she lay on her side. If he saw those stunning brown eyes and tasted her lips, they wouldn't leave the room the rest of the day, or longer. Despite only wanting that, his stomach disagreed. If he was fast, he could slip into the kitchen and return with breakfast before she realized he was gone.

Grazing his knuckles tenderly against her cheek, his cock twitched when she leaned her face into his caress. The sheet fell completely off at her movement, and it took every ounce of self-control to only stare at her beauty.

He carefully moved off the bed, the cool flooring nice compared to the warm breeze drifting in from the ocean. He'd forgotten to turn the air conditioning on the night before, and he didn't exactly take the time to do it after Ireland's impromptu appearance. He wasn't about to complain; it was a surprise he'd accept any day. He'd only buy her zippered dresses from then on if it meant she came to him for help.

The long curtains billowed, and he stopped long enough to look out to the light blue water on the shoreline. This was the type of paradise he could live with. He glanced over his shoulder and saw Ireland cuddle his pillow. *A pretty girl and a sandy beach. Nothing better.*

His smile dipped when he remembered reality. It could all crash down in an instant. He was determined not to think about what might happen off the island. For now, he'd be happy with… well, whatever they were doing. The logistics still needed ironing out. *But after food.*

Turning, he sighed at the clothes strewn around the room. Her dress—too tight for anyone but him to see, in his opinion—rested on the armchair at the bedroom entrance. His shorts peeked out from beneath the bed, but their underwear was nowhere to be found. He didn't mind one bit either; they merely got in the way.

After checking the time again, he pulled on a pair of black shorts and a T-shirt. *Hopefully no one else is up.* It wasn't that he was ashamed, quite the opposite. He wasn't sure he could keep his mouth shut if he saw someone else. Being with Ireland made him remember why he was drawn to her in the first place. She pulled him out of himself then and now.

He slipped on a pair of sandals and returned to the bed. Ireland hadn't woken yet. He almost wanted her to, if only to give him a glimpse of how she was feeling about him in the morning light. He bent down and placed a featherlight kiss to her temple, then slipped out the back door.

Food and water, then back for round… four, is it? He couldn't help but grin. Ireland's appetite was nearly as insatiable as his—a fact he hoped to exploit to its fullest.

***

The moment the door shut, Ireland rolled out of the sheets. She wasn't one to wake up with the birds, but once Gideon's warmth left her, the desire to stay put vanished. Scrounging around the room, she gathered her discarded dress and pulled it on fast. Her thong, on the other hand, was nowhere in sight. *Oh well, not like anyone's going to know it's mine anyway.* The attached bathroom tempted her, but she shook her head. A shower would have to wait, since she wasn't confident her brother wouldn't barrage the villa for a wake-up call like when they were younger.

Quietly, she snuck to the front door. Only after looking through the peephole did she slip outside and run toward her room. She barely made it before she heard voices outside. Hustling to the bedroom, Ireland's feet stopped at the reflection in the mirror above the dresser. Her normally straight hair was mussed in the most erotic way. The streaks of mascara were quite the sight, but she doubted Gideon noticed much. He was too preoccupied with other parts of her body to care about a makeup malfunction.

"Talk about 'just got fucked' hair," she laughed, pulling her long strands back. She found a hair tie on the dresser and wrangled the mass into a messy bun. She had to admit, the afterglow of Gideon suited her, a rosy hue lined her cheeks and her lips were extremely plump.

Tracing her swollen mouth, she recalled the three times Gideon made love to her. The first was fast and furious, as if they'd both been waiting their entire lives to collide. A tingle traveled to the pit of her stomach thinking about it. The other two times were slow, gentle, and put the term 'making love' to shame. She couldn't deny Gideon's feelings.

Ireland stripped off her dress and grabbed a robe before she headed to the bathroom. After cranking the knob for the shower, she stood back and waited until the water warmed up. Gideon's masculine scent intensified with the steam. He'd seeped into her very skin in the hours they were together. The delicious ways he took her played in a constant loop that was slowly driving her insane. All she craved were Gideon's arms tucking her against his chest and spending the day between his kisses.

Shaking her head, she stepped into the cascading water and let it drench her sore muscles. After the night she'd had, a massage was in order.

Or maybe another round or five.

***

"Where'd you run off to last night?" Krista asked, sitting beside Ireland at the table a few hours later.

Ireland took a bite of fresh fruit and hoped the subject would evaporate by the time she swallowed. No such luck, since Zavier also joined the table nearest the pool. "Uh, work. I had a late night. Sorry I missed it."

"Oh yeah?" Gideon took the chair opposite her and bit into a piece of cheese. "Hope the work wasn't too hard on you."

She wiped her mouth with a napkin and met his gaze. "Nothing I couldn't handle."

He smirked and tried to hide it behind the sandwich now in his hands. Gideon the morning after sex was adorable. He was cocky and all kinds of hot. She'd completely forgotten the boyishness.

Zavier glanced between the two of them. "You weren't at the rehearsal either, Tagg. Hmm, suspicious."

Shrugging, Gideon held up his cup and took a noisy sip through the straw. The man even made drinking a pop sexy. "All these activities really wear me down. I needed to lie low for a night," he said at last.

"Need another drink?" Krista asked with a laugh.

Zavier didn't seem to buy Gideon's excuse like his fiancée, but Ireland wasn't going to give him time to think it over. Seeing the Kellogg, Leighton, and Taggart parents at the lunch bar, she waved them over.

"Everyone ready for some beach time? The staff has surfboards, boogie boards, and a few floaties for those of you who'd rather drift along the water." She pointed toward the beach at the back of the resort. "Plus there are cabanas and plenty of chairs."

"Perfect, but I think I'll opt for a nice, cold Sex on the Beach," Joanna said with a smile.

Zavier and Ireland exchanged glances. Their mother wasn't a lush, but her time in Barbados thus far had been filled with more booze than usual.

"A nap on a lounge chair under a palm tree sounds nice," Kenny said with a wink to his kids.

Lance joined the group and slung an arm around Frances and Walt. "Hell no. I'm catching waves." He nodded to Ireland. "And getting babes."

Gideon's chair scraped along the tiled patio. "Doubtful."

The parents headed toward the beach, drinks in tow. Ireland was grateful Lance went along with them; she could only take small doses of that particular Taggart man.

Her eyes shifted to Gideon. *But I can handle more of him. Lots and lots more.*

"I better go grab my suit," Gideon said, moving the opposite direction. He looked expectantly to her.

"Oh yeah. Me too."

Zavier narrowed his eyes but didn't question them. "This is why I always wear my swimsuit." He pulled Krista in for a quick kiss. "Meet you at the beach in fifteen minutes."

Ireland nodded and did her best not to sprint toward the villas. Krista and Zavier were watching, plus the parents could pop up anywhere in the thick trees. Getting caught by one of them would be beyond mortifying. At present, all she cared about was getting her bikini on.

"Where ya heading so fast, darlin'?" Gideon asked, snaking his arm around her waist as she rounded the bend to the cove of villas.

"Hey." No other words came to mind once she met his eyes.

He kissed her forehead. "I was a little worried when you weren't in bed when I got back with breakfast."

"You brought food?" He nodded and she bit her lip. "Sorry, I needed to shower. And to send a few emails."

He brushed back her hair. "God, you smell so damned good."

Looking up, Ireland cradled his furry jaw and stared into his eyes. *This. This is what I've been chasing for six long years.* She hadn't realized until that moment. It was scary and exhilarating at the same time. When she was with Gideon, it was just the two of them and nothing else mattered. "What am I going to do with you?"

Gideon kissed her top lip. "A lot, I hope."

She giggled and pulled him toward her room. "We need to hurry. Zavier is suspicious."

"Zavier is always suspicious," he laughed, but followed her anyway.

Ireland's stomach jolted at his cute grin. For the first time in her life, the past didn't matter. It couldn't when she was staring at the future. Her future.

She stopped herself there. *What am I doing? Gideon lives in Iowa. I live in Barbados. Gideon and I could never work. I'm a fool to think—*

"Hey, Ireland, calm down," she heard Gideon say from the edge of her panic.

Her eyes flicked up to him. It was then she realized she was squeezing Gideon's hands a little too tight. "Oops, sorry." She dropped them and hurried toward her villa.

"Wait a minute," Gideon called, hot on her heels. His large hands wrapped around her hips, halting her retreat. "Don't freak out on me."

"How can I not? We're... what we just... Gideon, I don't...." She clamped her mouth shut, her thoughts jumbling together so much that a cohesive sentence was impossible. She was spinning out of control, and he was the reason.

Gideon moved in front of her and tilted her chin up with his fingers. "I've been asking myself the same things, but I don't want to overthink this. Us. We're great together. We always were."

"But you're only here until next week. After that, you'll… and I'll—"

"I know." He rested his forehead to hers. "Just don't pull away, Ireland. At least give us the week. Please."

It sounded heavenly. It'd be easy to be with Gideon again. *It already is.* But she was afraid of what would happen at the end of their beach fling. It'd break her heart again if they ended.

"Can we keep this friendly?" she finally asked. "Because if this doesn't work, I can't lose you as a friend ever again."

Gideon's lips pressed together beneath his beard. "I don't know. I want to say yes, but I can't make that promise."

"So then what do you want to do? Act like it never happened and carry on with our lives?" She held her breath, waiting for his reply.

"Fuck no." He shook his head. "What do *you* want? That's all I care about, Ireland."

Meeting his eyes, Ireland wove her fingers through his hair. "You. I want you."

He smiled and kissed her forehead. "All right then." Pulling back, he nodded once, then swatted her ass. "Get something skimpy on so I can fantasize about you."

"We can't be all touchy-feely around our families," she reminded him.

"No, but it'll be fun to hide it from them."

He jogged toward his villa. Watching him leave never felt so wrong.

***

Holy hell. Ireland in a bikini was jaw-dropping. Sure, he'd seen one on her before—and nothing on her the night before—but the way the orange two-piece hugged her curves sent his adrenaline pumping. Running on the beach in a bikini should have been outlawed unless no one else was on the beach except the two of them. Watching her chase a loose beach ball made leaving the water more impossible with every bounce of her luscious body.

They managed to keep a safe distance at the beach for the last hour, Ireland trying her hand at surfing while he watched from afar. As it turned out, she tackled the smaller waves like a professional. He, on the other hand, could barely get on his feet before losing his balance. From the first wave in, he opted for the safer boogie board.

"What's going on with the two of you?" Zavier asked, treading water beside him.

"Nothing." Gideon eyed his friend. "Don't you have a bride to watch or something?"

Zavier chuckled and waved at his fiancée on a beach towel. "Aw, come on, Tagg. We're on a gorgeous tropical island, and you and my sister have something between you.

It's obvious to me, so the rest of our families won't be far behind. Better tell me now or I can't help."

Clenching his jaw, Gideon switched to float on his back. He couldn't hear that way. *Well, at least not as much.*

When Zavier dunked him under the water, he decided the back float wasn't safe around his old friend.

"Jesus, Z, don't drown me." He shook his head to get water out of his ear. "Your sister would be pissed."

"Ha! I knew it. Tell me. Tell me now!"

They swam out of earshot of their families before Gideon said, "She spent the night with me last night."

Zavier whistled low and bobbed on the floatie. "Well hot damn. I knew the two of you would eventually end up in bed again."

"Yeah, but it's not all I want."

"Figured as much. You've always had a thing for her, even after she left." Zavier slicked back his hair with water. "Have you talked about it?"

Gideon watched Ireland tumble from the surfboard. She popped out of the wave smiling and splashing water on Krista on the beach. "Yeah, kind of." Zavier lifted his middle finger out of the water. "All right, so maybe we haven't discussed it."

"Well, I love you like a brother, but I'm *her* brother, so don't hurt her. I saw the aftershock of your last breakup, and I really don't want to see it again." Zavier playfully punched Gideon's arm. "Good luck," he said, then ducked under the water.

Watching the shore, Gideon accepted that his friend's

heart was in the right place. The thought of messing up a good time with Ireland over technicalities wasn't what he had in mind. For the time being, he was content with just being the person she fell asleep beside.

Three hours later, he wrapped a towel around his waist and padded toward the villas. Fish baked right on the beach was the best dinner they'd had so far on the island, but he didn't want to roast marshmallows. He had something else in mind for dessert.

Ireland's voice drifted to him the closer he got. She'd raced back to her villa after surfing to make a few conference calls. Toby tapping his toe on the boardwalk earlier didn't help slow her workaholic syndrome either. It was nearly dusk, and still she remained in her home away from home.

He walked up to the front door and saw it cracked open. Taking the incentive, he followed her voice until he reached the small living room. Her villa was laid out in the same way but held a different style, seashells and a plethora of other beach themes accenting the area. He peeked at the single bedroom and saw the bed still made to perfection. He smiled and decided to fix that before long.

Finding Ireland with her back to him, Gideon took in the sight. With her left foot resting behind her right ankle, hair flowing in the crosswind and nothing but that damn orange bikini to cover up, Ireland was delectable. She rattled on in what sounded like French to him, though it could've been Parseltongue and he wouldn't have known. A wizard had nothing on the smooth way her voice carried amid the tropical setting.

In that instant, he wanted to know more about Ireland's travels and when she'd learned French. *Hell, she probably knows more than one other language.* The little he knew about her biological parents was that they were avid travelers. It made sense that she'd continue their legacy.

There was always something about Ireland that didn't fit until she realized her lineage. Now he was afraid it might be the one thing that kept her away from him for good.

He leaned his left arm against the entryway to the living room. There was a lot about the woman across from him that he didn't know yet. Some of it he'd read about in the gossip blogs and magazines, but he wanted to hear the truth from her own lips. Despite his faith in Ireland, it nagged at him that she hadn't shared anything with him. He didn't count hand-me-down knowledge anymore where she was concerned.

As if sensing his presence, Ireland glanced over her shoulder and met his gaze. She kept up her conversation but managed to grace him with a shy smile. After another minute, she hung up and placed the smartphone on the counter.

"Hey. Done with swimming so soon?"

"Yeah, it was fun. Everyone's making s'mores on the beach. We missed you." He cleared his throat. "I missed you."

She scribbled something down on the planner in front of her. "Sorry, had to finish these agreements."

He had to admire her tenacity with her job, but even he knew when to take a break. They only had a short amount of time, and he wasn't about to squander it.

"Do you ever stop working?" He took a step toward her and tossed the beach towel on the nearby couch.

Ireland set down her pen. "Not really, no. It's kind of a must when you manage a bunch of charities and trusts, plus run businesses."

"What's it like?" She lifted one eyebrow, so he continued. "To be in charge of all that money."

"Stressful." She ran a hand through her hair. "But when you get to do something good with the money, it makes all the hard work worth it."

Gideon closed the distance between them and gently pulled on the string to her bikini bottoms. One half fell free. "Like the orphanages and group homes?"

"Yeah." She smiled. "Z mentioned you told him about those. How'd you find out?"

"I have my ways." He unlaced the other side and the strings fell loose against her thigh. He couldn't resist touching the smooth skin there, a complete contrast to his own. "What else have you been keeping from the tabloids?"

She took a shaky breath when his fingers moved to the top of her bikini. "You don't want to hear that stuff."

Gideon paused and looked straight into her eyes. "Yes I do. I want to know everything about you, Ireland. Not just the details you give everyone else but all of them. I want to know your secrets and dreams, because that's what makes you who you are."

"All right, I'll tell you about one, then." Ireland slowly licked her lips. "Toby and I came up with a charity over here that pairs abused children with a therapy pet. Dogs and cats mostly, but we did find a gray parrot for this one kid in the Bahamas. She loved it."

She applied the same organic lip balm, and he could almost taste it. "The kids are recovering from all sorts of abuse. It's sad that people can be so horrible. Anyway, they get to go to one of the centers to help train the pet and get to know them. They also have a mentor—a certified therapist or psychologist—who can help them through their healing process. If the kid sticks with it and makes progress, then after a few months they can take the pet home and continue the program there with monthly check-ins. Some of the kids end up in foster homes, so we try to find adequate alternatives if that's the case too."

"Wow, that sounds like a great program. I don't know where you get all these ideas." He pushed her hair behind her shoulders. "You really are an amazing person."

"It's no big deal. I have the ability to help people, so it's a waste if I don't."

Gideon nodded appreciatively. She'd always had a big heart. "Don't ever change," he said, shedding the last remnant of her swimsuit.

The cinnamon hue of her eyes lightened as she searched his face. "I wasn't planning on it."

Running his hands down to her breasts, he squeezed lightly. "Good."

While he wanted to hear more about her life outside Iowa, he was desperate to be as deeply in Ireland as possible in that moment. He walked her backward until she reached the built-in bookshelf that separated the living room and kitchen.

"I can't resist you, Ireland, and I don't want to. But if you're not up for this, I need to know," he said, withdrawing his hands. She whimpered at the act, and he held in a satisfied grin. He wouldn't pressure her with anything. It hadn't worked six years ago, and he wasn't about to repeat history.

Ireland's fingers brushed through his beard, then tugged on it, a blush creeping over her face. He'd witnessed it over the years, but right then it had a whole new meaning. "I want you, Gideon, more than anything. I don't want to be scared of what might happen. I just want right here, right now, with you."

Desire exploded in his veins, but he held off. He'd made all the moves. He always had. If she was serious about their island time, proof was what he needed.

As if hearing his thoughts, Ireland pressed her lips to his. Honey-flavored lip balm had never tasted better. He kissed her back, coaxing her mouth with his tongue until she opened to him. Cupping her ass, he pressed her against the hard length of him. "This is what you do to me every damned day," he confessed, kissing her neck.

"Really? Because right now I look—"

His lips muffled the rest of her words. "You are beautiful no matter what you're wearing." His eyes scanned her naked body. "Or not wearing."

She lifted her brows and pulled down his swim trunks before she grinned approvingly at what lay between them.

"Yeah, I like the view here too." Her fingers danced along his tattoos. "I never thought you'd get tattoos. I like them."

"Good. I try to keep you on your toes when I can." Grabbing her off the floor, Gideon groaned when she wrapped her left leg around his torso. He possessively kissed her, reminding her exactly whose arms she was in and how he'd never let her out of them again.

"Gideon, please."

He brushed a finger to the center of her thighs and shivered at the slickness there. Gently, he pressed one finger into her drenched core. Her breathy moan was more than enough encouragement to add a second finger.

As he pumped inside her, her breath hitched. "You're way too good at this," she managed, standing on her tiptoes now.

Nibbling her ear, Gideon pressed his thumb to her most sensitive spot. Her hips bucked toward him, encouraging more. "I have to keep you around somehow," he teased, biting her nipple.

"I never meant to leave," she said, and he looked up. "You. I never meant to leave you. It all happened so fast and I thought I could come back and pick up right where we left off, but too many years went by and I couldn't."

The truth was written in her eyes, and it broke his heart just a little. "Now that's something I never thought I'd hear."

Regret filled her face and she looked away. "I didn't think I could have both. After I told you about my biological parents, your reaction told me everything you couldn't say."

"We were both young and didn't know what we wanted."

Cradling her face in his hands, Gideon tenderly kissed her. "But I know what I want—*who* I want—and I'm not letting you slip through my fingers another time. Not if I can help it."

Ireland nodded. "Me too."

He kissed her again, and that time she reached between them to stroke him. Pulling back, he grinned. "Now, where were we?"

Guiding him to her center, her smile demolished his self-control. "Right here, I think."

Placing Ireland's feet firmly to the floor, he spun her around and fully sheathed himself in her. Her back arched and he grabbed her shoulder as he thrust into her sweet body again and again. The books rocked slightly from their movements, a few even teetering to their sides. Their coupling was anything but sweet. He'd more than make up for it later that night though, because he planned to have her at least four more times before falling asleep.

She moaned loudly and gripped the edge of the bookshelf. Her orgasm clenched him hard and wouldn't let go. Gideon kissed her spine, coaxing her pleasure to continue. She needed more. She deserved more, and he would give it to her.

"Gideon," she cried, her voice laced with longing.

He jutted into her once more before pulling out. Ireland cried out in rebellion at his departure.

"Don't worry, darlin', I'm not going anywhere," he promised, turning her to face him. Her lips. He had to taste them before he let himself release. Lifting her up, he propped his arms under her knees and pushed back into the only place that felt like home anymore.

"I hope you know how fucking gorgeous you are."

"I do now." Her greedy mouth bit down on the side of his neck and he had to brace himself. She drove him wild, and they were only getting started.

Her moans wafted to the open rafters, the sole sound echoing in his ears. She thrust her hips to meet him and screamed his name.

Fuck.

That sent him over the edge. He drove into her even after he came, marking her as his.

With the look in her endless brown eyes, he suddenly felt the urge to be as primal as possible.

She was his.

At least for today.

CHAPTER NINETEEN

"And next month, the apartment complex in Barcelona will finish construction. After the final inspection, the teens will move in." Ireland looked to Toby to make sure she hadn't missed anything. He subtly shook his head, and she smiled at the camera for the video conference with her latest investors. "Any questions will be answered by my assistant, Toby. Thank you for your time."

She skirted the room before anyone could speak up. While she loved meeting with people and networking, the question-and-answer part wasn't her forte.

Walking toward her office, she smiled at the mailman in the hallway before getting on the elevator.

The short ride passed in silence, and she nodded to the receptionist before turning right down the hall that had only her office and Toby's. The building held several Bourgeois companies thanks to her hard work the last four years. Even her grandmother was impressed when she visited the year before.

Swiping her keycard, she opened the oak door and inhaled the cucumber fragrance from the wax burner in the corner on a bookshelf.

The large office was complete with a stylish desk, chair, and small wet bar on the west wall beneath bold artwork from artists she met while abroad. Her desk was exactly as she'd left it, messy with a half-eaten pastry atop a merger folder, and notes with reminders scribbled in Toby's handwriting stuck to all sides of the desktop. She sank into the leather chair with a huff.

After checking emails, she noticed a new message from her mom. It was a photo of the wedding group all geared up and ready to parasail. Ireland pressed her fist to her lips to keep from cursing. Business came first for her, and the limited free time she had was spent on Gideon. She leaned back and stared out the large window. *And there's been plenty of* spending *over the last two days.*

She would've kept daydreaming about him if a knock didn't meet her ears.

"Come in." She pressed the button on the desk so it unlocked the door. The receptionist wouldn't let anyone past her unless they were approved—another added security measure she was getting used to.

Mason popped his head in. "Are you decent?"

"Unfortunately for you."

He chuckled and entered, closing the door behind him. "From what I hear, you've been plenty indecent these last few days with a certain farmer."

Ireland smoothed back her hair. "Er, well...."

Mason waved a hand and crossed the room to the window. "Don't worry, I won't tell our investors. Which reminds me, we do need to finalize those details."

"I know, I'm sorry. Zavier's wedding screwed me up." She dug out the file from her desk marked 'Straight and Leighton merger.' "What do you want to discuss?"

Clasping his hands behind his back and gazing to the water, Mason resembled the ideal partner in an old TV show. "How does Gideon feel about our partnership?"

"He's jealous of all the time we spend together." She stood and straightened her skirt. "But he understands it's business."

"I won't say I'm not disappointed that the two of you seem to be getting along well." He turned toward her, his eyes holding a stern gaze. "But you're not thinking of reconsidering our agreement, are you?"

Ireland stared toward the waves. "No, of course not, Mason. Business should always be separate from personal."

She glanced back to him in time to see an odd expression flicker over his face before he covered it up with a smile. "I suppose you're right. I'll get over my heartbreak," he teased.

"Then you are getting jealous?"

"Yes, in a way."

"Why?"

His brown eyes clashed with hers. "I have feelings for you, and I can't help it. I've tried to ignore them, believe me.

You're easy to fall for."

Remorse filled her stomach when he kissed both her cheeks. "Mason, I hope you don't think I—"

"No, you didn't lead me on, don't worry. You made it clear you had no soft and gooey feelings for me." He smiled. "I just felt like the first time in fifteen years, I might actually have a chance at love again." He kissed the top of her hand. "I suppose I should thank you for that renewed hope."

Ireland couldn't help but hug him. "There's some special lady just waiting for you, Mason. I know there is."

"You're right, of course. Please keep in touch, yes?"

She nodded slightly and heard him leave but couldn't watch.

Mason was a proud and shrewd business partner. A life with him would've been more of the same. Being with Gideon would be the complete opposite.

But will he leave Iowa for you?

***

Just when he thought he'd seen Ireland at her best, Gideon watched her open the orphanage in the heart of Barbados. Her entire family was in the crowd alongside a hundred others. The way she smiled over at him after cutting the ribbon made the noise disappear. He wasn't normally one for crowds, but for her, he made an exception.

"Well, what do you think?" she asked once she'd finished her duties. She met the group's huddle, her hair hanging freely around her shoulders. She could wear a flour sack and he'd still want her.

"We're so proud of you," her mom said, hugging her.

"Very proud," her dad added, joining in.

"Thanks." Ireland pulled back. "Helping the kids here is just as important as the other locations. This one is near my neighborhood, so it means a lot."

Gideon's parents hugged her next before the entourage followed the crowd to tour the home for children.

"You're stunning," he said, casually lacing his fingers with hers.

Ireland blushed. "And you're sweet."

"Not hard to be around you."

She grinned and pulled him toward the large house. He listened to her explanations of the rooms, split up by age and family if need be. *She thought of everything.* Watching her come alive as she spoke warmed his soul. Orphans had never crossed his mind until now. With Ireland showing him the kitchen large enough for the kids to learn how to cook and bake, Gideon couldn't imagine a better way to spend his time. Her smile and enthusiasm put all others to shame. When they reached the last door, he almost didn't want it to end. This was her element. A boardroom wasn't.

After the grand tour, including insider information about the project, they met up with their families on the street. As badly as he wanted to keep his arm around her shoulder, she stepped out of his embrace.

"We have some time before dinner if anyone wants to hit up the local shops." Ireland looked to Krista, who nodded enthusiastically. "All right. The cars will hang out until you're ready to head back." She led him toward a blue SUV parked on the street. "But you are coming with me. I want to show you my favorite spot on the island."

"Really?" He climbed in after her.

"Yep, really."

She shifted the vehicle into gear and they quickly picked up speed, heading away from the bustling city. The streets narrowed, and dense trees surrounded them the longer they drove. A sweet smell of fresh rainfall mingled with the earthy tones and made him miss Iowa.

Glancing over at her, Gideon simply watched her drive with one hand on the steering wheel and the other keeping time with the music on the radio. He could say for a fact that he'd never get sick of the sight.

Finally the SUV came to a stop in front of what looked to be an abandoned mansion. A tall metal fence surrounded the area but didn't stop Ireland from walking toward it.

"Where are we?"

She looked over her shoulder. "Farley Hill." She paused at the gate and hopped over.

He followed but stopped shy of the gate. "Should we be here? Kind of looks like they want to keep people out."

Ireland wiggled her brows. "Aw, come on, Gideon. Since when do you back away from an adventure?"

He eyed the signs warning trespassers to keep out. "Since we're in a foreign country and I'd like to go back to America someday soon."

Ireland threw her head back and laughed. "Don't worry, I know the owner."

His skin chilled. "Let me guess—Mason."

Instead of answering, she walked faster, nearly losing him completely. She wove between ancient trees and the soft ground almost twisted his ankles twice. By the time he caught up, Gideon realized why this location was her favorite. For a second, he stood enamored by the viewpoint. It couldn't have been more picturesque unless it was on a postcard.

"Wow. It's beautiful up here." He sat beside her on the bench that overlooked the ocean and valley below. Clouds floated above the trees, while mountains loomed in the distance.

"Whenever I feel homesick for Iowa, I come up here and just watch nature. It doesn't look much like Iowa, but it's not busy up here most of the time and reminds me of home. Sometimes I close my eyes and listen to the birds and wild animals chatter to each other. Up here, I'm safe, and nothing changes that."

Propping his arm on the bench behind her, he leaned over and kissed her cheek. "Thank you."

"For what?"

"I needed this. To get away from everybody." He inhaled and closed his eyes. It did remind him of Iowa in an odd sort of way. "The city and all the adventures have been a lot of fun, but getting out in nature was a long time coming. I love it."

She moved closer to him and rested her head on his shoulder. "Me too."

They sat speechless for several long minutes, merely

enjoying the splendor around them. He couldn't have asked for a better afternoon. A view and his girl were all he needed to be happy.

He peeked down at her serene face and semi-closed eyelids. Ireland stole his breath each time he looked at her. He didn't want it back either.

Scratch that. All I need is her.

Falling for Ireland was easy as a teenager. Falling for Ireland as an adult obliterated him in only the best ways.

Until reality washed over him like rain.

It should have been enough for him to be that close to her, to feel her warmth against him, but it wasn't. They wouldn't last beyond the trip, that much he'd accepted right after they made love and she curled into his arms to sleep. She'd always be his first, but the reality was she was destined to be someone else's last. That hurt the most. She belonged here, not in Iowa like he thought. He couldn't keep her away from her passion.

"Can we stay up here the rest of the trip?" he finally asked as the sun began its descent.

Ireland hummed. "I wish." The rumbling sound of engines pulled her out of his embrace. Craning her neck, she nodded toward the mansion. "But I'm guessing those trucks are here to set up for an event." She stood and waved at someone in the distance. "A wedding, if I had to bet. This is a popular spot."

Slowly, Gideon stood, eyes never leaving the horizon. "I can see why."

"We should get back to the house before our parents

send out a search party."

He wrapped his arms around her waist. "I wouldn't mind getting lost with you."

"Me either." She smiled sadly and walked toward the SUV.

Later that night, Gideon watched Ireland from a distance. It killed him to see she held back from him. He knew the reason, but he couldn't fix it. Only she could. He'd leave Iowa for her, he realized it the day after she left six years ago. He just didn't know if she'd do the same for him. Always giving and never receiving wasn't the type of relationship either of them deserved.

He just hoped he could handle it if they said goodbye for good.

CHAPTER TWENTY

"All right now, nobody say a word. Toby said Ireland would be at her condo this afternoon for a business call, so we have just enough time to crash the party and make her join us." Krista motioned the three families closer to the gated condo.

Gideon stood in the back of the group and hoped to God Mason wasn't inside with her. The last thing he needed was that dick to join their horseback riding on the beach. He scratched his chin. He still wasn't keen on the activity, but the bride-to-be had turned into a bit of a diva in the last week.

Toby waved from the front steps and a loud buzz sounded before the gate swung open. Gideon followed a pace back and watched the scene play out. He had to admit the condo was impressive. While Ireland had plenty of money, she didn't flaunt it on her home. *Probably because she has one in France too.* He nodded politely at Toby as they climbed the steps.

They entered the condo in time to hear Ireland sign off in French. Zavier paused at the steps leading to the living room, halting the group.

"Wow," he said a little too loudly. Krista glared at him while Lance jabbed him in the stomach. He didn't care. The sight in front of him was well worth the pain.

Cathedral ceilings opened to a large living area complete with contemporary artwork on the walls. A white couch and matching ottoman were to the left, nearest the huge bay window. A seventy-inch television was mounted on the wall across from it, and a twisty crystal sculpture sat on a white bookshelf brimming with books. From the look of the place, no one ever lived there, let alone Ireland.

Standing on his toes, he caught sight of the barstools in the updated kitchen. A small dining table sat off to the right, next to French doors that led to the veranda out back. The scent of coconuts and vanilla made him smile. Without seeing the rest of the place, he could guess it looked the same—clean, contemporary, and ritzy. There was no way he could keep a place like that. It'd be beige within a week.

"Surprise!" everyone except him yelled.

Turning his head, he saw Ireland come into view. Her hair was twisted into a braided bun, and he had to swallow when he saw the short blue romper with the left strap slouching down her arm.

"Oh my God. What're you all doing here?" She grinned when her parents wrapped her in a hug.

"Toby told us you had a free afternoon, so we thought

we'd snatch you up," Joanna said, still hanging onto her daughter. From the looks of it, she was serious about the snatching part of the plan.

Ireland scanned the group expectantly and her smile broadened when her eyes rested on him. "Great, what're we doing?"

"Horseback riding," Lance piped up.

"Yep, so grab your chaps," Zavier added with a nod toward Gideon.

Shaking his head, he was glad he opted to hang back. The heat creeping up his neck wasn't ideal in the warm climate.

"All right, let me grab some boots and we'll go."

Ireland disappeared, Krista and all three mothers following. The *oohs* and *aahs* from what he expected was the bedroom drifted out to the waiting men.

Why hasn't she brought me here?

He looked around and noticed a small picture frame on a side table. Walking over, he picked it up. It was a snapshot of Ireland and Toby on a beach somewhere. The sound of the surf caught his attention. Looking out the window, he noticed the private beach about three hundred yards away. *It was taken here, I bet.* Another photo caught his eye and he smiled at Ireland's broad grin while sandwiched between two elderly men who looked like tribal leaders in Africa. The baobab trees in the background gave away the location and he made a mental note to ask how many other locations she'd traveled to in her time abroad.

He carefully set it back down just in time for the women to return. Ireland wore the same outfit, but a stylish pair of boots fit for riding horses met his gaze when he looked at her feet.

"Everybody ready?" Krista asked, officially in charge of the troop.

No one objected, and an hour later, the three families were astride horses of every color. The Barbados native guide led them in two lines toward the beach. Waves licked at the hooves and he couldn't complain. The view was spectacular. On one side, the surf crashed against the sand, and on the other palm trees and greenery beckoned him to explore. The cool trade winds whipped his T-shirt, making him shiver despite the warm sun. It was the one time he was grateful he'd left his ball cap at the resort.

The Leightons rode in the front, chatting amongst themselves and the tour guide. It took a whole five minutes before Toby started flirting with the man in his early twenties. In a way, it made the afternoon easier. Krista's family picked up the rear of the group. The Kelloggs weren't the most athletic crew, so the trail guide in the back had to help them now and again.

Gideon watched his brother check out the girls among the waves. None could hear him even if he called, but it was just like Lance to scope out a pretty girl wherever he went.

Pulling the horse away from a patch of greenery, Gideon caught up with his parents.

"Enjoying your vacation?"

Frances lifted her sunglasses and grinned. "Yes! This is the best vacation I could ask for."

Walt snorted next to her, still getting used to the horse.

Despite growing up around the animals, he wasn't fond of riding them. "What about our honeymoon? We went somewhere tropical."

Frances shook her head and chuckled. "Florida isn't the same, dear." Walt shrugged and clucked his tongue to speed up. "How're things going with Ireland?"

Gideon watched his horse's mane flutter in the breeze. "What're you talking about?"

"Sweetheart, I'm your mother. You can't lie to me." She lifted her brows. That might've worked in junior high, but he didn't give in.

"It looks like she's having fun on her ride."

"Gideon." She said it in that mom voice, and he cringed. "The two of you aren't as subtle as you think."

He wrapped the reins around his left hand. "I honestly don't know, Mom."

"Aw, that's too bad to hear. You're the best couple I've seen in ages."

A yelp from behind made them stop their horses long enough to watch Krista's dad almost fall off his. Once he was situated, they started moving again.

"You have chemistry," his mom continued.

"All we have is chemistry," he said before she could go on. She'd do it the entire ride if allowed, and he wasn't in the mood for a heavy discussion. Riding on the beach and forgetting his problems was on his agenda.

"Oh sure. Well, I hope this doesn't change your mind about love, hon. If not Ireland then some other special lady out there."

Not to me. Thoroughly finished, he gave her a slight nod, then gently kicked his heels into the horse's side. The black gelding picked up speed quickly, hoofbeats coinciding with the rhythm of his heart. He passed Joanna and Kenny, who waved at him, and kept going. Only once he caught up to the guide and Toby did he slow. Glancing behind him, he scanned the upcoming horses and riders. Not seeing Ireland, sweat slid down his brow.

"Where's Ireland?" he asked Toby.

The smaller man jutted a thumb backward. "Last I saw, she was chatting up the family." He returned to his flirtations.

The horse trotting through the waves, his eyes skimmed the shaded faces. Panic started to spread through his body. *What if she was taken by a crazed reporter? What if her horse bolted when no one was looking? What if she fell off and no one noticed?* He pumped the brakes on those thoughts. Ireland knew how to handle herself, horse or not. Even though he knew there was a reasonable explanation, he couldn't stop the anxiety from zipping through his body.

"Everything okay, Gideon?"

"Aw, shit." He rested his hands on his thighs and lowered his head. From his position, he watched the clear water lap the hooves and the sand shift at the surf. Glancing over, he sighed in relief. "Yeah, everything's fine, Ireland."

She cocked her head to the left. "All right, cool. I had to find service to make a call." She waved her phone. "Business never sleeps."

"Which is why you weren't with everyone else," he said

more for his own benefit than hers.

"Yeah, I told the guides." She pulled off her sunglasses, her brown eyes searching his face. "Are you sure you're okay? You look flustered."

Prodding his horse closer, he grabbed the back of her neck and pulled her in for a kiss. Her gasp morphed into a satisfied moan and she clung to the front of his shirt. The urge to pull her off the horse and show her exactly how he felt overwhelmed him. He couldn't, though. *Not here.*

Easing back, he lingered over her mouth. "I'm good now."

Ireland ran her fingers through his beard and tugged once. "Good."

The sound of someone yelling met his ears and he looked over his shoulder. Their group of horses was much farther down the beach than he anticipated. "C'mon. We better catch up or they'll think we've run off to make out in the forest."

"Psh, more like have sex in the waves." She grinned sassily and kicked her horse into a trot.

Gideon let her get a head start before encouraging his horse forward. Every now and again, Ireland looked back, a broad smile on her cheeks.

If he didn't leave with her at the end of this trip, he'd never forgive himself.

CHAPTER TWENTY-ONE

"Um, Gideon, should we be here?" Ireland asked the next day, nervous for the first time in a long time. Her mouth dropped open as she walked farther into the hangar where a prop plane sat. The private airport was a frequent spot for her, but the size of the plane threw her off. She glanced over to Gideon. "An airplane?"

"Yes, ma'am." He smirked beneath his beard. "Ever been in one this small?"

"Uh, no." She looked toward the Cessna, then to the man who'd let them into the hangar. He merely grinned, then walked away. "Wait, you're flying this thing?"

Gideon checked the propellers and nodded. "As it turns out, yes, I am." He put his hand on the small of her back and guided her to the passenger seat. "Why? Are you scared?" He pulled the seat belt over her chest and snapped it in place, his bright blue eyes gleaming mischievously.

"I… well, I didn't know you were a pilot," she finished lamely. *This is the type of thing a friend would—no, should—know.* She suddenly felt extremely disconnected from the world she'd left behind.

He double-checked the belt, then carefully fitted a headset over her head, brushing back her hair so it didn't tangle. "Yep. It started as a part-time job crop-dusting to pay for college courses." Pausing, he kissed her cheek. "But sometimes it's fun to just get up there with the clouds and see the world." His lips hovered over her mouth. "Well, Iowa, that is."

Ireland glanced around the small cockpit. The aircraft was older, but looked to be in decent shape. "So, you… you sure you know what you're doing?" she asked when Gideon climbed in and started the engines.

He adjusted the microphone on her headset. "Do you trust me?"

All the trepidation disappeared from her mind when she met his gaze. If she said the word, he'd abandon this all. It was sweet how he'd set it all up. No doubt the cost alone for this little adventure was more than he could afford. "With my life."

Grinning, Gideon pushed in a flat knob, then moved a level between them. The plane lurched forward slowly at first until they cleared the hangar and made it to the maze of runways.

Ireland gripped the edge of the seat as they neared the end of the first path. The plane turned left, and he hung back to check in with the tower. Once given the green light, he looked at her one more time. She forced a smile and hoped it was reassuring.

The plane picked up speed, the propeller whizzing in front of them. Ireland's stomach jolted when the wheels lifted off the runway and into the air. "Holy shit." She let out the breath she'd been holding as they quickly ascended. The island shrank away little by little until the tall buildings looked like miniature building blocks.

"Well, what do you think?"

Ireland pressed her nose to the glass to see better. "It all looks so different. It's spectacular." The world below seemed foreign from the tiny plane. It was perfect in all directions. Blue water stretched along one side of the plane, while the shoreline stood out with its lush greenery and vibrant colors. "I've never seen it like this before."

"You have a private plane, Ireland." He gave her a disbelieving glance. "Don't you ever look out the window?"

She chuckled and shook her head. "Not usually until I'm way higher. Then there's not much to see." Her eyes shifted to the clouds overhead. It was surreal to be in between the land and clouds, never close enough to one for more than a minute. "I bet Iowa is a whole other sight."

"It is. I've grown fond of the plots of land and endless fields of crops. They look like puzzle pieces from above. It really is great." He contacted the airport over the radio, then looked back to her. "But this sight is the best I've seen yet."

Ireland blushed and rubbed her thumb against her bottom lip. "You do this all the time back home?"

"Yep."

"Wow. I'd never want to come back to solid ground again."

He turned the yoke to the right, allowing a new viewing angle of the island. "Most of the time, I fly around to enjoy the freedom, but eventually reality creeps back in." He chuckled. "I've had my fair share of panic when I noticed the fuel gauge was dangerously low."

Ireland watched him effortlessly guide the plane through a mass of clouds. Up here, he seemed completely at home. "My private jet is huge compared to this. I always thought bigger was the way to go."

She spotted a parasailer and a slew of tourist boats nearby. She'd yet to try that out, but after she'd been this high, she wasn't sure she could settle for a mere hundred feet above the water.

"But now I think I was wrong. You get to see so much more of life from this little plane." She laughed but stopped at Gideon's pained expression. *Damn, this isn't about flying anymore.* She offered him a smile, then asked about his pilot training, not that she listened.

The real-life comparison couldn't be helped. Gideon was equivalent to the Cessna—scary as hell but breathtaking when given the chance. And of course, her current lifestyle was the private plane, easy and comfortable, but not as beautiful or life-changing. *Did he mean for me to come to that conclusion?*

She snuck a glance at him. His lips moved beneath his bushy beard. There was something extraordinary about him. It wasn't the sex, which was mind-blowing all on its own.

It was Gideon. He cast a spell with those sky-blue eyes. His addictive lips reeled her in before she saw it coming. She doubted he meant for her epiphany, but she couldn't think about anything else right then.

An hour later, the plane's wheels touched down on Barbados once more. She would've stayed up there all day if they had the time. Sadly, the real world called her back.

"Did you have a good time?" Gideon asked, tossing the keys to the pilot at the hangar before they walked the short distance to her waiting SUV.

"I did."

"I thought you might." He grabbed the door handle and looped an arm through the open window. "But I was worried I'd screw it up."

She rolled her eyes. "Oh please. You never screw anything up."

"I'm going to disagree with you there." He pushed her hair off her shoulders and traced the braided strap of her tank top. "I screwed up more than you know, Ireland." He pressed his lips together and looked at his sandals. "Lance told you I tried to get on a plane."

"Yes."

"What he didn't tell you was that when I sobered up, I did get on a plane. I flew to Greece to see you and try to make things work."

Ireland's pulse quickened. *Surely, he doesn't mean….*

"I found you and some Greek guy." He looked up and grimaced. "Can't say I'd like to see your tongue in another guy's mouth anytime soon like I saw that day."

"Damn." She tossed her purse on the seat. "I'm sorry about that."

He ran his fingers through his hair, the result too adorable to consider messy. "It's okay. We weren't together, and you were free just like you always wanted. So I left, even though it killed me." He chuckled slightly. "If you love something, you set it free, right?"

Her phone rang but she ignored it. She couldn't think about answering a call when she'd realized Gideon was everything she'd ever dreamed of in a man. He may not have gone with her six years ago, but he did something better—he let her live wild and free. And now she didn't want to be apart from him. In a few short weeks, he'd pulled apart her neat plan for the future. The best part was she didn't care.

Moving closer, she caught his jaw in her hands and pressed her lips against his. "You need to not be so wonderful," she murmured.

His palm rested at the back of her head. "That's impossible when I'm with you, Ireland." His mouth found hers, tongue probing for entrance. She opened to him and sighed as their tongues met. Gideon pulled her against him, never once breaking the kiss. Her fingers slid through his hair, the distance still too great. She needed to feel him without the constraints of clothes.

"You're too good to me."

Gideon moved enough to run his thumb across her lower lip, his cobalt eyes searching her face intently. Just when it looked like he was going to speak, he leaned in and gently kissed her.

Ireland's heart tugged at his sweet embrace and everything they'd done since reconnecting. He didn't always say his feelings outright, but she could read between the lines. The truth tore her up inside.

"My, my, aren't you a fetching couple?"

Easing back, Ireland looked to her right and saw Mason with a wry smile on his handsome face. His black suit stood out among the tropical setting. Somehow, he pulled it off without looking cliché. The man was sheer perfection, just not hers.

"Mason, what're you doing here?"

Mason looked past her to Gideon. "My helicopter is due any moment."

"Of course it is," Gideon mumbled. He didn't release his grip on Ireland. Instead, he held on tighter.

"I'm taking a few prospective clients up for a sky-high incentive." He nodded to the group of men in business suits heading in their direction.

"Oh sure." She watched the two men size each other up. They were about the same height, but Gideon won when it came to muscle mass. He was bulky compared to the slender, yet fit physique of Mason Straight.

Ireland took a breath and tried to ignore the fact that both men were staring at her instead of each other. She struggled out of Gideon's hold and gathered her hair into a ponytail.

"Are we still on for this evening?" Mason asked, his voice smooth as caramel.

Meeting his brown eyes, she nodded. "Yeah. Toby put the reservations under my name."

"Lovely." Mason straightened his blue tie. "I'll leave you to it, then."

Once they were alone again, Gideon cleared his throat. "So, you're still meeting with him even though we're... whatever we are?"

She shrugged and climbed into the SUV. "He's about to become my biggest partner, Gideon. Meetings will be necessary tonight and many other nights to come. I'm not going to stop having business partners because you're jealous."

His brows rose. "Yeah, but he knows you're not interested in him, right?"

"I made it clear, don't worry. You have to trust me. It's not like I'd ditch you because he's rich." Ireland cursed herself when her statement made Gideon cringe. Still, he needed to have a little more faith in her. Her feelings for Gideon far outweighed his trust and that hurt. She stuck her keys in the ignition. "Let's go. I doubt you want to miss exploring Harrison's Cave. It's really spectacular."

For a second, it looked like he was going to argue. She was thankful when he walked around the vehicle and got in beside her. Explaining her business relationship with Mason to Gideon again would ruin their time. If Gideon could only give a little when it came to where he lived, they could be together. In the back of her mind, she didn't think he would. He didn't six years ago. Any future with Gideon would involve being landlocked once more. She couldn't do that again no matter how much she cared for him. Any future with him would involve compromise. *Neither of us are very good at that.*

***

Mosquitos buzzed in Gideon's ear, but he didn't swat them away. His focus was on Ireland as she spoke to Mason at the other end of the courtyard. They had recently returned from their dinner, and he itched to find out what they'd discussed.

Swinging his gaze away, he saw his parents lounging in the hot tub along with the Leighton and Kellogg parents. It was the one time he was glad they didn't extend an invitation. Lance and Zavier played catch with a football on the beach while Krista watched nearby.

And then there was him. He should've joined one of the groups, but when he saw Mason and Ireland stroll on the beach with locked arms, he couldn't tear his eyes away.

"They're such a cute couple."

Gideon looked over to see Toby beside him. "Yeah, I guess."

Toby pulled over a chair. Plopping down, he clucked his tongue. "Look, I'm Ireland's best friend, and believe me, she has feelings for you."

Gideon took the seat next to him. "But?"

"But she also has family obligations."

"You mean her grandmother."

Toby tapped the side of his nose. "Exactly, but I probably shouldn't tell you any more."

He placed a hand on Toby's shoulder. "Please, I need to know. She won't tell me anything, and all my thoughts are running wild not knowing what's true and what's not."

Toby's eyes narrowed with pity. "Oh, all right. You're adorable. I can't refuse that face." He snatched a drink from the table and lowered his voice. "Since Ireland is the next generation of the Bourgeois family line, her grandmother expects her to marry someone appropriate. Mason comes from a long and quite impressive lineage in England. His family has numerous connections around the world. Combine him with the dynasty of the Bourgeois and it's a recipe for mountains of money. Put two and two together and voila! The perfect power couple."

It made sense to Gideon then. "Mason is the ideal match for Ireland because of their families."

"Yeah. I'm sorry. It isn't that Ireland doesn't want you, because who wouldn't? You're a fine piece of arse." Toby brushed off his orange shorts. "But she'll do what's best for her future."

"But what if I am what's best for her?" Gideon stood and paced, the sand tickling his toes. "Ireland will do whatever she wants. I've seen it before. She's headstrong and gets her way no matter what."

"Oh yes, she'll always be a princess like that." Toby also stood and patted Gideon's bicep a little longer than necessary. "But that was Iowa. Ireland is different now. She's learned a lot more about the world."

Gideon clenched his jaw to keep from responding. Once Toby walked off toward the house, he cursed. *Of course, Ireland grows up when you're tilling a field on the other side of the world.* He kicked at the chair and stubbed his toe.

"Everything all right there, farmer Gideon?"

He recognized Mason's accent before he saw the millionaire. When he saw Ireland speaking to Krista out of earshot, he shook his head. "Are you really trying to convince Ireland to agree to a business marriage?"

Mason scratched his forearm. "Ah, I see Toby's been gabbing again. And as usual, he doesn't have all the facts correct."

"Answer me."

"That was Fiona's suggestion." He looked over to Ireland. "But we decided to move forward with just a business deal because…." He paused. "Well, probably because of you."

"I sure hope so." Gideon tried to steady his breathing when Mason shrugged. Part of him wanted to whoop for joy that the millionaire knew Ireland didn't want him. Another part of him didn't trust that, though. If he and Ireland couldn't work out their situation, she might end up with Mason or a guy like him.

Mason's eyes grazed over him slowly and he managed a small smile. "Gideon, Ireland and I don't know each other very well, but we have an agreement. One that involves a lot of dollar signs, castles, and a few vineyards." Mason loosened his tie around his neck and popped the first button on his dark green shirt. "Right now, Ireland is exploring her single life and I fully support that. She knows I'm here if things don't work out between you two." Gideon didn't move, even though he really wanted to sock the other man in the nose.

He didn't like the sound of any of those words. "Wait, so

you're just waiting around to see if Ireland and I work out? If we don't, you're just going to swoop in and be the hero?"

Mason's brown eyes met his. "I'd like to say no."

"But, you can't." He glanced over and saw Ireland laughing. "She needs more than what you'd offer. She needs love."

Placing a hand on Gideon's back, Mason nodded. "Why don't you let Ireland decide what she needs? She sees the world as it is. Love isn't a commodity to people like us."

Gideon's hands curled into thick fists. The guy was taking it all nonchalantly. Would Ireland as well? Surely she didn't think marriage was a business transaction. *Does she?*

He looked over and noticed no one else remained on the beach with them. Stifling his rage, Gideon pushed Mason's hand away. "Ireland wouldn't ever agree to that."

"Maybe, maybe not." Mason fixed his eyes to the ocean. "But she's not your responsibility, Mr. Taggart. You didn't work six years ago. Perhaps you should think about why."

"It's because—"

"Wrong." Mason faced him. "It's because she found out what happened to her biological parents. How her father's family disowned him because he fell in love with someone they didn't approve of. And then she was orphaned, and her family didn't find her until she was an adult. Think about it, Gideon. It's all I've done since meeting her. None of it made sense. Why would a wealthy family do that? They could've tracked her down immediately."

"Because they're assholes, obviously."

Mason stuffed his hands in his pockets. "Maybe. Or

maybe they did it to protect her from someone."

Gideon thought it over. It didn't make sense why her biological relatives waited to look for her until she was an adult. "But who?"

"Before I go into business with anyone, I do a thorough investigation. Part of that includes meeting the family members, researching criminal and personal history, and of course, checking for skeletons in the closet." Looking out at the horizon, Mason shifted his weight. "The Bourgeois family lost many investors when Ireland's father died without a successor. I have a hunch that someone was profiting off Fiona not finding her grandchild."

Gideon bristled. "Why would anyone do that?"

"I don't know to be honest. I think the answer lies within her parents' wills. Once she takes ownership of Bourgeois Investments, she'll do a complete overhaul on her business partners. Some may not be happy to lose out on money like that."

"Seems cold."

"Yes, it does."

"Knowing all that, why do you want the merger to go through?" Gideon felt a bead of sweat slide down his forehead. "Is it because you're in love with Ireland?"

When Mason didn't answer right away, Gideon wanted to be sick.

"No, it's because I got to know Ireland over these last months. She's the real deal in my opinion. Even if the Bourgeois family didn't know of Ireland's existence, the situation doesn't feel right to me. I want to buy out Fiona's shares so Ireland regains full power of the Bourgeois companies."

"Why?"

"It's what she deserves." Mason shrugged. "Plus, it's business, Mr. Taggart. Naturally, the added money is nice but being associated with someone like Ireland is good for business."

Gideon dug his shoes into the sand. "I only want Ireland. I don't care if she has money or not. I didn't fall in love with her because she's an heir."

"Duly noted." Mason chuckled and sized him up. "You know, I think we might've been friends had the situation been different."

He shook his head. "I doubt it." Gideon didn't bother to listen for the millionaire's reply. Now that he knew more about Mason's reasons for the merger, he felt a little better about Ireland. His gut churned. *Except for the part that Mason admitted he'd be waiting to see if we work out.* He didn't like that thought at all. Especially since it was more than plausible.

CHAPTER TWENTY-TWO

The crowd of reporters outside her condo made Ireland worry her bottom lip. It wasn't normally that bad. The paparazzi were getting bolder by the day. She even saw them trying to sneak into her office building under the guise of postal workers. When she told her grandmother about it, the woman didn't seem too worried.

Opening the back door, she let out a huff when more reporters lined the beach. Normally the condo association was good about the scoundrels. Not today, apparently.

She clutched her purse and headed toward the front door. *Might as well get it over with.* She paused at the entry and grabbed an oversized sunhat from the hat rack. A flurry of voices met her when she stepped outside.

"Ireland, are you and Mason Straight a done deal?"

"Let's see that million-dollar smile."

"Miss Leighton, what's going on with your brother's wedding? Why are you using Mason Straight's resort instead of one of your own?"

"Pose for a picture, sweetheart."

"Ireland, who is this Gideon Taggart to you?"

"How is your grandmother's health? Will you be inheriting more money by the end of the year?"

"Ireland, can you tell us which man kisses the best?"

More questions peppered the air at the same time and she lost count of which one to answer. *Not that I'm answering any of them.* If it weren't for the gated driveway, she was positive they'd push and shove until they got what they wanted.

Tugging the hat closer to her face, she obscured any photos they could get and climbed in the back of the SUV.

"Freaking vultures," she huffed, snapping her seat belt.

"Where to, miss?"

She thought about her office, but it was Sunday, so only the weekend staff would be there for mail. The resort sounded tempting, but she couldn't yet. "Mason Straight's office, please," she decided.

Once they were free of the reporters, Ireland watched the busy streets until they reached the large business complex. Mason's apartment was the penthouse, but she doubted he'd be anywhere but his office.

His personal assistant led her to a large corner office, and Ireland sat in the leather chair on the other side of the oak desk. If she thought her office was expensive, she had another think coming when it came to Mason's décor. She'd guess an interior decorator had their way with the space since it was chic, modern, and held an ungodly price tag.

A fireplace sat along the western wall. Nearby, four chairs were placed around a glass table that had an ideal view of the balcony large enough to hold ten people. With matching side tables, the gray-blue walls stood out against the brown pieces.

After five minutes, Ireland stood and made her way around the large space. One bookshelf held titles mostly in Italian, piquing her interest. Finally, she opened the door to the balcony and rested her elbows on the rail. Waves rolled in from the ocean at a safe distance, but she could still smell the salt in the air. "This view is incredible."

"And now you know why I built this building here."

She glanced over her shoulder and saw Mason close the office door. "I would too."

He set a folder on his desk and joined her. "But you're not here to discuss real estate, are you?"

She turned, back facing the ocean. "No."

"What ails you, my dear?"

"God, you're British." She chuckled at his faux shocked expression. "The paparazzi. They're a little out of control since we started being seen together."

"Mm, yes, I did notice that." His eyes scanned the horizon. "What would you have me do? I can increase security around the resort and have a few of my men switched to your service."

It didn't sound like a bad resolution, but it didn't answer the question burning in her brain. "Did you call them?"

"Who? The paps?"

"Yes."

He cleared his throat. "Well, I let my schedule leak so they'd be around whenever we're together, but I don't encourage the paparazzi unless I have to." His brows furrowed. "You don't think I'm trying to hurt you with them, do you?"

"Well—"

Mason clasped her hands within his, brown eyes searching her face. "Ireland, I would never put you at risk, whether it's with nosy reporters or a walk in the park. I hope you know that."

The sincerity in his eyes registered in Ireland's mind. "I do. I'm sorry."

Rubbing the back of his neck, Mason offered her a small smile. "We learn to put up with the reporters, but I can tell you I'm not a fan in the least." His eyes clouded. "I lost my fiancée many years ago, and I still blame the paparazzi for her death."

Ireland's stomach dropped at the sad story. "Oh, Mason, I'm so sorry. I didn't know. When I looked you up online, there wasn't—"

"There wouldn't be. I bought the paper the reporter belonged to." He squeezed her hand. "It's in the past. I try to keep it there. Since then, I control the paparazzi around my life. If that means I have my assistant give away tidbits of my life, so be it. At the end of the day, they'll leave me alone or they won't have jobs."

So that's his big secret. It's actually really depressing.

Noticing his pained expression, she kept the conversation moving. "Gideon isn't a big fan of being famous."

Chuckling, Mason kissed both her hands. "Well, if he can't handle a little inconvenience now and then from the paps, he chose the wrong woman."

"I guess so." She didn't like the thought, but it was true. Her life was a constant circus.

"You should know that your grandmother once owned a French media company."

"Wait, really?" She rubbed her lips together.

"Yes, the same one I lost my Brigette to, which is why I bought it. To prevent other lives from being lost so carelessly. Obviously, I don't believe your grandmother knew anything about it."

"Oh God, Mason." Her eyes instantly teared up. "I'm sorry."

She bit her thumbnail and thought over the paparazzi involvement in her life. She thought it happened when Mason was around, but that wasn't true.

"I think she's the one telling the reporters about where I am."

Mason nodded. "I think you're right."

"Shit. That sucks." She imagined her grandmother scheming and started laughing. Just the thought of it was ridiculous and more than believable. "Here I was blaming you when it was my grandmother of all people. Wow, I guess that's one way to learn about someone."

"It took me a little time to figure it out too." He handed her a tissue when tears rolled down her cheeks. "We all have a soft spot for family, love, and that isn't all that my investigator found out."

Deciding sitting was a better option, Ireland sank into a chair and listened as Mason explained what he'd found out. She hadn't questioned her grandmother about her parents or their wills. She just assumed the wills had been properly followed. It was one thing to bend the truth, but Fiona had lied straight to Ireland's face. *No wonder my parents left.*

"Come to think of it, she pressured me to not only move forward with you but to marry you. Now, I know it's because of money." She couldn't decide if she should laugh or cry, so she did both. "What should I do?"

"That's not for me to decide, Ireland. I still want to be your partner."

"Thanks, me too." She held up a finger and added, "Business partner."

"A man can dream, right?" he teased with a wink.

She chuckled but quickly sobered when she thought about her grandmother's meddling. She barely knew the woman if she was honest with herself. "There are probably more things she's hiding."

"It's a possibility, yes."

"Will you help me figure them out?" she asked after deeply inhaling. "I have a feeling there are more. Lots more."

"With pleasure."

"Great, thanks. I think it's time the Bourgeois companies were solely under my name. My parents would've wanted that, I think."

"Let me know what I can do." He walked back toward his desk. "I have a slew of attorneys if you need them."

"Good to know." She smiled. "I better get to the resort. I'm taking the ladies to a spa while the men go deep sea fishing."

"Sounds relaxing. Have a good time. I'm off to visit an old chum who owns a couple chocolate factories in Colorado and back home."

"I wouldn't mind a few samples. I could use some after today."

"Consider it done. Archer chocolates are the best." Mason walked her to the door. "I'll call you later." She paused at the door. "Thanks, Mason. You really are a great guy."

She walked to the elevator and waited for it to arrive.

Just the wrong one for me.

***

The clouds cleared just as the large fishing boat left the docks. Gideon watched the waves in the distance. They were still white-capped, but the wind seemed to have died down significantly since they left the resort.

"Who's ready to fish?" the captain asked.

A round of *yeahs* bounced off the waves and the boat picked up speed. They were headed toward a secret fishing spot, according to the captain. Gideon didn't mind either way. It was a relief to get on the water again. Plus, not having a certain distraction would do him good. At least that's what Zavier told him earlier.

Reaching the top-secret location, the captain tossed the anchor and helped the Iowans prepare their rods.

"So, are we doing a bachelor party?" Lance asked, casting out.

Zavier shook his head. "Oh no. Krista would kill me."

"Aw, have a little fun, son," Kenny chimed in, and everyone glanced at him. "What? I was young once."

They all chuckled, the sound of water lapping the boat putting them at ease. The captain offered tips to whoever would listen. Gideon listened to a few tips before focusing on his task. He'd been fishing since he could hold a pole. Deep sea fishing was different, but he wasn't expecting to score something big.

Gideon sat back in the raised seat and rested the rod in one of the holders on the side of the boat. Closing his eyes, he tilted his head to the Caribbean sun and sighed. No idle chatter was the ultimate prize of the day. He stayed like that for an hour before his dad reeled in a wahoo. The rest of the crew managed smaller fish, but Zavier eventually caught a barracuda.

The day couldn't have been better until his brother whispered, "We're kidnapping Z later for a night out."

Gideon glanced to the other man, helping Krista's dad with his line. "Nah, you heard what he said. Krista will kill him."

"Live a little. We won't do anything crazy, just go to a local bar or club or something." Lance pouted. "Please."

It wasn't a horrible idea. Zavier deserved a fun and safe

night before he tied the knot. "All right, fine, but just a few drinks."

Lance clapped and hooted until the rest of the fishermen stared at him. "Shit, sorry."

Settling back in the sun, Gideon wasn't disappointed when their excursion ended, especially after he caught two wahoo plus a few other smaller fish. *I can check that off my bucket list.* He smirked and helped his dad off the boat later that night.

"I wonder how the girls fared with their spa day," Zavier said, walking up the dock.

"Guess we'll find out," Gideon replied.

"But he won't until tomorrow," Lance added with a nudge.

Rolling his eyes, Gideon mentally prepared himself to be the designated driver for the bachelor shindig. It wasn't his favorite pastime, but it'd be plenty of fun.

***

Snuggling in her Egyptian cotton sheets, Ireland turned off the light next to her bed. She checked her phone but didn't see any new messages. After spending the afternoon at the spa with the ladies, she remembered a last-minute proposal to send to the Beijing office. She'd dropped off the very relaxed bride and their mothers before returning to her condo. By the time she finished a few changes, it'd been too late to go back to the resort.

Yawning, she rolled to the other side of the bed. Gideon sent her a text message four hours ago, saying he and

Lance were taking Zavier out for one last night on the town before he became an old married man. Even though Gideon didn't drink, Ireland worried about him. Barbados was safe compared to other islands, but there were horrible people everywhere.

Tell me when you get back so I can sleep, she had replied.

She turned to her other side and reviewed her afternoon. Mud baths, deep tissue massages, facials, and hot stones rounded out their spa experience. Her skin felt softer than it had in years. *I bet Gideon would like it.* She pushed that thought to the back of her mind and cuddled the empty pillow beside her. Their time was swiftly coming to an end, and she was getting more attached by the hour.

Her phone lit up with a new message. Grabbing it, she stared at the screen until it blinded her.

Gideon: Out front.

Ireland: On my way.

She hopped out of bed, sure to grab a robe since she didn't exactly want to show off her underwear to her brother and Lance. She didn't need Lance making a pass at her in his drunken state. It'd happened a few times over the years when they were younger.

Walking to the front door, she reviewed the security camera feed for the gate. Sure enough, her brother and the two Taggarts stood outside. Well, *stood* may've been stretching it for the two with rum bottles in their hands.

Pressing the button for the lock, she opened the front door and waited until they reached the steps.

"Do you need help?"

Gideon looked up and shook his head. "Nah, just need a place for these losers to sleep it off." He grabbed Lance's hand and guided him up the stairs.

"Oh my God, Ireland's here," Zavier greeted, hugging her. "My little sister is so pretty and rich. So freaking rich. Don't you think so, Tagg?"

Gideon didn't answer as she quickly locked up and waved her brother toward the spare room. "And you're drunk. I know just the bed for you." She looped his arm around her neck and led him to the room off the kitchen. "Here you go." Zavier plopped onto the bed, his snoring echoing before she shut off the light.

Shaking her head, she turned to see Lance wobbling on his feet and Gideon slapping his brother's hand from touching anything within reach. "Will he be okay on the couch? I only have two available bedrooms. The two downstairs are being renovated."

"A park bench is good enough for the way he smells." He chuckled and steered Lance to the living room. Guiding his brother to the couch, he carefully pressed him down and took off his shoes.

"Think they'll be all right?" she asked once she covered both men with blankets.

"Oh yeah, they'll be fine." He met her gaze, his blue eyes tired. "Thanks for this. I didn't want our families to see them wasted."

"You bet. I'm glad I was here and not at the resort tonight."

"For once I agree that your workaholic ways came in handy." He slipped off his shoes and sighed. "Did you have a good time getting pampered?"

"Yep. Got all relaxed. It was nice to have girl time."

Lance snored loudly, and she scrunched her nose. "Maybe we should finish talking somewhere quieter." Gideon followed her to her bedroom and shut the door. "How was fishing? Catch anything good?"

Gideon leaned against the door. "I did. Not a lot, but enough to make me want to go again." He rubbed his eyes and Ireland realized the time.

"I'm beat. Do you mind if we go to bed?"

His face relaxed. "That'd be great. I don't know how I kept up with them all night, honestly." He took off his shirt and pants. "Sleep sounds perfect."

Ireland switched off the light and patted the spot beside her. "I agree. We'll talk more in the morning."

Gideon slid under the covers and Ireland chuckled when he fell asleep as soon as his head hit the pillow. Tossing her robe aside, she snuggled under the sheets. Gideon's steady breathing lulled her eyes to close. Even lying next to him was satisfying. She couldn't say that about any other man.

She stared at his sleeping face. In her heart, she chose Gideon the moment she saw him again. It was her brain causing the problems. She'd followed her heart once and that resulted in losing Gideon. *If I do it again, who's to say the same thing doesn't happen?*

***

Cracking open his eyes, Gideon tried to focus on his surroundings. Sunlight shone through a window on the opposite side of the room, and somewhere nearby, somebody was snoring like a chainsaw. The night before flooded his memory, and he sat up quickly when he didn't see Ireland beside him.

"Ireland?" His heart pounded in his ears. He hoped she hadn't left him alone in her house.

Her cute face popped into view from what he guessed was a walk-in closet. "Hey, sleepyhead."

He wiped his eyes and relaxed back on the pillow. "Hey." His eyes grazed over the purple robe. It was sheer enough that he could see the only thing beneath was underwear. "What time is it?"

Ireland glanced to the clock by the bed. "Not too early. We'll make it in time for the wedding, don't worry."

"Shit, that's today, isn't it?"

"Yep."

He propped his head on his hand and watched her play with the rope holding her robe together. "So, when you say it's early, is it early enough for you to come back to bed for a few minutes?"

A shy smile crossed her face and she caught her bottom lip between her teeth. "Now why would you want to do that?"

"Come a little closer and I'll show you."

She giggled and neared the edge of the bed. Her hair sat in a bun on top of her head, messy after a night of sleep.

"Close enough?"

Gideon reached out and snagged his arm around her waist, pulling her down on top of him. "Much better."

She fingered one of his curls and smiled. "I wasn't sure if I should wake you when I got up. You looked pretty comfortable."

He leaned up and kissed her chin. "Always wake me up, Ireland. I'll never complain if I wake up to see you next to me, I swear."

"Hmm, so what if I did this?" She kissed the side of his neck. "Would that wake you up?"

"Nah, probably not."

Determination filled her face and she wiggled against him. "How about this?" Her tongue slid down his neck and swirled at the base of his throat.

If his body wasn't already awake, it would be now. "Maybe a little."

Ireland peeled off her robe and tossed it to the other side of the bed. Running her hands along his chest, she leaned down just enough so her nipples grazed his skin. "What about now?"

"I think I'd start to wake up after that."

Her lips traced his abs, and Gideon held his breath when she lowered. "How about now?" she asked, tugging down his boxers.

Meeting her mischievous brown eyes, he swore out loud when she freed him. "Yeah, I'd be awake."

She smirked. "Fully awake?"

"I think you can see how awake I'd be."

A red tint covered her cheeks and she nodded. "Good, now I know how to wake you up." She moved off his legs and toward the door.

"Whoa, whoa, whoa." He grabbed her hips and hauled her back to him despite her giddy shriek. Settling her beneath him, he brushed his lips to hers. "You're not going anywhere, darlin'. I'm not done with you."

She tilted her head to the left. "Oh yeah? And when will you be done with me?"

He moved down and traced her left breast with his tongue. "Never."

Goose bumps pebbled her skin at his words, encouraging him further. He shoved the soft sheets out of the way and dipped his tongue between her legs.

"Gideon!" She sat up fast and he grinned.

"What?"

"Your brother—*my* brother is on the other side of the door." Her eyes were alarmed, but that wasn't the only emotion lining the brown depths.

"You better be quiet, then," he said, laying her flat and settling between her thighs.

Her back arched when he licked the inside of her leg. "You know I can't."

Looking up, he smirked before returning to his preferred spot on her. The rest of Ireland's body was a wonderland, but the way she tasted here was his favorite. Her fingers clawed at his hair the longer he indulged in her. Feeling her muscles strain under his touch sent his body into overdrive. He couldn't get enough of her, couldn't taste enough of her.

He slipped a finger inside, and her moan washed over him.

"Oh my God, Gideon." She clenched around him and he quickened his movements. He didn't give a fuck where they were; he'd never give up on the way her body felt against his.

She muffled her cry of pleasure against a pillow, but he wasn't done yet. Locking her legs over his shoulders, he lifted her up to meet his mouth. She bucked against him, but he didn't back down, determined to make every part of their morning last in her memories. Their time was coming to an end, but he didn't want her to forget him. Ever.

"Gideon, please, I need you," she whimpered after another orgasm shattered her.

He carefully laid her legs back on the bed and leaned up to catch her mouth. Her tongue swirled against his, furthering his desire to never let her out of his arms. With one fluid movement, he entered her. Ireland's breath hitched, and he stared into her desire-glazed eyes. "Fuck, I love you."

She wrapped her legs around his waist and he closed his eyes. He couldn't imagine heaven getting any better than this. Slowly, he rocked their bodies until he found a rhythm with her hips. He wasn't going to last long if she kept it up.

"Stop being goddamn bunnies and get out here! I'm getting married today!"

Ireland's eyes went wide. "Shit."

Chuckling, Gideon yelled back, "Go wait outside, then." He didn't hear Zavier's response, but was glad when the footsteps went the other direction.

Looking down at her, he grinned. "I'm about to set a new record because I'm sure as hell not stopping."

She leaned up and kissed him. "Good, because I didn't want you to."

Thrusting into her once more, Gideon picked up his pace and clamped a hand over Ireland's mouth when she started to moan. Those sounds were for his ears only.

CHAPTER TWENTY-THREE

"Okay, we're all set," Ireland announced, clapping her hands. She smirked when Zavier and Lance winced. *Oops, forgot.* Their hangover wasn't quite cured after all.

The three families swung their attention to her. Excitement filled the air more than usual, and she took a breath when Toby waved at the caterer. He pinched her wrist, then walked toward the kitchen. A giant white cake followed the duo, and Krista hugged Ireland's arm.

Once the wedding was over, Ireland swore to never plan another one. The details involved were insane. Then again, the bride played a large part in the extravagance. Krista wasn't a bridezilla by any means, but she had tendencies, and was giddy to the point that it became intolerable. Others may like it, but it drove Ireland crazy. Even with a wedding planner, it was stressful.

"Krista, my stylists are waiting in the bridal suite."

She pointed to the large house. "They'll take good care of you."

The bride-to-be grinned, then grabbed her mother's hand and disappeared.

Ireland turned toward her brother. "Zavier, you and the best man need to change."

"What, I can't get married in swim trunks?" Zavier teased, sipping his beer.

Evidently it's not too early to start again. She cast a sideways glare at him. "Not unless you want to be divorced by the end of the day."

Zavier rolled his eyes and nodded to the villa nearest the pool, now dubbed the 'bachelor pad' by Lance so the men could get ready for the wedding in peace.

Try as she might to keep her focus on the list on her phone, Ireland still watched Gideon walk away. It would've been better if he'd have tossed a smile her way before vanishing, but he was off today, and she didn't know why. They had plenty of fun earlier in the morning. She shivered, recalling the way her innocent tease turned seductive. *Maybe it's because Z's getting married and he isn't.* She frowned at the thought of Gideon marrying someone else. Dwelling on that would only sour her mood, so she shook her head and focused on the activities from earlier. Those were the only thoughts she wanted circling her brain today.

"All right, the rest of you have about an hour before we begin." She reviewed the notes. "You can head over to the beach anytime. The seats are set up and ready for us, and the musicians will be here shortly." She scrolled the screen with her thumb, recalling the local reggae band she'd found the other day. They were exactly what the wedding needed to pull off the perfect beach theme.

Krista's dad and the Taggarts walked toward the beach, but Ireland's parents stayed behind.

"You've done a wonderful job preparing all this, princess," her mom said, hugging her.

"Thanks, but Toby did most of it." She looked toward the kitchen and heard her assistant yell something in Italian. "He keeps me together."

Kenny looped his thumbs on his belt buckle. Despite the warm weather, he wore jeans and boots. It was a wonder they got him to put shorts on at all during their stay. "I think somebody else is doing that these days." He nodded toward where Gideon disappeared moments earlier.

"Yeah, maybe so." Ireland's phone buzzed, but she ignored the call.

"You two were always good together, you know?" Joanna stated.

"Yeah, we really were, but I don't know if we could work a second time. We're too different now. He has a life in Iowa. I have one in Barbados. And my life is busy, complicated, and requires consistent travel." She shrugged. "I don't think Gideon wants that. He doesn't deserve that."

"He'll go back to Iowa and get a girl just like that." Her dad snapped his fingers.

Smoothing the front of the mint-green dress, Ireland silently applauded her father for trying to help. "I know, Dad. It'll suck if we part ways, but I'll eventually be okay with it. And we'll be friends after all this. I promise."

"Let's hope so," Kenny said, slipping his arm around Joanna's waist. "We'll head over for the wedding. See you soon."

She didn't bother to watch them leave. Her parents were always there to help, but today they'd done nothing but put doubt in her mind. She really needed to discuss all this with Gideon, but it didn't feel right on Zavier's wedding day.

Pushing her fears aside, Ireland focused on the next event. Her brother was getting married today, and she'd be damned if anything messed it up.

Ireland fanned herself with her hand, telling her it was the weather and not the memory of Gideon that morning. *Freaking tropics.* She knew it wasn't, though. Every time she slept with Gideon would forever be ingrained in her mind. *Does it really have to end?* She watched a butterfly land on a flower. *Maybe, it doesn't.* Her recent conversation came to mind. Gideon didn't deserve to be wifeless for weeks on end while she traveled for work.

"Ah, there you are," a deep voice called.

Turning, Ireland tried not to gape at Mason. He looked scrumptious, if that was possible. His deep brown skin and dark hair stood out against his beige suit. The blue shirt beneath was unbuttoned midway to his chest, showing a peek of tanned skin underneath.

Reaching her, he pulled off his designer sunglasses and smiled.

"I'm glad I caught you before the wedding began. Anything I can do to help?"

"Um, no. I think we have it under control."

"Wonderful." He glanced around the estate decorated for the happy event. "The place looks lovely. I couldn't put on a better wedding."

"Thanks. Toby is a wiz at this sort of thing."

Mason reached over and tucked her hand in his. "Oh, I don't doubt it, but this has hints of Ireland. I can feel it."

Remembering her manners, Ireland said, "Thanks again for letting us use this place. It's a dream come true for everyone. I've never seen my family and friends so relaxed."

"Good. Glad I had the place available on short notice." He led her through the house and to the full bar. "Now, are we going to discuss transferring the California vineyard before or after the wedding?"

Ireland took a seat on one of the barstools. "Mason, not now," she shushed. "It's Zavier's wedding."

Mason made a rum cocktail with pineapple and lime juice, garnishing it with a strawberry on the side of the glass. "I spoke with Fiona this morning. I think I should go back to France with you when you talk to her."

"Yeah, I could use a friendly face when I confront her about my parents' wills and the businesses." She sipped the drink. *Wow, this is good.*

"All right, now, back to that vineyard. I want it."

She rolled her eyes. Mason hadn't let up about her newly purchased vineyard in California. "And why would I trade it? I think I'd like California."

"So would I. A beachfront property near movie stars sounds more up my alley than yours."

She smirked. "Hmm, then maybe I want stock in that chocolate factory you were telling me about."

"Oh, now you're playing dirty. I like it." Mason walked around the bar and sat across from her. "Please, Ireland. Don't make me beg. I'll give you free wine for life."

Ireland chewed on the straw. "Well, if that's all you're offering as incentive—"

"Dear lord, you *are* going to make me beg." He got down on his knees and offered her a sad face. "Please, please, please trade me the vineyard and I'll give you twenty percent of my chocolate share."

"Forty."

He lifted one knee and rested his elbow on it and clasped his hands together. "Thirty."

"Thirty-five and I still get that free wine for life."

"You drive a hard bargain, Ms. Leighton." He chuckled. "I think I made the right decision in partnering with you."

"What the hell?"

Her eyes slid shut at her brother's familiar voice.

When she looked over, the smile on her face disappeared.

"Ah, gentlemen, you must convince Ireland—"

"Convince her to what? Marry you?" Gideon growled.

She didn't feel anything. Not the warm breeze on her cheeks or the touch of alcohol in her body. She looked down at Mason and inwardly groaned. From their viewpoint, it looked like Mason was on bended knee, proposing. "Wait, Gideon, that's not what this is. I swear."

She met Gideon's blue gaze that had gone black. While she expected a pained expression, she only saw acceptance, and that hurt even more.

"We're gonna be late to your wedding, Z," Gideon said, turning on his toes. "I knew it was too good to be true. Isn't proposing on someone else's wedding day a faux pas?" he muttered, walking toward the beach.

Mason stood, a forlorn look on his face. "I'm sorry, I think they misunderstood."

"Mason, seriously?" She glared at him. "You had to freaking beg me on your knees?"

"Sorry, I wasn't thinking." Mason cleared his throat. "I'll clear this all up."

She groaned in frustration and scanned where Zavier and Gideon disappeared to. Neither popped back in to let her explain.

"Forget it. I'll talk to him."

"Maybe this will encourage him to make a step in your relationship," Mason suggested.

"Or send him packing. I need to get to the beach." She couldn't be mad at Mason or even at Gideon. While there was nothing wrong with what she and Mason were doing, it hurt to think that Gideon instantly went to a dark place. He hadn't let her explain. *Almost like he expected it to happen.* She shook her head sadly. There was no way she could endure a lifetime of him not trusting her.

Moving in the beach's direction, Ireland held back the tears blinding her vision. The happiest day of her brother's life just became the worst of hers.

CHAPTER TWENTY-FOUR

The wedding went off without anyone tripping or the weather turning. Krista looked beautiful in a flowing gown, and nobody could wipe the smile off Zavier's face. Gideon stood to his friend's left and tried to focus on the couple saying their vows, but he couldn't. It was impossible with Ireland's scent on the wind.

Sneaking a glance over to her, he sucked in a breath. In a light green dress that rested midway on her thighs, Ireland looked gorgeous. She wore more makeup than usual, and her hair sat in a mass of curls at the nape of her neck.

So much for not upstaging the bride.

She flicked her eyes to him. They were sorrowful and begged to let her explain.

But I can't.

He stared at her for another few seconds before returning his gaze to the bride and groom. It was idiotic to think she'd turn down Mason for him. He was nothing.

Gideon scanned the crowd and saw Mason in the back, a pleasant smile on his face. *Dick.* Naturally, she attracted the person who could make all her dreams come true. It ripped his heart in more pieces than he thought remained. The millionaire was Ireland's best chance at happiness. *I'm not.* Even if she didn't love Mason, she could have a fresh start.

Zavier turned to him and held out his hand. After finding the small metal circle in his pocket, Gideon handed over the wedding band. He was being one shitty best man right then. He hadn't heard a word the pastor said the entire ceremony. All he could think about was what a fool he'd been. He tried to keep it in his pants, and nearly had until she came to him for help. He wasn't strong enough to turn her down then, or earlier that morning. Not to mention, his body had a mind of its own where she was concerned.

From that day forward, he didn't resist his feelings for Ireland. *But I should've.* He was paying the price today. Seeing Mason down on his knee solidified the fact that he really didn't know Ireland anymore. Years ago, sure, but not even close now. She'd marry Mason because it was best for her life. Gideon would come to terms with it eventually.

"You may kiss the bride."

He looked over and watched Zavier kiss Krista until she blushed and the small group of family members clapped and cheered. He'd never understood the fascination. Then again, he was a quiet guy and didn't want undivided attention from a large number of people. He just wanted it from one person.

His eyes met Ireland's as they linked arms to walk down

behind the married couple. It was her attention he wanted, and hers he couldn't have. *Not anymore.*

"Gideon, I need to talk to you," she started, but he shook his head. "Mason didn't—"

"I don't think that's a good idea." He followed Zavier and Krista toward the house where a feast sat waiting. It didn't even tempt him.

"Let me explain."

"I think Mason on his knees did enough explaining." He dropped her arm. "I need to… you know what, I need some space." She reached out, but he lowered his voice. "Give me space, Ireland. I sure as hell gave you plenty."

Pain shone back in her brown eyes, the complete opposite as six hours earlier. "Fine."

Turning around, he moved against the crowd. The casual suit suddenly felt like it was choking him. Being anywhere near Ireland suffocated him.

Not looking where he was going, his shoulder collided with another man's. "Sorry," he mumbled.

"Quite all right."

Gideon cringed at the accent. "Of course it's you." He glared at Mason. As much as he wanted to slug the guy, he couldn't. He had no reason to hate the millionaire other than they both vied for the same woman. "Take care of her, okay?"

"Gideon, you don't—"

"I know what I saw. Maybe you didn't propose, but you will eventually. You can give her everything I can't. Now promise me."

Mason's eyes met Gideon's. "All right, I promise."

"And make sure she knows every day how special she is."

He nodded once. "Of course, but—"

Satisfied for the moment, Gideon brushed by him and held back the urge to sprint into the crashing waves and never surface. He was officially done with Barbados. He never wanted to leave Iowa again. It only brought heartache when he did.

***

"This is all so va-va-voom," Krista gushed, hugging Ireland. She pointed to her dress. "I never thought couture and sand would go together. Thank you so much for helping us."

Zavier wrapped an arm around his wife's waist. "Yes, thank you. Being here has been wonderful."

Ireland pasted on a smile. "Of course. Don't forget you have the next week here too." She looked around to the small dance floor where the parents were grooving to Elton John. "I think you've earned some alone time."

Krista's bubbly laughter grated on Ireland's ears, but she fought through it. She had a sister now, after all. She'd have to get used to it whenever she visited Iowa again.

"Oops, looks like cake time," Zavier said, nodding to the table with a decadent cake on top.

"Have fun." Ireland hugged them before the newlyweds headed toward the lemon-flavored concoction. She placed a cream-colored envelope on their table. Inside was her present to the newlyweds. A week each year in Barbados was the least she could do. Every couple needed to recharge now and again. She had a similar envelope for her parents, though theirs wasn't limited to Barbados. She'd talk to them later about it all. She couldn't think clearly while things were unsettled with Gideon.

Deciding dessert could wait, she went in search of Gideon. After checking the villas, it didn't take long to locate him, his jacket lying on the sand beside his bare feet. From her view, he looked remarkable. His wide shoulders and tall stature stood out against the setting sun behind him and cast him as the ideal fit to the scene. The once perfectly gelled hair was mussed, as if he'd run his fingers through it. His shirt was untucked, fluttering behind him in the breeze.

Quietly approaching, she slipped off her heels and let the warm sand overtake her feet. She'd never get sick of the feeling. She caught a whiff of Gideon's soap. *Just like I'll never get sick of that.*

"He didn't propose. He was begging me to trade stock for my vineyard in California," she said above the waves crashing on the shoreline.

Gideon folded his arms over his chest. "I don't care."

She watched the water recede from the sand. "But I do. Mason and I are business partners. Friends. That's it."

"But you like him, don't you?"

"As a person, sure, but not like us." She laid a hand on his forearm. "I've never felt this with anyone else, Gideon. It's always been you."

He slowly shook his head and turned to face her. His blue

eyes instantly drowned her with the intensity there. "That's the problem, Ireland. I've always known this, but you…." He let out a frustrated breath. "You go six damn years without saying a word to me, and then after a couple weeks, you think I'm the man for you."

She twisted her arms together. When he said it out loud, it didn't sound very good.

"You're selfish and spoiled, Ireland. Always have been, and judging from our recent reunion, you always will be." He loosened his tie and tossed it to the ground. "And I'm done being the play toy you want in small doses. That's not what I want in a relationship." He leaned closer and brushed his nose against hers. "I deserve better than to be yanked around again and again only to have my heart stomped on when you leave. Whether Mason proposed or not isn't the real issue here."

Tears streamed down her cheeks and she didn't bother to wipe them away. It was the ugly truth no one else would say to her face.

"I never meant for this to happen."

"I don't care if you meant for it or not, but it did. I didn't want to fall in love with you, but I did. I fell for you so fast, and I can't imagine a life without you. I meant every touch, every kiss, every word I said, even if you didn't."

He lifted his hand to her face but then pulled back, as if the temptation to touch was too great to give in to. "But I'm done, Ireland. One hundred percent finished. Don't call me. Don't text me. Don't smile at me. I can't handle it. Just like I won't be able to handle it when you accept that millionaire's proposal and marry him all to make your life easier."

"But I—"

"You will. Maybe not today or tomorrow, but I know you." He chuckled, but it was strangled in his throat. "Go live in your French castle, princess. I have a farm to run, and you don't fit with me. We always needed an ocean between us. Now I know why."

Gideon walked away after his words met Ireland's ears. She couldn't look back to watch him disappear even if she wanted to. Her tears were too thick.

CHAPTER TWENTY-FIVE

The smell of coffee woke Ireland abruptly. Her eyes popped open and she noticed the china cup on the side table. Yawning, she sat up and rubbed her eyes. A gentle breeze filtered through the screened window, her hair tickling her neck.

Standing, she looked out the window and saw crisp autumn colors in all directions. She'd never thought France could be more beautiful than Barbados, but right then, that's exactly what she thought. Her grandmother's estate wasn't massive, but it was large enough to get lost in at times.

She retrieved the coffee and slowly drank it while she watched sheep graze in the fields to the south. The trip to Bourgeois Castle wasn't planned, but after the way Gideon left, she needed time away from the tropical paradise. Luckily for her, a trip to France was necessary for administrative duties.

The thick evergreen trees reminded her of the woods in Iowa, and tears pooled in her eyes before she could stop them. She'd been in France for three months, but the sting of Gideon's words remained fresh in her heart.

A blue light flashed in the upper left part of her phone, stealing her attention from the French countryside. Unlocking it, she reviewed the orphanage plans for a rural city in Cambodia. *Looks good.* She'd go over everything with Toby later in the day.

Swiping through her phone, she clenched her jaw at the background picture. *I really need to change it.* Seeing Gideon and her smiling on the beach every time she opened it wasn't helping her demeanor at all.

Her thumbs hovered over the messaging app. Texting him was too tempting. Instead, she opened the music app and hit Play. *Some fresh air and music are all I need.*

She put the phone on the dresser and pulled on a pair of athletic pants and a matching long-sleeved top. The steady beat of Maroon 5 echoed to the vaulted ceiling until she plugged in the earbuds.

Hustling through the castle, she grinned when she reached the rear exit. The hum of the leaf blower motivated her legs to start moving. After cracking her neck, Ireland set out at a steady pace across the lawn leading to the nearby forest. No doubt the inground hot tub would come in handy after her jog around the grounds. She made a note to grab her swimsuit when she returned, then focused on the music pounding in her ears.

It wasn't long before she was lost amid the ancient trees

and overgrown shrubbery. This was her first extended trip to France, and she liked the country more and more with each passing day.

France in the fall was quickly becoming her favorite. The tourists went home after a festive summer and the year-round residents finally had peace. Plus, after confronting her grandmother about the paparazzi and her inheritance, this place was her haven, and she didn't know if she'd ever leave.

She jumped over a fallen tree and waved at a curious squirrel poking its head out of a hollow tree. Though she didn't run much, it swiftly became therapeutic ever since she arrived. She couldn't run from her feelings for Gideon, but she could run to clear her mind. It worked for a few hours, at least.

Sweat dripped down her forehead, but she didn't stop to wipe it away. It wasn't as if she'd let Gideon go without a fight. She'd tried to talk to him before he boarded the plane back to Iowa, but he wouldn't budge. He wouldn't even look at her.

Her family was no help either. *Not like they actually know the whole story.* She took a sharp left turn down the hill. While her parents were supportive of her, they didn't offer much assistance when it came to Gideon.

So she'd let him return to his farm. No texts, emails, or phone calls from him, and none from her either. While she promised herself not to get involved, she couldn't stop herself. The phone call and subsequent wire transfer to the bank were the last attempts she made to reach out to Gideon.

She made sure it wasn't traceable, and talked the banker into allowing him to keep making monthly payments on the loan even though the money would simply go into a savings account.

Gideon was stubborn, and he wouldn't accept a handout, so she worked around it. *What he doesn't know won't hurt him.* After he repaid the loan, the funds would be released back to him. Then and only then would he know what she'd done.

Ireland glanced at her phone to see how far she'd gone thus far. *Four miles. Not bad.* Any other time, she would've given up on running more than two miles. Ever since she left Barbados, she pushed herself more each day. The same could be said about her businesses.

Thankfully, Toby stayed on the island to keep control of her business ventures there. From the calls and email updates, it appeared he was doing fabulously and didn't need her help any time soon.

Which is good, because from the sounds of it, I need to be here a while. Fiona's façade crumpled the instant Ireland and Mason met with her three months ago. She was indeed the person behind the mass of paparazzi during Ireland's time abroad. As to why, it appeared one of Fiona's oldest business partners didn't want Ireland to take over the family businesses and threatened to come forward about Fiona's lack of attempts to find her granddaughter.

As it turned out, Fiona did seek out her son's daughter, but once she realized the Leightons already adopted her, Fiona left Ireland to enjoy a life without the pressure of her biological family name. At least, until she was old enough to understand and handle it. Once Ireland found out, she made sure the business partner was addressed appropriately before cutting all ties with the wealthy man. While she couldn't condone Fiona's actions, she realized her grandmother did them for what she believed were honorable reasons.

Ireland had the chance to review her parents' wills and as of last month, she ran every business with the Bourgeois name associated with it. The success felt good, but also drained her. She was never more thankful to have Toby and Mason by her side to help. Fiona profusely apologized for not telling Ireland about any of it. Eventually, Ireland forgave her. She didn't trust her grandmother like she once did, but the woman was family and Ireland swore to never turn her back on family again.

Turning around, she paused and wiped the sweat from her face with the hem of her shirt, then carefully stretched her calves and thighs. She still Skyped her parents and made it more than once a week this time around. Their time together was precious, and she wouldn't squander it even if they were still upset with her for how things ended with Gideon.

She checked her phone for the time and her eyes widened. She had less than an hour to make it back, shower, and meet Mason for brunch. *Better get my butt in gear.* Over the months, they became closer as friends and colleagues, but she had an inkling that Mason wanted more.

When she saw the castle looming in the distance, Ireland sprinted the rest of the way back. Her heart beat wildly and sweat drenched her clothes, but she'd made it. She passed the hot tub and mourned not having enough time to enjoy the warm water. *Another day.*

After a quick shower, Ireland made it to the dining area right as her grandmother entered the room. The woman was well in her eighties, but she looked fabulous.

"There you are, my sweet." Fiona kissed both of Ireland's cheeks. "You look beautiful." She took a seat. "Must be all this country air."

"I'm sure it is." She noticed the empty place setting. "Mason's not here yet?"

Fiona's brown eyes glanced to the spot beside Ireland. Before she could answer, Mason strode into the room. "There is the lady of the hour."

"Well, when you didn't return my call, I thought you fell off the planet," she teased.

He chuckled and scooted his chair to the table, his dark eyes sparkling with mischief. "Not at all. I flew to Morocco straight after our meeting last month."

"Any update on the Tokyo investments?" she asked, pouring tea. She looked up and saw Fiona curiously watch them. She already guessed what the woman would say. Ignoring her nosy grandmother, Ireland focused on the conversation. An hour passed, and she noticed Fiona waning.

"Why don't I meet you in the library later?" she suggested.

"I think that's a wonderful idea. Perhaps, I'll get a nap

in as well." Fiona smiled at both before toddling out of the room.

A moment of silence passed before Mason suggested, "How about a walk around the garden? It's been a while for me."

Standing, Ireland nodded. "Sounds good to me."

They fell in step even after they reached the small but eloquent garden in the rear of the castle. The gardener paused his winterizing of the roses and waved at the two as they walked by. The garden truly was gorgeous in the fall, with cheery mums lining the walkways. A majority of the flowers were grown in the greenhouse up the road and transferred to the estate. Roses were her grandmother's favorite, so an array of colors dominated the area in warmer months.

"How was Morocco?"

Mason glanced over at her and smirked. "Busy, but when isn't it?"

They reached a large fountain in the middle of the shrubs sculpted into a horse. "Are you still interested in something deeper between us?" she said at last.

He paused, clearly trying to choose his words carefully. "This is unexpected. What brought it on?"

"Plenty of self-reflection, I guess."

Mason looked to the colorful leaves on the ground then back to her. "I wouldn't be opposed to it, but that's not what you're asking, is it?"

The koi fish swam slowly in the small pond beneath the fountain. "No." She sighed. Thinking about marrying anyone except Gideon sounded horrendous, but when she considered Mason after the last months, it didn't seem as bad.

Sitting on one of the benches nearby, Mason met her gaze. "Do you want to marry me? Oh, and that wasn't a proposal, just a question."

Ireland nibbled on her thumbnail. What she desired didn't matter anymore. The one man she wanted didn't want her back.

She took the spot next to Mason and cleared her throat. Just when she opened her mouth to reply, a small plane flew over the castle. Instantly it reminded her of the flight she shared with Gideon at the helm. That memory, as well as hundred more, flooded her.

She took a deep breath, hoping it'd clear away all thoughts of Gideon. She needed to move forward. For her sake.

"Mason, I need to—"

"See if he loves you too?" he finished for her.

She grinned. "Yeah. I can't move on until I try everything to get Gideon back."

"Even move back to boring Iowa?"

She laughed. "Yeah, even that."

"Well, it sounds like you know what you want." He stared up at the sky. "Go back to Iowa. See if he loves you."

"You really think he'll listen?"

"Yes, really. You're worth the trouble, Ireland." He searched her eyes intently. "But if he doesn't feel the same for you, and you're still entertaining ideas of us, I'll be around."

"You're a fabulous friend, you know that?"

"Unfortunately, I do."

***

Sweat dripped from Gideon's face and he grunted at the sight in front of him. While he'd managed to harvest a hundred acres, he was only halfway finished. He wiped his face with the back of his hand and turned the combine to the next row. If he pushed hard, he could complete this field, but chores at the farm beckoned him to call it quits for the night. He mulled it over for a minute before he turned off the engine and grabbed the key.

Climbing down from the giant tractor, he sighed. The weather was cooperating, but the hotter-than-normal autumn made sitting in the rig all day uncomfortable. He adjusted his hat and reviewed the fields. If all went well, he'd have plenty of money to give the bank next month.

Shaking his head, he thought back to his unexpected meeting with the bank when he'd returned from Barbados ready to sell his soul in order to not lose the Taggart farm. To his surprise, the bank manager himself shook Gideon's hand and told him they'd extended the loan. The man even offered him a tumbler of whiskey. It had been the weirdest exchange of his life, and it still didn't sit right with him.

After he successfully secured the farm, Gideon broke the news to his parents and brother. He didn't want to run the business anymore. His dream was and always had been to be a veterinarian. He couldn't have his dream girl, so he opted for his dream job instead. His apprehension flew out the window when his parents hugged him and said it was about damn time. Once the harvest was complete, he'd focus his attentions on building his own office and reaching out to new clients. He'd never looked forward to winter more.

A breeze ruffled his hair and he closed his eyes. The lingering scent of coconut and vanilla clung to him. Just like that, he was back in Barbados. Back in Ireland's arms. Back to fighting his feelings for her. And back to the heartbreak.

Opening his eyes, he winced at the bright sunlight. He hadn't heard anything from the brown-eyed heiress in three months. It was partly his own fault. He'd told himself not to look back anymore; she was the past, and he should only focus on the future.

His phone rang in his pocket and he saw a text message from his best friend.

Zavier: Dinner?

Gideon's thumbs hovered over the keyboard, his stomach grumbling. He could use a good homecooked meal. Ever since his parents headed to Florida last month, he hadn't bothered to make much at all. TV dinners and frozen pizza were all he and Lance had lived on recently.

Although the newlyweds were building a house on the Leighton land, they still lived in the original farmhouse until the construction was complete. Ireland hadn't been there in months, but her memory hung around the house so much that he'd avoided it completely since returning.

Gideon: Rain check. Busy tonight.

Zavier: Yeah, whatever. You'll just watch TV and

hang out with your dogs.

Ignoring his friend's jabbing response, Gideon rubbed the small of his back. Every inch of him hurt. It didn't matter how in shape he was—harvest time always pushed his limits, especially when Ireland kept creeping into his mind long enough to distract him.

Walking along the freshly cut rows, he picked at stray weeds the combine missed. Any other year, he stayed fixated on the upcoming months. With his vet clinic on the horizon, he should've been happy, but he wasn't. Not completely. He could barely see beyond the morning he left Ireland in Barbados. He'd disappeared just like she had six years before. *Irony at its best.*

Gideon kicked a lump of soil. That wasn't the worst thing about leaving her behind. The worst part was that Ireland's perfect perfume went everywhere with him. He showered and washed his clothes twenty times, but he smelled warm vanilla when he least expected it.

He rubbed his sternum, the thoughts of Ireland physically hurting him. Sleeping without her beside him hurt. Not seeing her gorgeous face hurt. Love hurt.

For the first month, he was pissed. Pissed at himself for putting it all out there again to receive next to nothing. Pissed that Ireland had a rich guy waiting for her whenever she was ready. Gideon thought he'd come unglued when he saw Mason on his knees. It didn't matter that Mason and Ireland denied any romantic affections. He couldn't handle watching them knowing that Mason would be her fallback.

Gideon let out a noisy breath. Month two, he seriously

considered hopping on a plane to shake some sense into Ireland. He'd heard from Zavier that she'd spirited away to France not long after the wedding. He could only guess her grandmother had something to do with her sudden departure.

By month three, he simply accepted that Ireland wasn't coming back. Not in the way he wanted her to. Try as he might though, Gideon couldn't stop loving her. That part sucked the most. The few web searches he dared make about her didn't yield anything he didn't already know.

Until today, when his email notifications showed a photo of Ireland and Mason in Marseille, France. The snapshot of the seemingly happy partners at a ribbon cutting ripped directly through his soul. Ireland was gone. A snooty bitch had replaced her. He couldn't deny she was always meant for greatness, but he'd stupidly hoped he would be at her side.

He neared the end of the row and froze when he looked ahead. Squinting, he tried to make sense of it all. *It's just a mirage.* When he returned to her face, he realized it wasn't. Keeping his hand over his heart, Gideon willed it to slow its tempo. It couldn't be real. She couldn't be real. He was simply overheated.

He blinked and pushed up his ball cap. Sure enough, Ireland was walking toward him with her long hair flowing in the breeze like a scarf behind her. Her skin looked darker, no doubt thanks to the French sun. Just enough thigh showed beneath her paisley dress to make him appreciate her long legs. The brown cowboy boots were new but couldn't look out of place on her.

When she reached him, Ireland kept a few feet between them. It didn't matter—he could smell the perfume on her. *The same damn vanilla that keeps me up at night.*

"Hey," she tentatively began, meeting his eyes.

Gideon resisted hauling her into his arms, barely. He'd done enough of that when they were together, only to get his heart pulverized. "Hey."

She locked her fingers together. "Looks like you're getting a lot done."

"Yep." Shaking his head, he shoved his hands into the front pockets of his jeans. *Small talk. Great.*

She shifted her weight, keeping her gaze on the field behind him. "I bet you'll get done early this year."

He'd never minded chitchat until that moment. If she wasn't going to say something, he wouldn't continue to torture himself. "Look, Ireland, I need to get back. I have a couple patients I need to look in on, plus chores." He walked around her, careful not to inhale her essence.

"Gideon, wait." She caught his arm, spinning him back to face her.

"What do you think I've been doing?" He clenched his jaw when she looked to the ground. Swallowing the rest of his confession, he took long strides toward his truck. He wasn't one to cry, but today he just might let his emotions free for once.

"Go back to what makes you happy," he said over his shoulder.

"I did." She caught up with him before he realized.

"And it's you. You make me happy." He lifted his brows and she rushed on. "I thought I could forget like I did six years ago. I figured once I was back in France, I would be content with business."

Gideon's jaw ached with how hard he held it shut. He needed to hear her out before he said his piece.

"But I wasn't. Honestly, I couldn't even go a day without thinking about you. About us." She met his gaze, and he inhaled at the clarity in her brown depths.

"What're you doing here?"

"I'm here because I love you, Gideon. I loved you six years ago, and I fell back in love with you this summer."

His heart thudded in his ears, but he didn't budge. If he was dreaming, he'd kill his subconscious.

Ireland leaned forward and tilted up his hat. "I love you," she whispered, lips grazing his.

"Well I don't feel the same." He pushed her back, hating himself even more. "We can never be a couple. You're an heir to millions, if not billions," he pointed out. "And I'm a farmer who moonlights as a veterinarian and—"

"And who flies prop planes to see the world."

He nodded and stared at his boots. "This won't work. We're from different worlds now. I can't leave, and neither can you. What you do for other people is too important to give it all up for a farmer like me."

She reached for him, but he shook his head. "Go home, Ireland. Go back to France. To Barbados. To Mason." He swore he was actually ripping his heart out with the emotions coursing through his body. "I don't ever want to see you again."

Her eyes welled with tears. They flowed freely down her cheeks, further etching the scene in his mind. "I just flew four thousand miles to see you."

"Well you wasted your time." He started toward his truck again. "I'm done with you."

"Gideon, please."

Her strained voice was too much to handle. This was all he'd dreamed about since she left all those years ago. He dreamed she'd come home and want him and only him. But after finding out what her life could be without him, Gideon wouldn't let her waste it. Her future was better without him, and he'd push her away over and over again if that was what it took for her to realize the same thing. She would hate him if he let her give up everything for him. He could live with a lot of regret, but helping her loathe him wasn't a burden he could bear.

Opening the truck door, he chanced a look over his shoulder. Ireland stood in the middle of the field, hair tumbling in her face that was red with agony. It ate at his resolve, but he wouldn't give in. She was an heiress, after all, and he was a farmer. One who swore to never fall in love ever again.

CHAPTER TWENTY-SIX

Ireland had never felt more defeated. Staring out the window of Rome's La Pergola, her heart pounded in the most forlorn way. She'd done it. Professed her love to Gideon, only to get shot down. *Awesome.*

She sipped the vintage wine—her second glass—and looked out at the ancient city below. The last thing she wanted to do was have dinner at the most romantic restaurant in Italy. Despite her mood, she'd promised to meet Mason here. Her hunt for love in Iowa was over.

"Ravishing as ever," Mason complimented, kissing her cheek before sitting across from her. "I'd ask how your trip to the States was, but your face tells it all." He placed his hand over hers on the table, dark brown eyes searching her face. "I'm sorry it didn't work out."

"It is what it is." She attempted to smile, but it wouldn't stick.

He glanced around the full room. "Come on, I have a surprise."

Quickly finishing the wine, Ireland stood and smoothed the black Vera Wang dress before slipping her arm through Mason's. He led them to the outside eating area where a lone table sat overlooking the great city of Rome. Champagne chilled in a bucket nearby, and a lone candle accompanied the white tablecloth and dining set.

"This is gorgeous," she murmured as Mason pulled out the chair for her.

"Even though we aren't in love, I wanted to make this special, because maybe someday we will be. I consider you a great friend and you deserve the best." He knelt in front of her and opened the tiny box with a large diamond ring inside.

Her throat dried at the sight. Looking between the ring and Mason, she wished she had something stronger than champagne at her disposal.

Meeting Mason's eyes, she couldn't deny he truly was a romantic person at heart.

"Ireland, will you be my partner in and outside business?"

She straightened her back and pushed her hair out of her face. Holding out her hand, she nodded as he slid the ring in place.

I can do this.

She had no other choice.

***

Scratching behind the goldendoodle's ear, Gideon chuckled when the dog's leg thumped on the floor.

"Give her these antibiotics and she'll be ready for show season," he said, handing the bottle of medicine to the dog's owner.

"Thanks, Gideon. I'll be sure to give your name to my dog show group," Mrs. Rainer said, rattling the meds.

Seeing them out, he waved once they settled into the luxury Cadillac before flipping off the overhead lights. His phone buzzed in his pocket, reminding him to get a move on. The blind date in an hour wouldn't go well if he didn't show up.

Before locking the door, he double-checked the litter of Siamese kittens recently found near the interstate. They were huddled together in the cutest clowder of white and brown fur. If he didn't already have ten cats hanging around the barns, he might've kept one for himself.

As he stepped outside, a chill hung in the air. With the holidays right around the corner, snow would be along any day. He yanked up his hooded sweatshirt and started toward the farmhouse. His plans for the vet clinic were slow since he hadn't found an affordable plot of land, so he kept on with his makeshift one on Taggart property until the time came to build.

"Hey, Tagg, did you hear?"

Turning toward the voice, he noticed his brother piling firewood in his arms. "Hear what?"

"Ireland's getting married in the spring."

Gideon didn't miss the edge in Lance's voice. It was

the same one he felt in the pit of his gut. "That didn't take long," he mumbled under his breath. Picking up his pace, he tried to push the thought out of his mind.

"She got engaged three months ago, Tagg. Are you really that disconnected with social media?"

"Yes, and I prefer it that way." He saw a snowflake land on his brother's head. "I need to go. Don't want to be late."

"How'd you pay for the farm again?" Lance asked, shifting gears.

That time he didn't stop, merely turned to walk backward. "It doesn't matter. It's paid. End of story."

Lance caught up with him. "And you didn't bother to see where the money came from? I bet that guy Mason paid it off to make sure you stayed away."

The cold outside felt like a heatwave to the frigid temps in his veins. That thought gnawed at him since he'd found out, but he couldn't dig deeper. He didn't want to know if it meant Lance was right. "What the hell are you implying?"

"That you gave her up for money." He shifted the wood in his arms. "Why else would you let her go? Hell, she came to Iowa to see you, bro, and you rejected her love."

He shook his head, frustrated at the infiltration in his otherwise complacent day. "Shut up, Lance. You don't know what you're talking about. There's an ocean between Ireland and me. Even when we're in the same room, it's there."

"Then build a goddamn boat." Lance dumped the wood in the pile near the side of the house. "We joke around a lot, but I know a good thing when I see it. You and Ireland are the best combination."

Gideon shoved his hands in his front pockets. "I'm going to be late for my date. We're done here."

"The hell we are." Lance grabbed his arm and spun him around. "I'm going to be your big brother for a minute, so shut up and listen."

Deciding it was better than fighting him, Gideon stood still.

"Do not lose Ireland to some rich guy she doesn't even love." Lance brushed wood chips from his jacket. "I've watched you the last three months. You act like you're happy, but you're not. You go out on these dates, but you're not really there. You're with Ireland. I may give you shit about your relationships, but if I were in your shoes, I wouldn't stop until Ireland Leighton was mine. She's a pain in the ass, but I'd bet my life that she's worth it."

Snow fell more frequently then, dusting Lance's hat. It wasn't normal for his big brother to act like one, especially when emotions were involved. Gideon shifted his weight and studied the brown grass around them as he mulled over Lance's words. It'd be easy to let Ireland go. He'd done it once before. No, twice. He wasn't sure if he could handle a third time.

Patting Lance's arm, Gideon nodded. "Thanks. I'll think on that." He stepped around the wood pile and to the back porch.

Lance cursed under his breath just as Gideon opened the door.

He couldn't take the advice. She was too far gone.

CHAPTER TWENTY-SEVEN

"Ireland, darling, are you ready for the evening?" Fiona asked from the doorway four months later.

Clasping the earring in place, Ireland looked in the mirror one final time. "Yes, I'm all set."

She stood and lightly kissed her grandmother's cheeks before linking their arms together. "How're you feeling?"

Fiona patted Ireland's hand. "Oh, darling, I'm fine. The doctor said I'm on the mend. Plus, I didn't want to put off your engagement party again. It'd be the third time."

Ireland focused on walking down the long hallway. A crowd of people waited at the other end, and she needed to give them a show. After agreeing to marry Mason, she'd returned to France to let Toby plan a gaudy wedding. Due to her grandmother's health, the year-end wedding gala didn't happen, but their spring wedding date quickly neared.

"I'm sorry your parents couldn't make it."

"It's okay. They came the first time." She smiled reminiscently of the quick trip the Leightons took three months ago. Since Fiona fell ill right before the event, Ireland had a chance to take her parents on a tour of Paris and the towns surrounding the castle.

"They'll come for the wedding, yes?"

Ireland thought about the text message she'd received earlier that day. Zavier and Krista were expecting—*honeymoon baby, big shocker there*—and the baby was due in the late spring early summer.

"Hopefully, yes."

"Well if not, Mason's entire family will be there."

They reached the large double doors and Ireland rolled her shoulders back. Ever since their engagement hit the tabloids, she'd been tossed from one family get-together to another.

Two men opened the doors at the same time and light flooded the hallway. Ireland's gasp was drowned out by the sheer magnitude of the ballroom, glittering from floor to ceiling with lights, diamonds, and gold sparkles in the flooring.

"Wow."

Fiona chuckled and patted her granddaughter's hand. "This will be yours someday, my dear. Though Mason owns it, you will run it."

Ireland smiled and searched the crowd for the man of the hour. When she spotted him, a blush crept up her neck. He completely stopped his conversation and stared at her. His mesmerizing eyes clicked with hers and his lips spread in a wide smile.

"Have a good time. I'll check with you later," Fiona said, moving toward a group of ladies to the left.

By then Mason had reached her, taking her hand and kissing the back of it. "I don't know whether I should bow in front of you or simply weep from your beauty."

Blushing harder, Ireland resisted the urge to roll her eyes. "You, sir, are going to spoil me."

He tucked her hand in his. "Good. Then you'll never leave."

"Don't worry, you're stuck with me."

His gaze slid down the front of her formfitting white gown with gold threading. It was as close to a wedding dress as she'd worn thus far. Her neckline was modest yet hinted at her cleavage, a fact she noticed Mason approved of.

"You are bewitching. I swear, you'll need to pinch me every now and then or I'll think you're a figment of my imagination."

That time Ireland did roll her eyes. "Let's mingle. I'm starving."

Mason guided them toward the center of the room where his family congregated. Small talk turned to laughter, and laughter turned to dancing. To her delight, the night didn't drone on as she suspected it would. Mason was the ideal match in every possible way. *Well, except one.*

Toward the end of the night, guests made toasts to the happy couple and she enjoyed every second. But each time she looked to her left, her smile waned. It wasn't Gideon beside her as she'd hoped. Mason was her business partner and friend. Surely, they could make an amicable marriage out of it.

"Ireland, remind me again. Your country bumpkin thoroughly tossed you out on your arse when you visited him, correct?" Mason asked, pulling her aside after a waltz.

"What the hell are you bringing that up for?" She dug her nails into his wrist.

Mason winced and nodded toward the balcony door. "Because if my eyes serve me, that's him."

***

Fuck, I shouldn't have come. The tie around Gideon's throat felt like a boa constrictor the longer he stood in the doorway. Men and women dressed in expensive clothes surrounded him. A select few spoke French around him, which only made the pounding in his ears worse.

He looked at his phone and then back up. It was the right place, but he hadn't caught a glimpse of Ireland yet.

"Well, slide me into Speedos and call me an Olympic swimmer." Toby's British accent met him, and Gideon almost hugged the small man.

"Toby, you're here."

"Of course I'm here. I'm Ireland's best friend. Where else would I be on the night of her engagement party?" He eyed Gideon warily. "Why are you here? That's the million-dollar question."

Gideon felt his pocket. The ring was there despite the fast change in the cab on the way there. "I made a mistake."

"Obviously."

"I can't let Ireland marry Mason."

Toby picked at his cuticles with a disbelieving face. "Mmhmm, and why should I believe you now and not months ago when you left her alone in a cornfield?"

Gideon stared at his rented tuxedo and shiny shoes. He was every inch out of place in the mansion, but he didn't care. He'd even trimmed his beard and slicked back his hair to impress Ireland.

"Because I need to tell her something."

"And?"

"And I love her."

"I assumed as much." Toby offered him a glass of champagne, but he waved it aside. "I mean, why else would you be all spiffed up and in France?"

"I don't know what I'm doing." He stopped himself before he ran his hand through his hair. "I rented a tux, caught a flight, and don't even remember the rest."

"Aw, how romantic." Toby pushed him toward the center of the room. "Tell her, not me."

"I can't just tell her in front of everyone. This is her engagement party." He wiped his hands on his pants. Apparently sweating was his newest hobby.

Toby scanned the giant room before he turned Gideon toward the opposite doors. "There she is."

Gideon's breath caught in his throat. If he was ever face-to-face with an angel, Ireland would still outshine the heavenly being. He hissed out a breath, the sight of her almost too painful. She was stunning. *No, elegant.* He shook his head. *And way out of my league.*

"Second thoughts?"

He met Toby's humored eyes. "More like terrified that I'll make a fool out of myself."

"You won't know until you try."

He took a step forward, then paused when he watched Mason guide Ireland onto the dance floor. "What should I do? Cut in?"

"That depends. Do you know how to waltz?"

"Um, no."

"Then I'd wait." Toby led him toward one of the tables lined with food. While the shorter man grabbed a plate, Gideon couldn't focus on anything except the fluid way Ireland sailed across the golden floor.

"What'd you need to tell her anyway? Or was it simply the love declaration?"

Gideon waited until Toby finished with the table to answer. "My farm loan was paid off."

The hors d'oeuvre stopped at Toby's lips. "And you think Mason is trying to pay you off so you'll stay away from Ireland?"

"Sounds crazy, but I could see it. I asked where the payoff came from, but all the bank would give me was an account in Europe."

Rich laughter filled the air as tears filled Toby's eyes, trying to stifle his sounds with his hand. Waving away one of the waiters, he wiped his cheeks.

"Toby, what're you laughing at? This is serious."

"Sorry. It's just... you know what, I'll let you figure it

out." Toby hugged Gideon tight and giggled. "Oh my! Is that a ring box, or are you happy to see me?" He shoved Gideon to the crowd. "Go away, and don't come back until whatever is in your pocket is on her hand."

Realizing he was all alone in this venture, Gideon squared his shoulders and started toward Ireland. He could handle her answer either way. If she wanted Mason after what he told her, then they truly weren't meant to be together.

***

"Gideon, what're you doing here?" Ireland resisted the desire to reach over to first smack him and then kiss him.

His clear blue eyes glanced around the crowd anxiously. "I need to talk to you." He looked to Mason and his cheek twitched at their proximity. "Privately."

"Gideon—"

"It's fine," Mason said with a gracious smile. "I'll chat with my university chums for a bit."

She forced a smile and nodded. Once Mason stepped away, she grabbed Gideon's arm and pulled him toward the veranda. The chilly weather and snowflakes would've been a shock if she wasn't boiling mad.

"What the hell were you thinking coming here? And at my engagement party, no less." She threw her arms wide, no doubt looking like a crazed woman from afar.

Gideon closed the French doors behind them and leaned against the rail. The terrace itself overlooked a vast garden during the warmer months, but today it was cold and unwelcoming.

"You look beautiful," he finally said.

Raising her brows, Ireland shook her head. "So you hopped on a flight to tell me that? Great, you can leave now."

"You're such a brat sometimes." He chuckled. "And the sad part is all I want to do is kiss you."

"Wh-what?" She took a step away from him and crossed her arms over her chest.

Taking off his suit jacket, he walked over and carefully placed it over her shoulders. His breath showed on the night air, and she cautiously lifted her eyes to meet his face.

"I came here to tell you that Mason's a no-good snake."

"Gideon—"

His fingers muted the rest of her words. "But then when I saw you, I realized it didn't matter. He didn't matter."

Ireland licked her lips and felt the effects of the cold for the first time.

"You matter." He smiled slightly. "You and me."

"I'm confused." Ireland pushed his chest to escape. "I went to Iowa, told you I was in love with you, and you told me to leave." She looked out at the garden to clear her eyes of the tears.

"I was wrong and stupid. Typical guy, right? I thought you were better off without me. That I was better without you."

She didn't laugh. She could barely breathe without crying. *Of all days for him to show up, it just had to be today.*

"I think you should leave. Go back to Iowa and be happy with someone else." She moved to the door that led to safety, but he beat her to it.

His solid body stood directly in her way now.

"Move."

"No."

"Fine, I'll walk around the whole damned castle, then," she huffed, turning the other direction. Stone stairs awaited her, and she cursed her heels.

"I don't want to be happy with someone else, Ireland." His voice sounded closer, but he didn't try to stop her.

Ireland reached the bottom of the steps and paused. Some part of her wanted to hear the rest of his reasoning for flying four thousand miles just to ruin her night.

"I want to be with you. If you're not mine, I'll never be happy. That's what I've learned since the last time we spoke."

"You're a farmer who lives in Iowa, Gideon." She faced him and wished she hadn't. He looked glorious, standing at the top of the balcony. His tuxedo fit every bulge of muscle in only the best way. She'd never seen him so dressed up before. His usually wild beard was trimmed and combed, and the gel in his hair deserved an Emmy for keeping back his thick curls and making him look flawless. But it was his eyes that made her heart lurch to her throat. Those idyllically blue eyes were filled with admiration and hunger. Hunger for her.

He stepped down one stair. "Actually, I'm not a farmer anymore."

"What?"

"I sold my half of the farm to Lance." He descended another one. "I'm a veterinarian full time now."

"When did you decide that?"

"Not long after I discovered somebody paid my farm loan off." He reached the bottom of the stairs. "I thought it was Mason trying to bribe me to stay away, which was partly why I came." He shook his head and licked his bottom lip. "But that's not what happened, was it?"

The time for running was over. She couldn't do it anymore. "No."

He cupped the side of her face and the minimal distance between them shrank. "You paid off the loan and convinced the bankers to keep their mouths shut, didn't you?"

"Yes."

He leaned closer, nuzzling his nose to hers. "Why?"

Gideon's scent intoxicated her more than any glass of alcohol. She bit her lip, telling herself not to kiss him.

"Because I loved you."

A slow smile crossed his face, his beard tickling her cheek. "Is it still true? Do you love me?"

Ireland thought back over the last nine months. From resisting Gideon to falling for him, she didn't regret one moment of it.

She nodded.

"Oh no you don't." He tilted her chin up and stared into her eyes. "I need those perfect lips that I want to kiss every damn day for the rest of my life to say the words."

Her body trembled, whether from the chill in the air or

the electricity between them, she didn't care. "I love you, Gideon Taggart."

"Damn right you do." He grinned and captured her mouth with his. Ireland wrapped her arms around his neck and clung to him, coaxing for more. She didn't want any part of this man to ever leave her side. She'd known since she was a teenager but couldn't accept it until that summer.

"So, should I tell everyone to leave, or do you want the paparazzi to find the two of you making out in the backyard?"

Ireland pulled away long enough to wave Toby away. When her best friend didn't get the hint, Gideon hauled her against the side of the balcony, kissing her hard. Ireland giggled when she heard Toby make a catlike growl before his footsteps echoed his retreat.

"What're we going to do now, Dr. Taggart?"

"For starters, I've been carrying this ring around for six years, just hoping I could give it to you. It never seemed like the right time until now." Gideon pulled a small box out of his pocket.

"You've carried that around ever since I left?" Tears brimmed in her eyes at the thought. He'd never stopped believing and the proof was right in front of her.

"Yep. Every damn day. And I'd do it all again because I love you." He dropped to one knee and held up the stunning ring. "Marry me?"

Placing a hand over her mouth, she hid her smile. With his hair tangled from her fingers and the moonlight glimmering in his blue eyes, he wasn't a business mogul or from a royal family. He was the boy next door she'd fallen for, except now he was all grown up and exactly what she needed.

"Every day for the rest of my life."

EPILOGUE

"I swear to all things holy, if you make me watch you give birth to that child, I'll hate you forever."

Ireland laughed despite the contraction racking her body. "You're such a baby, Tobes."

Toby waved his hand over his face, sweat glistening on his brow. "I'm the baby? Are you serious? I'm the one who's standing next to you, watching you go through agonizing pain while your stupid hunky husband is flying his stupid sexy plane."

"Okay, I'm sensing a lot of hostility here. Maybe we should take a break," the nurse suggested.

"It won't help." Ireland glanced to the window and breathed through the next moment of pain. "Toby's the godfather."

The nurse nodded but didn't look impressed with the person who'd be around Ireland's child for the rest of its life. "I think I'll go check on the doctor. He should've made it by now."

After the nurse left, Ireland watched Toby pace in front of the window. If she could stand upright, she'd do the exact same thing. She checked her phone but didn't see a message from Gideon. *He's flying, Ireland. He's fine.* She pushed back her braid and focused on the sound of the surf in the background. If he didn't hurry up, he'd miss it all.

She hadn't expected the baby to come early, which was why she encouraged Gideon to fly to Jamaica to check on the orphanage there. That had been two days ago. Now she hoped the tropical winds hadn't grounded his plane.

"He's fine, right?" Toby pushed off his straw hat. "Yeah, he's fine. God, why am I so worried? He's not my husband."

Sitting back, Ireland guessed her best friend wasn't only worried about Gideon, but also the man who'd gone with him. Raul wasn't Toby's boyfriend, but that was because Toby kept turning him down.

"Raul is fine too, Tobes." She held her stomach as the next contraction strengthened. "You need to tell him how you feel."

"And put myself out there? Hell to the no."

She ignored his finger snap. "Don't be like me. Please. If I hadn't been stubborn, I would've been with Gideon a long time ago and we'd have five babies."

Toby chewed his thumbnail. "All right, all right. Enough cute puppy dog eyes from you."

Ireland giggled and watched him check his phone again. It was hard for her to imagine any other life since rekindling her relationship with the Iowa farmer. After a very difficult conversation with her grandmother, she and Gideon eloped to Paris. They more than made up for the hasty wedding when they took their families on a vacation to Fiji the following summer.

Horns honked in the distance, and she was glad they'd built a house farther up the coast with a beach where Gideon could fly in and out whenever he needed to check on his animal clients in other parts of Barbados. Having a veterinarian for a husband kept him away some days, but she planned her business trips around Gideon's so they could be home together as often as possible.

A cat meowed from the other side of the bedroom door. Pets were another perk to Gideon's traveling clinic; he picked up injured strays and nursed them back to health. Over the years, a few even called their house home. The familiar whine of Gideon's Australian shepherds from the living room made her smile. Of course, he had to bring Dallas and Diesel to Barbados. The duo even flew with him on select trips.

With Gideon, her life opened to bigger and better ventures. They started several animal shelters in the Caribbean, along with vet clinics that he bounced between. She never thought helping animals would be fulfilling, but it was. They traveled to the South Pacific to open three more orphanages the year before she found out she was pregnant.

Since she'd broken the good news, Gideon didn't try to

keep her from continuing her passions, but he also made certain she never overexerted herself. The fear of becoming a mother vanished with Gideon. Together, they would get through anything. If their past was any indicator, they had plenty of experience.

Ireland sent another text message to Gideon, then one to her grandmother. Though Fiona was initially disappointed with Ireland's choice, the matriarch didn't stay upset long. They stayed in France each summer, and Fiona was more than excited to welcome a new generation to the family.

When a crack of thunder split across the sky, her eyes went to the door and she held her breath. The familiar buzz of Gideon's Cessna was the next sound she heard. Sighing in relief, she waited for the splash of the floats before she sat up. It'd only be minutes before his handsome face would appear.

It's all going to be all right.

"Ireland?" Gideon called, bursting through the screened door. He rushed over to the bed and knelt beside it. "Are you okay? Is the baby okay? What's going on?"

She tilted his ballcap up and smoothed back his mass of curls. "I'm fine." She gripped his hand. "All right, so maybe not fine, but I'm better now that you're here."

Worry lined his face, but he nodded. "I'm not going anywhere."

"The doctor is still with his other patient," the nurse said, returning to the room.

Ireland exchanged a knowing glance with the nurse. The time had come and gone for a hospital. It was now or never.

"I got this," Gideon said, standing and rolling up his sleeves. He met Ireland's eyes. "Do you trust me?"

"With my life."

***

Gideon pulled back the lightweight blanket and stared at the wrinkly skin of his newborn daughter. She smelled even better than she looked. He delicately traced her tiny face with his finger. He didn't think he could love anyone as much as he loved Ireland, but with one strong cry, their baby had completely stolen his heart.

He never imagined he'd bring his own child into the world, but he was damned glad he hadn't missed it. He didn't want to miss any part of his life with Ireland.

Rain beat on the house outside, but he didn't hear it. His gaze finally lifted when Ireland stirred on the bed. "Hey, darlin'."

She offered him a weak smile. "Hey, yourself."

"I was thinking Odette. What do you think?"

A tear raced down her cheek and she nodded. "After my mom. I love it."

He placed Odette in her bassinette and carefully climbed into the bed next to Ireland. "How'd I convince you to marry me, again?" He brushed back the wisps of hair that had fallen loose.

She kissed his neck. "You flew to France and stole me."

"Oh yeah." He chuckled. "I like that story."

"Only because you won." Ireland smirked and stroked his beard.

"Maybe a little." Gideon turned to face her. "But the best

part of that story is what happened afterward." He lightly kissed the tip of her nose. "How we started a life together and never looked back."

"Well, when you kiss me like that, I lose all control over my mind."

"Good, because I'm gonna kiss you again." He kissed her cheek. "And again." His lips drifted over her neck. "And again." He paused at her lips and gazed into her brown eyes full of love. "Until you know how much I love you."

Ireland smiled dreamily. "And how long will that take?"

"The rest of my life."

"I think that'll work for me."

"Good, because I wasn't giving you a choice."

Gideon pulled her close and shut his eyes. An ocean couldn't keep their love away. He swore Ireland would never leave his heart, his soul, or his bed ever again.

He'd given up hope, but the universe hadn't. Their love was always meant to be, Iowa farm or Barbados beach.

Without a doubt, she was an heiress worth waiting for.

THE END

Thanks for reading *Oceans Away*. I do hope you enjoyed Ireland and Gideon's story. I appreciate your help in spreading the word, including telling a friend. Before you go, it would mean so much to me if you would take a few minutes to write a review and share how you feel about my story so others may find my work. Reviews really do help readers find books. Please leave a review on your favorite book site.

Don't miss out on New Releases, Exclusive Giveaways and much more!

Join my newsletter:
WWW.SKYEMCNEIL.COM

Like me on Facebook:
WWW.FACEBOOK.COM/SKYESTHELIMITWRITING

Join my reader group:
WWW.FACEBOOK.COM/GROUPS/287389708375366

Follow me on Twitter:
WWW.TWITTER.COM/SKYE_MCNEIL7

Follow me on Pinterest:
WWW.PINTEREST.COM/SKYEMCNEIL

Follow me on Goodreads:
WWW.GOODREADS.COM/SKYEMCNEIL

Follow me on Instagram:
WWW.INSTAGRAM.COM/MCNEILSKYE

Visit my website for my current booklist:
WWW.SKYEMCNEIL.COM

I'd love to hear from you directly, too. Please feel free to email me at SKYESTHELIMITMCNEIL@GMAIL.COM or check out my website WWW.SKYEMCNEIL.COM for updates.

ACKNOWLEDGMENTS

Many thanks to my publisher, Hot Tree Publishing, my editors, beta readers, cover designers, fellow authors, reviewers, and readers. I'm blessed to have you all supporting me.

ABOUT THE PUBLISHER

Hot Tree Publishing opened its doors in 2015 with an aspiration to bring quality fiction to the world of readers. With the initial focus on romance and a wide spread of romance subgenres, we have since opened Tangled Tree Publishing, our crime, thriller, and suspense imprint.

Firmly seated in the industry as a leading editing provider to independent authors and small publishing houses, Hot Tree Publishing is the sister company to Hot Tree Editing, founded in 2012. Having established in-house editing and promotions, plus having a well-respected market presence, Hot Tree Publishing endeavors to be a leader in bringing quality stories to the world of readers.

Interested in discovering more amazing reads brought to you by Hot Tree Publishing? Head over to the website for information:

WWW.HOTTREEPUBLISHING.COM

www.ingramcontent.com/pod-product-compliance
Lightning Source LLC
Chambersburg PA
CBHW061045190726
48286CB00006B/1613